'A rip-roaring adventure' F...

'Pure Household and beautifully done . . . a great read
Los Angeles Times

'*Rogue Male* . . . has achieved deservedly classic status.
It's an exciting story, told in a crisp, no-nonsense style
reminiscent of John Buchan' *Mail on Sunday*

'Household . . . helped to develop the suspense story into
an art form' *New York Times*

'*Rogue Male* remains as exciting and probing as ever, un-
touched by the topicality that made it so popular in 1939,
and the reason lies as much in its incisive psychology and
timeless crispness of language as in its sensational plot'
The Times

'Household is a storyteller in direct line of descent from
Daniel Defoe and Robert Louis Stevenson' *New Yorker*

'*Rogue Male* must forever remain a classic' John Gardner

'A great book about an assassin who's a big game hunter
and goes to Europe on the eve of World War II . . . It has
the best opening page I've ever read and is not nearly as
well known as it should be' Robert Harris

By Geoffrey Household

The Spanish Cave

The Third Hour

The Salvation of Pisco
Gabar and Other Stories

Rogue Male

Arabesque

The High Place

A Rough Shoot

A Time to Kill

Tales of Adventurers

Fellow Passenger

The Exploits of Xenophon

Against the Wind

The Brides of Solomon and
Other Stories

Watcher in the Shadows

Thing to Love

Olura

Sabres on the Sand

The Courtesy of Death

Prisoner of the Indies

Dance of the Dwarfs

Doom's Caravan

The Three Sentinels

The Lives and Times of
Bernardo Brown

Red Anger

The Cats to Come

Escape into Daylight

Hostage: London

The Last Two Weeks of
Georges Rivac

The Europe That Was

The Sending

Capricorn and Cancer

Summon the Bright Water

Rogue Justice

Arrows of Desire

The Days of Your Fathers

Face to the Sun

Born in Bristol in 1900 and educated at Magdalen College, Oxford, Geoffrey Household worked all over the world, including Eastern Europe, the USA, the Middle East and South America, as, among other things, a banker, a salesman and an encyclopaedia writer. He served in British intelligence in the Second World War. His other works include *A Rough Shoot*, *Watcher in the Shadows*, *Rogue Justice* and an autobiography, *Against the Wind*. He died in 1988.

Fellow Passenger

GEOFFREY HOUSEHOLD

An Orion paperback

First published in Great Britain in 1955
by Michael Joseph Ltd.
This paperback edition published in 2013
by Orion Books,
an imprint of The Orion Publishing Group Ltd,
Orion House, 5 Upper St Martin's Lane,
London WC2H 9EA

An Hachette UK company

1 3 5 7 9 10 8 6 4 2

A CIP catalogue record for this book
is available from the British Library.

ISBN 978-1-7802-2406-0

Typeset by Input Data Services Ltd,
Bridgwater, Somerset

Printed and bound in Great Britain
by Clays Ltd, St Ives plc

The Orion Publishing Group's policy is to use papers that
are natural, renewable and recyclable products and
made from wood grown in sustainable forests. The logging
and manufacturing processes are expected to conform to
the environmental regulations of the country of origin.

www.orionbooks.co.uk

Fellow Passenger

THERE IS SATISFACTION in being imprisoned in the Tower of London. It seems to set a man, however undeservedly, in the company of the great. I wonder if criminals feel the same about Dartmoor. It is likely. After all, a sentence of twenty years, served in Dartmoor, does mean that one has reached the summit of one's profession.

I wish I could claim that the blackness of my crime was worthy of the grandeur of my prison, but the fact is that I do not know whether I can be found guilty of High Treason or not; nor does a somewhat embarrassed State. That suits both parties. The Government is in no hurry to decide what shall be done with me. I, so long as they continue to keep me safe from newspaper reporters, am in no hurry to leave. The food, while uninteresting, is at least as good as that of the average English hotel, and the service suggests a club in which the rules are rather too stringent and the staff a little too ceremonious in manners and dress.

There is also the blessing of leisure, as well as a strong tradition for its use. So, for my own amusement, I shall emulate Sir Walter Raleigh and Archbishop Laud. Like me, they were innocent of High Treason but thoroughly deserved the accusation. That, I think, is a combination which lends itself to literature.

I have no intention of justifying myself, for I do not feel in the least ill-used. If I were of pure English birth and shared the national gift for solemn indignation I should probably write to *The Times* – assuming that from this institution one is permitted to address the other – and kindle the sympathies of those excellent citizens who fret themselves about the eccentricities of birds and the injustices of bureaucrats. But I spent my youth in Latin America, and I am too much in love with the world as it is to bother about what it ought to be.

My father, James Howard-Wolferstan, emigrated to Ecuador in the early nineteen hundreds. He was, he said, the last of his line, and I have only heard of one other bearer of the name. He never told me why he left England. At any rate he was right to choose a small country where his flamboyant and kindly character would not be lost.

Ever since I can remember him he was the most dignified exhibit of Quito, dressed as if he were a fashionable clubman in a London June of 1908. But probably I underrate the formality of the time. Dressed, I should say, as if he were off for a week-end in the country during which he was likely to meet King Edward VII at lunch. Invariably he had a carnation in his buttonhole, and a white slip under his waistcoat. At race meetings and bull fights he would sport a grey top-hat. He would have nothing to do with the small British colony, but preserved proudly his British passport. So have I – or I shouldn't be where I am.

He cannot have arrived in Ecuador with any capital, and I have no idea what the qualifications were – beyond personal charm – which permitted him to obtain the hand and dowry of my mother. Thereafter he lived a life of gracious idleness, buying and selling concessions on the eastern side of the Cordillera. He was always at ease with politicians – indeed I often think he might have been Vice-President of Ecuador if he had cared to surrender his nationality – and foreigners, especially North Americans, were impressed by his appearance and undoubted influence.

I loved my mother dutifully, what there was of her to love. She was his absolute opposite. Dressed in unrelieved and dusty black, she spent her days and nights creeping rapidly between the Convent of the Sacred Heart and the Cathedral. In early days there must – since I exist – have been occasional exceptions to this routine, but I remember none.

She would, of course, have been happily fulfilled in a nunnery, but her parents, who carried the blood of the Incas, preferred that their only daughter should increase the lay population rather than the clerical. I suspect that my father was far from their first choice as a son-in-law, but it was said that only he was persistent, perhaps over-persistent, in his attentions to her. Lest I appear unfilial, let me add that it was never said in my presence – or only once, and by my second cousin who was a lieutenant in the glorious army. I slapped his face and, though already under the civilizing influence of Oxford, shot him in the leg (I aimed for it, too) at the comically ceremonious meeting which followed. But I have no doubt that his libellous statement contained a certain element of truth.

My mother, poor dear, had little influence on my father and myself. I do not think she found any tragedy in that. She was entirely absorbed by the salvation of her soul – not selfishly, but in the firm belief that we could be saved from eternal torment by her prior arrival in the next world and her careful employment of political influence with its Authorities.

My father died two years ago. He had known for some time that his fate was on him, but never allowed me to suspect it. Only when his doctor told him it was that week or the next did he break the news to me, and then with the very minimum of solemnity between his first and second brandy.

When he saw that I was wholly overcome by sorrow – for in moments of extreme emotion I cannot help being as Latin as I am English – he told me to restrain myself and to relight my cigar. I can remember his exact words:

'Everybody's father has got to kick the bucket sooner or later,' he said. 'What's so bloody astonishing about it?' You'll miss me for a month, I trust, and I'll miss you for the next forty years or so – if there's anything in all that stuff of your poor, dear mother's, which I rather hope there isn't.'

Then he told me that very little would remain for me after his death, and that the various companies of which he was chairman or president had only been kept in apparent prosperity by his reputation and the aid of a really clever auditor. We had lived well, and I would not have reproached him even if it had entered my head to do so.

'The auditor will skip with his savings as soon as I am under the daisies,' he assured me, 'and my advice to you is to follow him pronto. I've got a few hundred pounds in gold, and I want you to take them now. Book your passage home, and as soon as you've planted me – for I'd like you to be there – clear out before they start to settle up the estate.'

My father had never lied to me – though there were, of course, things which he found unnecessary to be described in detail. I therefore placed absolute trust in the story which he now told me, especially as it amused him. He was capable of being amused up to the end. His last conscious act, a fortnight later, was to wink at me.

'I have never mentioned to you,' he went on, 'the old home of the Howard-Wolferstans, and I don't propose to discuss it now. It was the manor of the village of Moreton Intrinseca. Go upstairs to the attics on the third floor. In my day a pack of servants used to sleep there, but from what I read in the

4

English papers there won't be many of them now and they won't sleep under the tiles.

'Turn to the right at the head of the staircase. The third door to the right leads into a small attic with a dormer window giving on to the parapet, and a fireplace. About three feet up the chimney you'll find enough capital to settle you in any respectable business. My advice would be to look up your old Oxford friends and buy yourself a partnership in a firm of stockbrokers. But if you prefer a racing stable, that's your affair.

'And, whatever you do, don't try burglary!' he added. 'Make friends with the present owner of Moreton Intrinseca. Stay a week with him. Marry his daughter, if you must. It doesn't matter whom a man is married to, so long as he has enough money to keep his temper.'

His instructions, on their face value, belonged to a fairy tale, but I knew him: the mere fact that there was some sardonic jest which he hugged to himself made it certain that he was in earnest. He did not encourage me to question him, nor did I wish to. He had just told me that he was going to die, and attic chimneys were a wretched irrelevance. I only asked why on earth his money should still be there. He replied that he had good reason to think it was, and why wouldn't it be? Even in his days no one ever lit a fire in the attics, and he was prepared to bet they hadn't since. Early Victorian architects, he said, always built a fireplace, whether it was likely to be used or not. It was part of the room, like the wallpaper.

When my father's funeral was over, I obeyed him and sailed for England. The financial disaster was just as great as he had feared, though not in the eyes of the public. That was because the concessions which he and his companies held were so enormous that they could be valued at any sum which the Government agreed; and agreement was easy since the politicians were heavily involved. Nor was the hushing-up wholly a question of money. My father was a much loved man, and nobody wanted to take revenge on his memory.

I was partly educated in England, for my father wanted it to become my country. Though he himself could never be bothered to return, he profoundly enjoyed all the second-hand impressions which I could give him. I used to record for him any incidents and characters with the sort of richness he appreciated. After his death it seemed to me that there were few to record, though whether it was I or the nation which had changed I could not tell. I had not been out of Latin America since 1939.

The after-war years I spent in idle movement for the sake of sport or exploration or wild-cat mining. I had some excuse for relaxation since, during the six years of war, I had been employed as a clerk, ostensibly Ecuadorian, at various airports, and as a guitarist in the Callao café which was the favourite of the German colony. My cover was never broken, and the less I talk about it, the better for me. Anyway, service to the State will not get you out of the Tower. It never did. The most it could ensure was that you would be beheaded instead of hanged – a doubtful advantage if you happened to meet the headsman on a day when he was off his drive and trusting to short approaches.

By the time I had settled into a small furnished flat in London I found myself with about five hundred pounds in the bank which vanished at the devil of a pace. I was not being at all prodigal, but it takes time for anyone with Latin tastes to adjust himself to contemporary England. Merely to eat and drink as well as a prosperous peasant is a shocking extravagance. So it was not long before I went down to Moreton Intrinseca.

There was no kindly retired colonel with whom I could make friends; no daughter to tell me how different I was from the average Englishman. The manor had become a damned hostel for scientists. I had lunch at the local pub and discovered that the house, for as long as anyone remembered, had belonged to two old maiden ladies, and that after they died it had remained empty for three or four years until it was requisitioned by the War Office. The War Office had passed it on to the Ministry of Supply, who used it to house a sort of upper middle class of experts from the atomic plant some five miles to the west. The real upper class were at the universities or where they pleased. A lower class was, I gathered, confined in the huts of the plant itself. But the chaps who really administered the plant were entertained in the ancestral mansion of the Howard-Wolferstans.

Back in London, I went to work to find an introduction into this specialized monastic world. I was, of course, under the impression that a man of standing and good education could still go more or less where he pleased. Before the war, if I had wanted, for example, to have a look at our latest tank, I feel sure that I could have found someone at my club to show me round the factory. One's loyalty was taken for granted. Security applied only to foreigners.

I could not get in touch. That upper middle class of cyclotronic monks seemed to have no background. Its world nowhere overlapped my own, which was social and commercial rather than scientific. However, I had academic contacts, too, and I looked up old friends and tutors. My innocent enquiries must have been a bit too frank. I was gently warned – so gently that I might only have been questioning a point of Greek grammar which had been settled for ever in 1892 – that perhaps I was drawing too much attention to myself. It is sometimes a handicap that in looks I take after my mother.

The English will never assume reliability in a too bronzed complexion.

I gave it up. After all, I had no idea what was in the attic chimney. My father had not told me, and, as the whole matter seemed faintly distasteful to him, I had not asked questions. I made a note of his directions, but very reluctantly and only because he insisted that I should.

A satisfactory job was difficult to find. For one thing, I was thirty-seven and had been too many years away from the conventional ladder; for another, I found it hard to say what I had done in the war. Unofficial, unpaid service in South America. I myself would distrust anyone who came to me with that yarn and no proof of it.

At last I got on to a really sound business proposition. I was offered a partnership in a firm to be founded by men of my own sort who knew the Latin American markets, the politicians and their exchange difficulties. We were out to persuade manufacturers to entrust their export business to us, very much as they would give their advertising to professional advertisers. It was a job after my own heart, allowing me to live and prosper with one foot on each side of the Atlantic. But it needed capital, and that, if existing at all, was at Moreton Intrinseca.

There was an excellent country hotel within two miles of the village, and there I stayed for a week. The earnest young scientists from the manor would occasionally drop in and become noisy in the bar. It wasn't drink. They were competing for the attention of an athletic and over-painted young barmaid-secretary, and behaving like a visiting rugger team. They did not seem to know how to set about seduction quietly. It was easy enough to make acquaintances among them, but none asked me to visit him at the manor.

Towards the end of the week I found that two genial

strangers were paying me drinks. I was accustomed to that. Police employed on security duties are all the same – German, Spanish or English. Their job must be far easier in American countries, north or south, than in England, where they are always up against the convention that one stranger does not normally ask questions of another.

So that was that, and I returned promptly to London to think out some new method of approach. It was all very well for my father to tell me to avoid burglary. He did not know that I had had a good eye for entries and exits ever since I was nearly caught with the archbishop's god-daughter at the age of thirteen, and had to pretend tearfully that I was only looking for my mummy. The outer ring of security, protecting the Ministry's secrets and stretching all over England, was evidently efficient; but the inner, more material ring around the manor was derisory. There were merely a twelve-foot brick wall, topped with barbed wire, and a gate with a doorkeeper on it day and night. After all, there was no reason for more. Burglars do not raid the simple bedrooms of scientists; and spies, I imagine, prefer to contact them on more neutral ground.

People have told me that I have a natural leaning towards lawlessness. I do not think that is true. I did consider at great length what a really English Englishman would do. He would undoubtedly write to the Ministry of Supply, giving every possible reference for his respectability, and ask permission to search for and recover his family property. I was instinctively unwilling to take this step. My father's conception of property, while never dishonest, had a certain originality, and – since all my enquiries had led nowhere – I found it hard to prove what the connection of the Howard-Wolferstans with Moreton Intrinseca really was.

A chestnut tree, growing in the manor garden, appeared

to me less futile than correspondence with the Ministry. It extended a noble branch into an open field, passing a clear ten feet above the wire-topped wall. I bought a length of good, light rope and attached a heavy hook to the end of it. With this and other simple necessaries in a small ruck-sack, and myself attired as a hiker out for serious exercise, I departed from London in a motor coach and got off it at a cross-roads some eight miles from Moreton Intrinseca.

It was a hot evening in early May, when a temperature of seventy feels like ninety. The hawthorn was out; the hay was growing; and the scent of the countryside was as deliciously overpowering as anything I have known in the tropics. This island remains inhabited, I think, merely for the sake of that week in May; another, probably, in June; and a third, reason-ably certain, in September. I walked across country to the edge of the downs above Moreton Intrinseca, and waited for darkness.

When the night was velvet black I circled round the vil-lage and found – after a couple of bad shots – the manor field and the chestnut tree. My first swing at the branch failed to catch and made a noise much more alarming than it really was. However, a wood-pigeon obligingly flew out, and under cover of her clatter, as she swerved towards the house through the little plantation inside the wall, I made a second swing at the branch and the hook caught.

I climbed the rope, pulled it up after me and stayed quiet for several minutes. Everything else was quiet – wood-pigeons, dogs, scientists and the village itself. The thick, smooth trunk of the chestnut looked as if it would be impos-sible to climb on my way out; so I shifted the hook to a firm hold on the garden side, curled up the rope in a fork and left hanging from it a piece of string by which it could be pulled down. When I had dropped to the ground, I attached the end of the string to a twig above my head. I reckoned that it would never be noticed even in daylight.

Once in the garden, I undid my pack and changed into pyjamas, dressing-gown and bedroom slippers. I did not know how many people lived permanently in the manor, but it stood to reason that there must be occasional distinguished visitors staying the night. A figure glimpsed on his way to the bathroom, with his face partly obscured by towel and dressing-gown collar, was most unlikely to be questioned even if he could not be immediately identified.

The luck, to start with, was all with me. On so warm a night the french windows to the lawn were open, and two men were strolling on the paved and very weedy terrace – one of them in sweater and trousers, the other, like me, in dressing-gown and pyjamas. Though it was after midnight there were faint lights in several windows, as if the cloistered scientists were reading or writing in bed.

I could not be sure what eyes might be looking out of the darkened house, so I moved from cover to cover slowly and meditatively, with the air of one seeking new experiments with which to tickle up a bored universe. When the two strollers had their backs to me, I nipped in through the french windows.

The room turned out to be the dining hall. I escaped from its uncompromising bareness into a lounge or common room, from which a fine oak staircase rose into the darkness. The lights were all off except for a single naked bulb at the foot of the stairs. The Government had certainly put the interest of the taxpayer before the comfort of its servants.

There was no object in hesitation or reconnaissance, so I ran silently up two flights with dressing-gown flying. On the second floor, at the end of the landing, I saw a small, mean staircase which had to be that leading to the attics;

but to reach it I had to pass an open door, flooding a strip of passage with light. I locked myself in a bathroom, peeping out at intervals, until the occupant of the room returned and went to bed.

Keeping my feet close against the wall to avoid the abominable creaking of the stairs, I went up to the attics. So far all had been so easy that I began to feel light-heartedly sure of success. I turned right and opened the third door to the right and found myself in just such a room as my father had described. Below the little dormer window was a parapet.

There were no bulbs in any of the lighting fixtures on the attic floor. My torch showed that the room was packed with junk – all the utterly valueless debris of a home which the old ladies had stowed away and no one, after death and auction, had ever bothered to clear out. The fireplace was there, but covered by a ruinous old dresser in front of which were piled fenders, fire-irons and decayed basket chairs from the garden.

I could only go slowly and hope that there was a heavy sleeper underneath. I managed to clear all the odd lots to the other side of the room in reasonable silence, but then came the dresser. The sole practical method of shifting that was to lift one end out and drop it, and then the other end out and drop it. The lifting and dropping, six inches at a time, made no noise, but the squeaking and scratching of the legs on the opposite side were intolerable.

I rushed the last of the job before anyone could come and investigate, and shoved my arm up the chimney. Nothing. Not even any soot. I looked up it and shone my torch up it. Still nothing. I was bitterly, desperately disappointed, but had, as it were, no time to be. Steps were climbing the stairs. I took refuge under the pile of basketwork.

Two men, one young and one younger, came straight to

my attic and dropped something which they were carrying on the floor.

'It's not usually in this room,' said a positive voice.

'The furniture has been moved,' answered the other in an excited half-whisper.

Well, it had. I did not see why he should make such a point of it.

'Peter was up here looking for owls or rats or something,' explained the younger.

'There aren't any. The War Office gassed 'em. And since the Ministry took this place over, the food has been too bloody awful to tempt 'em back. Now, we do not want to inhibit the phenomena, so we'll leave this and clear out. It will record the temperature readings for the next two hours. Meanwhile we can sit in my room and note the times of any audible disturbances.'

That was the elder man, and, though an enthusiast, he sounded responsible. The other had the infallibility of youth.

'Note my backside!' he said. 'If you can prove (*a*) that there are poltergeists, (*b*) that their action is accompanied by a drop in temperature, bang goes the second law of thermodynamics!'

'A mere working hypothesis,' answered the elder. 'We all know we've got the universe upside down, only none of us dare say so.'

Instead of noting disturbances they spent the next quarter of an hour arguing about the second law of thermodynamics. It was interesting. I love to listen to the learned so long as they avoid algebra; and I never knew that the case for poltergeists was quite so good. I concentrated furiously on their debate, for I had to keep my mind from brooding on the probability of a sneeze. The dust under those basket chairs was getting into my nose.

At last they set their thermocouple by the light of a small pencil torch, and went downstairs.

I must admit that after being mistaken for something that went bump in the night I was not as relieved at being left alone as I might have been. I put myself in better heart by the thought that if the other creator of disturbances was also a Howard-Wolferstan we had at least so much in common. After extracting myself from the chairs with the least possible noise, I examined the instrument left on the floor. The thermocouple at once recorded the heat of my torch on its revolving cylinder, so I made some little pattering noises to prove to the listeners below that poltergeists sent the temperature up, not down. It was the least I could do for the second law of thermodynamics.

I made a last thorough examination of the chimney just to ensure that I had not overlooked an envelope, a key or anything tiny but promising, and then, no longer buoyed up by the hope of capital gains free of income tax, set imagination to the duller task of removing myself to London. I did not dare tackle the creaking stairs again while two ghost-hunting scientists were on the floor below, wide awake and timing every sound. At my third attempt I found an attic window which would open quietly, and went through it on to the leads.

The manor was an oblong, late Georgian house without wings or additions, and as simple as if it had been built out of a child's box of bricks. While running up the main staircase I had clearly seen both ends of the landing on the first floor; and on the second floor, where I had more time to explore, I confirmed that the ground plan was as I thought. Now the house, seen from the roof, appeared larger outside than inside, but I put that down to the vague profusion of attic dormers, low gables and chimney stacks. In any case I was in no mood for cool measurements. My whole enterprise had gone wrong. Instead of wandering freely about the house as an amiable stranger in a dressing-gown, I was in the most unwelcome position of a cat burglar on the roof.

A handy drain-pipe at the extreme west end of the house would have offered a route from the parapet to the ground if only it had not struck off at an angle half-way down. I can tackle a perpendicular pipe as well as my neighbour, but not a sloping one. However, the perpendicular stretch passed close to a balcony on the floor below. There were french windows on to the balcony, and they were open. I listened. The room was dark, and a sound sleeper gave an occasional heavy snort. I scrambled down the pipe, losing a slipper on the way, gained the balcony and peered into the bedroom. It was occupied by a tousled, an immense, a very major scientist. I averted my eyes – for one should never allow one's illusion of woman to be destroyed by a mere accident – and fled through her door into the passage beyond.

It was lit by the usual ministerial naked bulb, and horribly empty of cover. The position was becoming plain. There were female scientists – dozens of them perhaps – and this west end of the manor was their nunnery. The ends of the landings had been blocked up, precisely to keep out gentlemen in pyjamas and dressing-gowns. The Lord only knew what might happen to me if I were caught, or how many psychiatrists might be turned loose upon me with indecent questions.

At that moment a door opened, and an extremely intellectual female – I judge her only from her hair, her vertebrae and a far too transparent nightdress of revolting green – began to say soft and interminable good nights to someone within. I panicked. I turned very quietly the nearest door handle, popped inside and closed it behind me. The room was pitch dark. The curtains were drawn in spite of the heat. A most attractive voice, with a shade of merriment in it, said:

'Horace, you *have* been long.'

What on earth was I to do? One answer was obvious. But I have never been able to believe those delightful fourteenth-century stories where the hero takes the place of husband or lover in the dark. At any rate, I trust that few other lovers could ever be mistaken for myself.

There was no time for any thought. The only deliberate act I remember was wiping my hands, all dusty from the drain-pipe, on my dressing-gown. I can only attempt to analyse – and that at a regrettable distance – my instinctive deductions. Horace was a bore. Horace hadn't really been expected to come. He had perhaps been dared to come. Something of the sort I guessed from her voice. And she? Probably forbiddingly scientific, but certainly not cold. A little quick tenderness was indicated – to kiss her hair or something, on my way to the window.

I tried it. I never said a word. Lord, but Horace wasn't going to be allowed to get away so easily! I responded. What else could I do? She was delicious, and the May night was amorously scented. It seemed as if Boccaccio must be right after all. But perhaps Horace had never kissed her before, and she hadn't much to go on. I did not dare say a word except the lightest breath of a whisper. The pace slackened, and it looked as if I would have to say something at last. That had to be avoided at all costs. I did what I hoped Horace would have done. This supple and passionate scientist had something of the scandalous attraction of the dedicated. She was startled rather than offended. She suddenly pushed me away and said:

'Peter, you beast!'

Contempt? Mingled with amusement? It was hard to tell.

But if I had been Peter I should have thought the tone highly propitious. Perhaps this wing was where he was bound when he pretended to be up in the attic looking for rats. I was about to do my very best for his reputation when the door began to open. I ought to have had half an ear listening, but the complications were too absorbing. I jumped behind the curtains a little too late. Peter? Horace? Which of them was it?

It was Horace.

'I heard something,' he remarked stolidly. 'Is this a joke?'

She was marvellous. I shall never again say a word against the higher education of women.

'How dare you come here?' she whispered fiercely. 'Just because I said I wished we could go on with our talk! You must be mad!'

'There's a man behind those curtains,' said Horace.

His lack of tact was really astonishing. He had no right whatever to be there – or only, let us say, the very smallest – and it was no business of his if she liked to have ten men behind her curtains. Also he was about to commit the extreme indecency of turning on the light. I bounded out, hit him hard in the wind and vanished through the open door.

'A burglar!' she yelled. 'Stop him! Stop him!'

She had not seen my face. She still thought I was Peter. And of course she was reckoning that Peter would be able to get clear away before the hunt started, and that then he could join in it. I do not think she would have aroused the whole manor if she had known how gravely it would embarrass me. My first impression of her was – admittedly on slender evidence – that she was a woman of taste and that she should never have been confined to a routine where her heated imagination had only scientists to dwell upon.

Horace was after me with the speed of light as soon as he

had straightened himself out. I expect he was glad that such a very awkward situation had ended in a chance for him to play the hero. Meanwhile I was charging down the private staircase of the nunnery, and using my faithful towel as well as I could to hide my face.

On the ground floor I ran into a dear old boy, full of distinction in spite of his heavy flannel pyjamas, who peered out of his room and asked me what all the excitement was.

'Trouble up in the harem again,' I answered. 'Just listen to this!'

And I took him by the arm and led him back into his bedroom.

'The harem! Ho, ho!' – he had a laugh like the bark of a small terrier enjoying itself – 'that's very good. And my poor room at the foot of the staircase. The chief eunuch. Ah, well!'

Someone dashing down the passage shouted rudely that it was that little bitch of a metallurgist again.

'Bitch?' protested my rescuer thoughtfully. 'Bitch? Well, I suppose we must admit it. But when you are my age, Mr . . . er . . . you will find that bitches are so much more polite to you than the others.'

'And we must all remember,' I added sternly, 'that she is an excellent metallurgist.'

'You would really say so? Is that your branch, Mr . . . er . . . ? I am afraid that without my glasses I find it increasingly difficult to recognize faces.'

I told him that, yes, indirectly it was my branch. He seemed satisfied. His rooms were highly civilized – a comfortable study lined with books, and a bedroom and bathroom leading off it. I had a feeling that he was a good deal senior to anyone else in the place: a sort of unofficial dean, perhaps, or an occasional and eminent visitor from one of the universities.

Outside this pleasant oasis of scholarly peace, the hostel was humming. I have noticed that those who are bored with living by their brains usually seize upon any opportunity to prove themselves men of action. The scientists were baying and rampaging all over the manor. I did not hear the voices of any females. Possibly they had their own opinion about that burglar. My delightful little metallurgist was unlikely to be popular with colleagues of her own sex.

'It all began,' I explained to him, 'with those two young idiots ghost-hunting in the attics.'

'Ah,' he chuckled, 'the second law of thermodynamics! And did they alarm the harem?'

'They did indeed.'

'And so – forgive me if I jump to conclusions – you were compelled to decamp so hurriedly that you left behind a bedroom slipper with the Scheherazade of the moment?'

This mixture of acuteness and wanton imagination was alarming.

'Sir,' I said, 'I trust to your discretion.'

'Sir,' he replied with an echo in his voice of Dr Johnson and senior common rooms, 'you might well do so if I knew your name.'

I hesitated a shade too long over my reply. He had a window opening on the lawn, and all I wanted was to open it and run.

'May I give you your glasses?' I asked. 'And then, I think, you will recognize me.'

A bit mysterious, perhaps. After all, I was not very likely to be the Minister of Supply himself or the Director of Military Intelligence. Still, it kept the ball rolling, and gave me a chance to stroll in the direction of the window.

'Certainly,' he replied. 'Thank you. They are on the ledge in the bathroom.'

His voice sounded so courteous and natural that I actually went to the bathroom instead of the window. And then he slammed the door on me and locked it.

He started calling for Peter. Peter again! This random personality dogged me. I might have guessed what he was. Who else would be checking up rats in the attics? Who else would have a perfect right to wander about the nunnery passages after dark? The security officer, of course!

Peter let me out of the bathroom with a damn great pistol held unobtrusively – so far as it could be unobtrusive – in his fist. A fine figure of a man, certainly. But her impulsive guess that I was Peter could never have lasted more than a few seconds. Even in the dark he would have smelt of snooping. I am quite sure she could never have said a word which would allow him to think that on his nightly round he might open a door which had been left unlocked for a friendly and comparatively innocent chat with Horace.

My dressing-gown and pyjamas seemed to bother Peter. He insisted on knowing where my clothes were. I was tempted by the vision of him searching very tactfully for my trousers through every blessed bedroom in the nunnery; but it wouldn't do. I had to behave responsibly. So I offered to tell him where my clothes were on condition that he sent someone to fetch them and allowed me to put them on.

I think the case might have been dealt with quite informally if I had admitted an overwhelming passion for atomic scientists. It might not even have been necessary to specify the sex. It was obvious, however, where suspicion would fall, and I could not possibly allow a government metallurgist to be so badgered with questions that she would mistake uranium for platinum, and plutonium for a bit of grandmother's bedstead.

'My name,' I said, 'is Claudio Howard-Wolferstan. My

family were at one time lords of this manor of Moreton Intrinseca, and I am here to recover certain family property.'

'And exactly how did you propose to recover it?' asked
Peter, with a nasty lift of his voice at the end of the sentence.

'By the only means open to me,' I replied.

'What were you doing in Dr Ridgeway's bedroom?'
Horace asked.

I had seen just enough of him – while he hesitated at her
door – to recognize him, but he was worse than I imagined.
I could not conceive how I, dark, eager, and of bronzed complexion, could be mistaken for a pale, sandy streak of futility.
However, to the touch we might have felt alike, for we were
both clean-shaven, narrow-faced and smooth-haired.

I said I had not been in any blasted doctor's bedroom.

'Dr Cornelia Ridgeway,' he explained, stressing the Christian name.

'Will you permit me to conduct this enquiry in my own
way?' Peter thundered at him.

'Look here, I was in that confounded wing entirely by accident!' I protested. 'I dropped off the roof on to a balcony,
and you'll find my bedroom slipper under it. I went through
that room into the passage, was nearly seen and popped into
another where I hid behind the curtains. Unfortunately I
disturbed some old lady in making my escape, and she yelled
for help.'

Horace was not very bright. He started off to say something and then saw that he was going to give his own
movements away. I don't believe he cared a damn about darling Dr Cornelia. He had a long way to go before reaching
the mental acuteness of my aged and sympathetic captor.
The old boy, who had been basking in quiet approval as if
some experiment of his had revealed perverse and entertaining behaviour of the proton, met my eyes with a mischievous

expression of innocence which he evidently meant me to appreciate. He had no more need of glasses than I.

My clothes, with some difficulty, were found, and I put them on. When Peter handed me over to the police, dressing-gown, pyjamas and towel were stowed away in my pack. I looked a respectable holiday-maker, but I was at once recognized as the man who had been staying at the local hotel a fortnight earlier and asking too many and too suspicious questions.

In the morning I was driven to Saxminster, and came up before the local beaks. The bench was at first favourably impressed. I was, after all, a citizen of known antecedents with a club and friends to whom reference might be made, and a bank balance – though it was mighty small, and I could not claim any source of income. But nobody could remember that there had ever been any Howard-Wolferstans at the manor, and my statement to Peter was treated as bluff or a mere impertinence. I thought it best to give no more details.

The justices remanded me for further enquiries, and were very ready to grant me bail. They had quite an argument with the police about it. But then Peter called up reinforcements – a very military-looking gentleman who had not opened his mouth in public and was continually having violent, whispered conversations with the superintendent of police. The superintendent passed on a whisper to the magistrates' clerk. The clerk whispered to the justices. They announced gravely – though looking impatient – that in view of the Importance of the Establishment into which I had broken, bail could not be granted.

All went well in gaol. I won't pretend I enjoyed it; but if a man is to live his life to the full, he must expect occasional loss of liberty, be it in cell or hospital bed. For the first five days I was treated genially as if it were a foregone conclusion that my behaviour could be satisfactorily explained. Then came a subtle change in the attitude of my warders.

I thought I must have broken some taboo. Had my normal social gaiety been mistaken, I wondered, for insolence? In so ancient and traditional a country as England there is a proper manner for every situation, and one knows it or should know it by instinct. In the Tower, for example, I find that a distant courtliness, a melancholy humour are much appreciated. But in a plain, respectable prison the right note for a first offender was hard to strike, especially since I was accustomed to conditions in the less formal countries of Latin America. There a prisoner is free to chat, to cook his food if he can get any, to catch his own lice and to pass the time as best he can in the easy society of well-mannered thieves and murderers. I have never been able to understand why Victorian England decided that confinement in a cell was more progressive.

The disapproval of my warders, however, had nothing to do with any traditional subtleties of behaviour. No, their inexplicable coldness merely showed that they had learned through the police grapevine of the enormity of my crime. Myself, I never suspected it. I had not even employed a solicitor to advise and defend me. I felt that the complexities were such that only I myself could be sure what to admit and what to suppress. In gaol I had had plenty of time to think, and it had occurred to me that the manor, as I had pictured it, did not fit the social habits of its day. The horde of maidservants, passing from the domestic offices to their attic bedrooms, would have to go up the main staircase, which was most improbable. The likely answer was that the Ministry had blocked up the western ends of the landings on the first and second floors to form the nunnery wing, that the nunnery stairs had originally been the back stairs and that they carried on up to the attics at some point which I had not discovered in the dark. If my father had been thinking of this second staircase – I repeat that I always had the utmost confidence in what he chose to tell me – then his nest-egg might still be where he said it was and I still had a hope of regaining it. Obviously I did not want any solicitor insisting that I should produce it and prove my title to it.

The magistrates' court was crowded. I had a good look round from the dock. Peter and Horace were both present, and at a decent distance from them was Dr Cornelia Ridgeway. She was sternly dressed, as befitted a scientist, and a man without my keen appreciation of women might have had to take a second look before realizing that when she wished – in her bedroom or in Bond Street, for example – she could be alluringly feminine. As my acquaintance with her had been purely spiritual – or, let us say, spiritually tactile rather than coarsely visual – I might not have recognized her; but, when our eyes met, she produced a scintillating, exquisite, gorgeous carnation of a blush. There was also a tremor of the lips. I think she may have intended a distant smile, a mere politeness to show that she was above embarrassment. But I had, of course, to look away.

The case for the prosecution opened. Peter gave evidence and very wisely kept Horace right out of the story. So did Dr Cornelia. I had passed through her room and woken her up. She had screamed for help. That was all she knew. As she left the box, modest, serious and glowing with the inner consciousness that she had aroused the chivalrous admiration of every man of taste in court, I was able to express my apologies in a respectful bow.

Then came my old professor. I had been right about him. He was of immense distinction, and he spent as much time at Cambridge as in the suite of rooms opening upon the manor lawn. He was Sir Alexander Romilly himself.

He had evidently decided – for he knew almost as much of possible human beings as possible universes – that a fuss was being made about very little. He pointed out that Mr Howard-Wolferstan (no nonsense about calling me the accused) had offered him no violence whatever and had indeed – ho, ho! – engaged his sympathies by conversation. So far as his experience permitted him to judge, and unless he had been grossly deceived by outward appearances, he felt as sure of Mr Howard-Wolferstan's loyalty as of his own.

Loyalty? Well, I supposed it would be investigated, but I was so precious innocent and confident that I was startled when the word was openly mentioned. I fear I returned Sir Alexander's little nod without the full courtliness which springs from an easy mind.

I am not, I am quite sure, more Ecuadorian than English. But put it this way. I had been brought up in a country where a man of substance and family could do more or less as he liked, short of murder. Such eighteenth-century liberty was, of course, unthinkable in England; but the nearest thing to it was the charitable attitude adopted, before the war, to the peccadilloes of high-spirited but essentially honourable young men at the older universities. And that had been my chief experience of England – two years of school, four years at Oxford and a fifth as a gilded and irresponsible youth in London. Thus I was idiot enough to expect that my breaking into Moreton Intrinseca manor – in the absence of any evidence of theft or intended theft – would be treated as an eccentricity in the worst of taste, and that I should be let off with a tremendous lecture from the magistrates and a heavy fine. I had also, I fear – for youth in the Americas endures so easily – forgotten that I was thirty-seven not twenty-two.

When I was called upon to tell my story, I put it very simply. I said that I had no witness except my father who was dead. He had told me that there was a considerable sum of money in the house – I claimed that it was gold coin and in a deed box, for I dared not weaken my story by saying I hadn't the faintest notion what it was – but that the box was not in the attic where he said it would be found. I strenuously maintained that I had passed through the wing set apart for female scientists by the purest accident.

The Crown had employed an eminent Q.C. to deal with me. He seemed a very ferocious iron-grey sledge-hammer to crack a harmless nut, but I supposed, uneasily, that his presence was just bureaucratic routine. He asked me whether I seriously expected my story to be believed. I answered that I did not and that, all the same, it was true. I rather hoped that he and the magistrates would suspect me of telling a gallant lie. Dr Cornelia was clear on my evidence and Peter's of all possible complicity, but I might well have been enamoured of the intellectual in the green nightdress.

Counsel for the prosecution ignored those attractive byways. He asked me whether, a fortnight earlier, I had been in the district asking questions about the atomic establishment and the accommodation at the manor. I admitted that I had, and that it was natural enough. I hoped, I said, to be invited to eat a meal, and had not realized that an invitation would be so difficult to obtain.

'You did not appreciate, perhaps,' he asked me, 'that the establishment would be so security-minded?'

'No, I did not.'

'It had not occurred to you that some of the administrators might be working at night on papers classified as Most Secret?'

'No.'

'Sir Alexander Romilly, for example?'

'I am sure Sir Alexander would never take back to his

rooms any documents which would be safer at the Establishment,' I answered.

As a matter of fact, the old boy's desk had been covered by a mass of official-looking documents with some kind of test report in the middle of them and a formidable sheet of calculations. But I was not going to give him away. He had proved himself a lot more capable of looking after secret papers than any amount of security officers and barbed wire.

'Have you any political affiliations?' Counsel asked.

'None whatever.'

'You are not a member of the Communist Party?'

'Of course not.'

'Have you ever been a member?'

Good God, I had completely forgotten it! It was no more important to memory than whether I had worn a red tie or a yellow one. So much had come between. Youth passing into middle age. Six years of exhausting service to my country. The death of my parents. It seems to me, now, impossible that I could have forgotten. Yet I had. The communism I knew was comparable to my other social or anti-social activities. In my conscious mind there was no association between the real, objective communism of every day and my own early follies. Suppression, because I was ashamed of them? It's possible. In any case I had done my own brain-washing with an efficiency which startles me. How many other discreditable episodes have I conveniently forgotten?

'Yes,' I answered him, utterly horrified.

'When did you resign from the party?'

'I don't know.'

'I put it to you that you never have resigned.'

My expression must have been guilty as hell – exactly that of a spy who had trusted that his political allegiance would never be ferreted out. In 1938, when I was twenty-one and up at Oxford, communism was a mere protest against Hitler and Mussolini. A fashionable protest. A jest, though an angry one. Some of my contemporaries, I suppose, must have taken it very seriously, for since then they have solemnly exposed the struggles in their blasted consciences. I have no conscience – politically, I mean.

It was hopeless, in the atmosphere of to-day, to explain that I had never resigned my membership because I did not think it of sufficient importance. My silence was damning. I will give the rest of this appalling cross-examination verbatim. I can never forget it.

'When did you join the party?'

'In 1938.'

'What were your activities?'

'None – except that I once hoisted the red flag on Magdalen Tower.'

'Secretly?'

'Of course – though everyone knew I had done it except the authorities.'

'That was on the instructions of the party?'

'Lord, no! They were very angry. They said it was an irresponsible, diversionary activity.'

'But they did not expel you?'

'I don't know. Not at that meeting, anyway.'

'Why not?'

'They probably thought I might be some use to them in Ecuador.'

'And were you?'

'No. The war broke out soon after my return, and I was much too busy to bother with them. I suppose they lost track of me.'

'What did you do in the war?'

'I formed and led an organization of dockers and airport workers on the Pacific coast of South America.'

'For what purpose?'

'Counter-propaganda and other pro-allied activities.'

'And of course you found communists the most useful? Just as in Greece and Jugo-Slavia, for example?'

'No. As a matter of fact we didn't touch the communist organizations at all. Most of my men were catholics, in name at any rate.'

'From whom did you take your orders?'

'May I write down the name?' I asked.

The court was full of newspaper reporters dashing off sheets of shorthand in hysterical excitement. I did not want to compromise the unsuspected and respectable Peruvian citizen who had been my immediate boss.

I was permitted to write the name down, and it was handed up to the magistrates. The prosecuting counsel, through whom it passed, looked disappointed. I knew what was coming then.

'And above this gentleman?'

'Christopher Conrad Emmassin.'

That was the end of me. Chris was a brilliant but irresponsible diplomat who ought to have been a soldier. Sitting at a desk – though it must have been a fascinating desk – exasperated him. After the war he simply disappeared without scandal, without excitement, and turned up again quite openly in Moscow. I only met him half a dozen times, and I have no reason to believe he was a communist then. It may have been close acquaintance with the negro worker and the Indian peon which upset him. He was watching Latin America through the eyes of a too liberal, too sentimental Englishman.

Counsel for the Crown just looked at the magistrates and

sat down. Myself, I hadn't anywhere to look. By accident I met Sir Alexander's eyes, and he must have seen the despair in mine. He shrugged his shoulders and slightly raised one white eyebrow. I suspect he meant that he was inclined to believe me, but that not even the Almighty could do anything for such a lunatic.

I allowed myself a last glance at Dr Cornelia. To my astonishment she was anxious to catch my eye, and blazing with indignation which a slight gesture of her hand directed at the Court. By what feminine clairvoyance she had persuaded herself that I was innocent I cannot imagine. She may have felt instinctively that no communist would fall so far from earnestness as to interrupt his mission by the little courtesies I had offered her.

The Court sent me for trial on a charge of entering to commit a felony, and it was suggested that further charges might be preferred. I do not think there was much doubt in anyone's mind that the indictment would be High Treason by the time my case came on the Assizes. In my mind there was no doubt at all. I was only praying that I could reach Ecuador and remain there, like my father, for ever after.

My case had taken up the whole of the afternoon. The pubs were now open and the court cleared very quickly. It was a warm, clear evening after rain. Thirst, regret and desperation combined to keep me keenly aware of my last moments of freedom and of any chance of prolonging them. It seemed a remote chance. I was handcuffed to a constable, and I had in attendance a plain-clothes detective. We remained in a sort of condemned cell below the dock until the magistrates and officials had gone, and then marched out through the empty courtroom.

It was a friendly little court, so far as architecture was concerned; it had no private and underground door through which to hustle the unfortunate back to gaol. Everyone came and went by way of the spacious, stone-flagged, mediaeval hall. The public used an imposing flight of steps to the street. Prisoners and police used a narrower flight which led to a side courtyard where the Black Maria was parked.

On and below the steps of this discreeter exit I could see the pack of press photographers; but they had to wait. A door opened on the opposite side of the hall, and a young man, whom I recognized as one of the reporters in court, beckoned excitedly from inside the room. There was a photographer with him. My detective whipped us through the door and shut it.

I can usually recognize a bit of roguery when I smell it. That detective had struck me as a crook from the start. I don't mean that he could be bribed. He was too unctuously smart to risk it. But he was the sort of careerist who would always be working at some scheme for getting himself noticed or rewarded by means which would make any decent policeman sick.

'Son, we've got to make it snappy,' the reporter said to me. 'Here's my card!'

The Sunday paper which he represented was the one which specializes in sanctimonious filth. When its readers complain – in pitifully sincere and illiterate letters – the editor publishes their opinions and adds a footnote to say that it is the duty of a British newspaper to publish the facts without fear or favour. That shuts the poor little blighters up.

'Want us to pay for your defence at the Assizes?' he asked.

'I don't mind if you do,' I said, looking cautiously over the lay-out of the room.

That bright young reporter had been scattering his employers' money around. The porter ought to have been in the room, and he carefully was not. The detective and the constable – he was looking a bit uneasy – should not have been there, and they were. The porter's uniform coat and overalls hung on pegs. There was a half-open broom cupboard, full of untidy brushes and cleaning materials. A wide lattice window gave on to an inner courtyard where the bicycles of the municipal employees were ranged in racks. The window could not be more than twelve feet above the ground, though God knew what there was directly underneath.

'Sign that,' said the reporter, 'and we'll get you the best Counsel available.'

By habit I glanced at the contract which he slapped down in front of me. He seemed surprised at my reading it with attention. He even addressed me by name, instead of 'son'.

'It just gives us the exclusive right to print your life story, Mr Howard-Wolferstan,' he explained.

I reckoned that I had better appear a sporting prisoner – elastic, easy and with a proper British respect for 'avin' me nyme in the pypers. It surprised me that they should want it. Spies, after all, come a good second to sex, and are not sympathetic to the average reader. I suppose there was a shortage of material. For the last week or two there had been no spectacular murders, and neither Canterbury nor Rome had had any eccentrically erring priests.

I signed his contract without protest, for at bottom he was a man of enterprise after my own heart; he would have been entertaining in a bar or as a companion in any illegality. But I could not stick his tame photographer, who had the artificial good-fellowship of some mackerel living on the earnings of a prostitute, and just the right face for it. However, I was polite, even cheerful. I did what he told me and showed an interest in his camera. Thank God I had the sense to put on a wide, film-star grin!

There was half a plan forming. I played the publicity

hound. The reporter, who had seen me and listened to me in court, was puzzled, but the photographer naturally assumed that I had a mind like his own. I asked if I couldn't make a picture of both of them.

'A new idea,' I said. 'You can plaster it on the front page. Our representatives taken by the accused himself.'

The detective believed in keeping in with the press. He was all for it, so long as we wasted no time. He told the constable to turn me loose, and the photographer gave me his camera. They all stayed pretty close, however, although I was obviously a harmless and model prisoner.

I took a snap, and then complained that I did not think heads and shoulders were going to be really effective. So I grouped them round the door – to allay any possible suspicion – and myself went to the far corner of the room. At last I quickly tried them sitting at the table, with myself at the side of the window. That, I said, was perfect. And then, without any warning, I fell backwards out of the window, grabbing the upright to steady myself.

I am no acrobat. I do not think I could either have planned or taken the risk if I had not been overcome by the atmosphere which surrounded me – of a certain slimy kindliness, of petty crookedness, of British tastes as reflected in the papers which the masses are supposed – wrongly, I think – to admire. All that, far more than the shock of finding myself a spy and a communist, drove me into not caring if I broke my neck.

As it was, I merely twisted my right arm and bumped my head. The municipal ash-cans were underneath. The one I hit had its lid on, and I practically bounced off it on to the nearest bicycle. The detective hit an ash-can with its lid off. It took him a couple of seconds to climb out.

There was an alley leading out of the yard into one of the

main streets of Saxminster. I took it, just missing the bumper of a horrified driver. Corners, as in most country towns, were close together. I turned three of them at random, and then looked back. There was no one in immediate pursuit. I turned a fourth corner, and found myself in a narrow road with backs of ancient buildings on one side and an endless row of cottages on the other. Here I was certain to be trapped if I tried mere speed; so I propped my bicycle against the kerb outside a greengrocer's shop, with the delivery boy's bicycle to keep it company, and dived into a narrow archway which passed under the buildings on my right. Two minutes since I hit the ash-can? I do not think it can have been more.

The passage led into the cathedral close. There were already signs that Saxminster resented the affront to its administration. Huddled against the wall, I watched a constable dash into the saloon bar of the leading hotel. He didn't want a drink; he was alerting the authorities. An excited group poured out of the bar into the street. Had I really been a communist I should have described them as typical fascist hyenas; they'd have sat on my head at once, and that, to judge by the expanse of some of their riding breeches, would have been the end of me. The Black Maria – no time yet to call up any other police car – was cruising between the cathedral lawns and the lovely fat houses of church dignitaries. A constable was at the corner of the next street; another was running to take his post at the main door of the cathedral. I don't know whether I was expected to take sanctuary or hide in it or blow it up, but evidently the close was the net into which I was to be driven. Naturally enough. If the main outlets from the town were blocked, all other roads led to the cathedral. And there, in fact, I was.

Within the next minute someone was sure to go through the dark length of the passage and discover me. My only possible refuge was a door with a brass plate on it, marked CHAPTER OFFICES. I entered with reverent assurance, as if I had been booking orders for a cheap line in chasubles. The attitude was wasted, for there was no one to receive me. On the ground floor were two offices, from one of which came the sound of a typewriter. The other had a little frosted glass window and a notice: *For Attention, Please Ring*. I decided against Attention, though considering it as a possibility. In these canonical offices no one would know my face, and with a good enough story I might have been allowed to sit down and wait for the Dean. The bicycle – an old, black one – was unlikely to attract attention, and, with luck, it would not be found and identified by its owner for some hours.

The stairs, however, were more tempting. I went up. There were three doors on the landing. Two of them looked businesslike and unceremonious; but the third, a double door of black oak, was ecclesiastic. You could bet that there was emptiness behind – in a worldly sense, I mean. I opened it, ready to retire hastily with an excuse, and found a very fine seventeenth-century hall with a long table down the middle. There the Dean presumably presided over his chapter.

It was too late for any directors' meeting, and so, if canons kept the same hours, their board-room seemed to offer shelter for the night. But there was no cover. The curtains, of faded magnificence and rich in folds, would not do; it might be somebody's duty to come in and draw them. From the walls portraits of seventeenth- and eighteenth-century churchmen looked down upon me. They had the casual air of aristocrats who had merely dressed up in bands and black for the purpose of being painted. I was fortified by their approval.

At the far end of the room was a gallery with a little curving staircase leading to it – a real, Carolean show-piece, with all the balustrades delightfully carved. I explored it, stepping over a rope of red velvet which hung across the foot of the stairs. Against a side wall were a few stools and benches – probably for musicians – which would do for a hiding-place so long as the person who pulled the curtains and gave the hall its good-night inspection did not deliberately search for me. At the back of the gallery and in the centre of its panelling was a small door. I thought I had better make sure that no one would come in by that, so I turned the wrought-iron handle and gave a firm pull, slightly lifting the door to keep it silent.

It was locked, but the mortice which projected from the panelling seemed to be loose. One is always vaguely fascinated by doors which are supposed to be secure, and are not; so I fiddled with the mortice and found that it could be lifted out of its seating. The flange at the bottom, which should have been sunk into the wood to a depth of two or three inches, had been filed away so that only an eighth of an inch remained.

The door led to a deep, cool cupboard in the thickness of the stone wall, fitted with racks for bottles. The set-up was obvious. The chapter's butler or the Dean himself kept the key of this little cellar, but somebody else had decided that the servant was as worthy as the master. His neat bit of jobbery, which showed signs of considerable age, had never been detected. It was not surprising. Who in so smoothly run an establishment would tug or rattle at the door – which might have torn the lower flange of the mortice clear out of the wood – or who would lift the door, as I had done, and spot that the mortice was loose? Like had spoken to like across the decades.

I looked for whisky. When a man is hot, thirsty and distracted, there is nothing else. It is the sole creation of the

British Isles of universal, irreplaceable value. Parliamentary government? For most countries, an illusion. Bits of machinery? Every sane man wishes they had never been invented. Shakespeare? We could get along very well with Cervantes and Rabelais. But a world without whisky would be the poorer by an essential pleasure.

That is by the way. A mere remembering of my disappointment. There was no whisky. The cellar made no concessions whatever to hot and thirsty vulgarians beyond a tap for rinsing glasses. Three-quarters of the bins were empty. The rest contained only port and Madeira, and I never had any great opinion of either. On principle I disapprove of the dry, fortified wines beloved of the English, and the prejudiced Spanish half of me refuses to admit that the Portuguese know anything of wine. But I now apologize, sincerely and from the depths where lives the palate, to our oldest alliance.

One bin of Madeira bore the date of 1851. There were only four bottles left. In a calmer mood I should not have dreamed of depriving the Dean and chapter of the last of their treasure. I must have been feeling more of an outcast from society than I realized. Or was it the power complex of a man on the run? At any rate, I opened a bottle, decanted it – a last clinging to the decencies of civilization – and restored myself.

Oh, but my dear Dean, my reverend chapter, what a noble wine have you there! If ever, in your weekly mourning for the missing bottle or in the regret that steals upon your souls while listening to Bach upon the organ after evensong in summer, grief is more poignant for the thought that it vanished down the unthinking gullet of some housebreaker, let me assure you that, after the first careless swallow, I sipped it fasting, as it should, I think, be sipped, with no disturbance but the excellent dry biscuits from the tin upon the shelf.

And never was it more gratefully appreciated, never did it make so generous a return. By itself, it called me back to a proper mood of urbanity in which a charge of High Treason resumed its place as a mere triviality in the normal and genial nihilism of mankind.

No more agitated movement was demanded, no skulking under furniture. I had only to drink Madeira and eat biscuits. But one drastic action I had to take. I picked up a brewer's mallet which was on the shelf and slammed back the lock with a sharp blow. Nobody paid any attention. Probably the noise was not so loud as it seemed to my agonized ears. Thereafter I was free to go in and out by using the latch only.

I replaced the mortice and shut myself up in the cellar, keeping close to the large keyhole in order to listen to the evening routine, whatever it should turn out to be. I had little fear of discovery. It stood to reason that the person who tampered with the cellar lock had done so before the war. In these days of high prices and church poverty no Dean and chapter could possibly be robbed of their liquor without noticing it.

After an hour or so, someone entered the hall, drew the curtains and went out. Then all was silent and I emerged into the darkened hall. The double doors had been locked for the night. That suited me very well. The police could busy themselves heavily in the streets while I was tucked up under the wing of the Dean. I had some more biscuits and finished the bottle. With an optimism entirely due to Madeira I slept under the great table until the first light woke me up in a panic.

The dawn mood was not so cheerful. My wholly unjustifiable confidence was overwhelmed by the practical difficulties. I had no money and only the conspicuously well-cut suit in which I was dressed. It had been brought to me from my flat, at my own request, that I might appear at my best before the justices. If I had ever considered that I might be on the run – and, Lord help me, I hadn't even thought that I should be sent for trial! – I should have appeared in the windbreaker and shorts which I was wearing when handed over by Peter to the police.

And where to go if ever I got clear? Ecuador was a sure refuge, for all my friends, including the Chief of Police, would have hailed it as the jest of the year that I should be accused of communism. But was the rest of my life to be spent there in exile? Divided loyalties are hard to explain. In every way Latin America suits my taste and my character. Yet England is more deeply my country. Even its police and justices are in my blood, indispensable – to say nothing of the great Alexander Romillys and the little doctors of metallurgy. Put it this way. I take it that any man or woman would rather be at a generous party of congenial spirits than elsewhere. But you can't make a home of a party.

However disastrous the future, the game now was to see as much as possible without being seen. The gallery appeared fairly safe. Whoever locked up the night before had not bothered to climb the steps, and there was evidence that he seldom did. The balustrade was dusty; so was the pile of ancient stools and benches against the wall. I concealed myself among them. Through the gap between two of the close-set, heavily carved posts I had a perfect view of the hall below.

At half-past eight precisely the porter or caretaker unlocked the door of the hall and set down his brooms and polishes. He was a tall, thin man, with fifty years of respectability and indigestion stamped upon his face, in shirt-sleeves and trousers – blue trousers with a line of black braid down the sides which suggested that, when he had finished his morning chores, he would put on a uniform coat or gown.

He drew the curtains and dusted the window-sills perfunctorily with a feather brush. He then settled down to a serious
and quite unnecessary polishing of the table, which was obviously his real love, and finally placed upon it a cardboard
notice: *Please Do Not Touch.*

I had visualized the Dean and chapter gathered daily round
the table, with sheets of blotting-paper in front of them, to
settle the affairs of the cathedral. But that was clearly wrong.
The beadle went out and returned with a folding-table and
a formidable oak collecting-box, which he set up near the
door. *Chapter Hall Fund. Visitors are Urged to Contribute to the
Repair of the Ancient Timbers* – which harboured not only me
but death-watch beetles. A third notice, CLOSED, went up at
the foot of the stairs to the gallery. Quite rightly. They would
not have stood half a ton of visitors.

This changed the direction of such vague plans, or hopes
rather, as I had. It was clear that I had taken refuge in a
historic monument, used on occasion for its original purpose – witness, the cellar – but normally a mere show-place
for the public. Thus it was a fair gamble that I could live
for a few days between cellar and gallery until all search for
me in the town had ceased. There were water and biscuits
and a cheap port – reserved, perhaps, for the more evangel-
ical clergy – which I might reasonably use for sustenance.
It would, I felt, be an outrage upon the Dean's hospitality
to continue the consumption of Madeira. What had been
excusable at my agitated arrival on his premises would be
mere insolence now.

When the beadle had gone, I considered returning to the
cellar. I found myself reluctant to do so. Sitting there in the
dark was safe, but led nowhere. If ever I were to get a space
of daylight between myself and the horde of angry officials
who were spending their morning in explanations why a

dangerous spy had got away and why they hadn't caught him, I had to be sensitive to my environment.

And pretty sensitive I was a moment later when the police arrived. I ought to have expected them. The bicycle left in the road outside the chapter house passage showed – when at last the greengrocer reported it – that I had probably gone through the archway. A constable and a sergeant accompanied the beadle. He was now wearing a long blue livery coat with brass buttons, and held a silver-topped staff of office. That all helped. It was somehow unthinkable that a criminal should approach the ward of such a personage.

They came up to the gallery, treading with care. The sergeant asked about the door, and was told that it gave access to the service cellar of the chapter and the Dean held the key. 'Service Cellar' sounded magnificent; it implied another vaster cellar, a veritable cathedral crypt, from which every year or so the service cellar was restocked. If I had believed the beadle I might have permitted myself another bottle of the 1851 Madeira. But I didn't. He was only keeping up the prestige of the Established Church.

They neither saw me nor looked for me – though they had only to move a couple of forms. The hall gave such an impression of clean and lovely emptiness that the one spot where it wasn't empty was taken for granted. They discussed me at length. The constable was of opinion that I was hiding in the cathedral. The sergeant, pretending to knowledge of mysterious worlds within worlds, snubbed him and said that Politicals went Underground. This amused the beadle, who pointed out that Cecil Reyvers was the only Communist in Saxminster and that *he* wouldn't be much help to any underground. The sergeant was not so sure. With the full responsibility of his rank he suggested that Cecil Reyvers' bookshop might be a blind and that Chris Emmassin – God

rot the newspapers which publicized him! – had his organization all over England and could spirit a man away to
Russia as easy as kiss your hand.

As soon as the police had gone, I found an overwhelming
reason for movement. The needs of nature were imperative.
I leapt back to the cellar and its empty bottles; and, once
there, there I had to stay for the morning. Sightseers were
arriving at irregular intervals, and I never could be sure of a
free half minute in which to leave the cellar and settle myself
comfortably under the pile of forms.

It was a safe bet that the hall would be closed during the
beadle's lunch hour, so at half-past one, when he was reasonably certain to have his feet under a table, I resumed my
position in the gallery. The afternoon was busy and at first
enjoyable. The beadle had dignity. His tone as he explained
the dates and named the master craftsmen was sepulchral,
fruity, and quite unlike that of the ordinary pattering guide.
Conducted parties of visitors went on and on, and by the end
of the day I knew his little lecture by heart. In moments of
boredom the thing still runs round my head. I wish I could
drive it out by listening to one of the Tower wardens at the
same game; but state prisoners are not exhibited to the public.
A pity. I wouldn't mind coming to an arrangement with my
gaolers whereby I could be examined for half an hour a day
at a pound a head, and we would split the proceeds.

When the day was over and the hall locked up, I ate a few
biscuits, drank curate's port with water and tightened my
belt. The only shadow of an idea which had come to me was
that of borrowing the beadle's livery coat and making my
way through the town in disguise. It seemed worth a trial.
The double door of the hall was easy enough to open from
the inside; I had merely to pull up the bolts which secured
the second half of it.

The chapter offices were empty. On my floor was nothing of interest except a little pantry for making tea, with a large slice of stale cake in it. I ate that – all but a bit which I left, pitted and crumbled, to put the blame on the mice. There was also a box of matches which was invaluable, for I dared not turn on the lights.

Downstairs in the passage was a notice board. The hall was open to visitors from ten to twelve-thirty and two to five, except on Tuesday afternoons when the chapter meetings took place. That meant that my cellar was safe till then, and probably longer – for it was unlikely that bottles and glasses would be produced for routine weekly meetings. In the room bearing outside *Ring for Attention* was the beadle's coat and tricorne hat. I put them on and walked out, leaving the front door on the latch in case I wanted to return in a hurry.

It was a little after ten, fairly dark and not too late for a respectable official to be on the streets. My plan was to work round the cathedral in the shadows and thence, by any lanes which looked deserted, to the outskirts of the town. Crossing the close, I was hailed from a distance as 'Erbert, and asked if I were spy-hunting. I vanished with dignity into a porch and from there slipped round the east end of the cathedral. Out into the reach of dim street lamps again, I was greeted by some cheery soul who waddled out of a pub twenty yards away and asked 'Erbert for the loan of 'is 'at. The only way of escape from him was among the noble eighteenth-century tombstones. In my enthusiasm for any sort of trick which might get me unrecognized out of Sax-minster, I had forgotten that everyone in a small town knew everyone else's business. I fled from cover to cover back to the chapter offices without any further attempts to imitate the walk and bearing of 'Erbert. Almightily thankful that no one had been near enough to be sure that I was not the beadle, I replaced his garments on the hooks and returned to the hall.

That second night I could not sleep. The floor of the gallery was hard and I was very hungry. I was also ashamed of myself. I had proved myself only half an Englishman when my safety depended on being awake to every nuance and custom. I should have known perfectly well that the beadle's coat and tricorne came off punctually on the stroke of five. A Latin American functionary would wear his uniform all night in any café or public place as a matter of course, but nothing would persuade an Englishman to do so – once he had passed the age of ten.

On the Friday morning, after I had eaten the last crumbs of biscuit with more curate's port, I took my place under the benches. Business was brisk and the beadle less fruity than usual. He did his best, but he could not help catching the boredom of his customers. Three-quarters of them were doing the cathedral and chapter house because it was part of their coach tour and they had paid for it – the remaining quarter, younger and more earnest, because it was their self-imposed duty. The collecting-box did well, especially from a party of North Americans who were far more fascinated by the beadle than the architecture. And quite right, too. I sympathized with their transatlantic humanity. I once spent six months in Madrid without ever entering the Prado. Shameful, of course, but I was so occupied by enjoyment of the living that I never had time.

One man remained sketching while parties came and went. He was of a type strangely common in these days, with a fleshy, full face of coarse complexion, and black, untidy hair that looked as if it had never been combed by anything else but greasy finger-tips. Yet the breed is pure British without a trace of Mediterranean blood. I have a theory that many of them are dark Scots who have taken to the arts, eaten too much starchy food and gone to seed.

He was wearing a dark-blue turtle-neck sweater, with coat and trousers. It was a coat and they were trousers, and that was about all you could say of them, for they had neither definite colour nor shape. He was not concentrating on his sketch. Whenever the hall was empty, he padded across to the open door, looked out and listened.

At the lunch hour he had a word with 'Erbert and was permitted to stay on and finish his work. Having seen his restlessness when he thought he was alone, I did not altogether like that. Sketching was not his real interest, though, as I could see when he had his back to me, he was thoroughly competent. He had two different styles – one architecturally exact and one unintelligible. Both seemed to me dull.

As soon as the hall was closed for lunch, he whipped a pair of cotton gloves out of his pocket and set to work on the collecting-box with a skeleton key. The box had a general iron-bound air of being built to withstand the mediaeval thief, but possessed a quite ordinary lock. Though my artist had not, I think, any professional qualifications as a cracksman – beyond some practice and a draughtsman's neatness of touch – he had the box open in a couple of minutes.

The position was obviously packed with opportunities for my escape, though how to take advantage of them I did not yet know. I jumped up from the pile of furniture, regardless of minor crashes.

'We've had our eyes on you for some time, my lad,' I said, advancing down the stairs with the kindly, confident air of the police. After all, I had had some time to study them.

My shot went right home. He didn't protest or ask for pity. He just sank into himself, burning and sulky and resigned to the inevitable.

'It's not as if I were robbing an individual,' he said, with a good, educated accent.

'And all right so long as it goes into your pocket, what?'

'If you put it like that, yes,' he answered, looking at me with sudden insolence.

I remembered that I was unshaven for at least a day longer than he, and that my suit was a good deal dustier than that of a plain-clothes detective.

'And what about all the church offertory boxes?' I asked him. 'I tell you, I'm sick of sitting up all night for you under pews and tombstones.'

After that I had him where I wanted him – running through in imagination the prison sentence ahead. He obeyed without question when I told him to take off his gloves and lock the box up again. It occurred to me that I was a far more likely criminal than he, and that the guilt had better be settled before we went any further. I forced down his fingers on the inside of the box before he shut it up.

'I'll tell that to my solicitor,' he said.

'But the magistrates won't believe it of Saxminster police,' I assured him.

I told him to pack up his drawing-board and pencils and to precede me up the stairs to the gallery. He, of course, assumed that we were going out by the cellar door. So we were – but my difficulty was to prevent him seeing that it led nowhere.

He waited opposite the door for me to turn the handle, and I pretended to think that he was meditating escape. I ordered him sharply to turn round and lock his hands behind his head.

'You don't want another six months for resisting the police, do you?' I asked in the reasonable, firm tone that was so familiar to me.

While he stood with his back to me, facing the hall, I opened the door.

'Six paces backwards – march!'

He obeyed, grumbling. It was luck that he had never been in the hands of the civil police before, but I think he may have had trouble with the military. At any rate he shambled backwards into the cellar as if he were used to meaningless severity. I then turned him about, and shut the door on the pair of us.

'Could we possibly have some light?' he complained.

I found it hard to be polite to a nasty piece of work which lived by robbing collection boxes. An honest burglar – whom, of course, I could never have deceived for a moment – would have been far more congenial company in the cellar. However, there was nothing for it but to use a sympathetic approach. A struggle in the dark might be overheard, or end with the wrong man being hit over the head by a bottle.

'You're a very lucky fellow,' I said.

'And why?' he sneered.

'Because I am not a detective.'

'My opinion of the police is restored. Shall we go on?'

'We've arrived,' I answered. 'There is no on.'

That made him think a bit. It was pitch dark and he was at the far end of the cellar. All he could feel were stone walls. I myself was in the little bay where the wine was kept. He could tell by my voice that I was in some other passage, but he could not possibly guess that the space was as confined as it was.

'Are you hungry?' I asked him – not that I had anything to offer, but I wanted to know with what sort of man I had to deal.

'Not particularly.'

'Then why the collecting-boxes?'

'Because I myself am a more deserving charity than ancient timbers. What's your racket?'

'Very simple. I want your clothes in exchange for mine, and your sketches and drawing-board.'

'You won't get 'em.'

'Yes, I will. I'm a deserving charity, too.'

'By God!' he exclaimed. 'You're the escaped spy!'

'Quite right. And you're shut up in the dark with him in a place he knows and you don't.'

'Try that game, and the noise we'll make will be the end of you.'

'End of you, too. I'll bet you left your fingerprints on a dozen church boxes before you took to using gloves. Besides, be reasonable! What do you care whether I'm a spy or not?'

'Well, I don't much. And that's a fact,' he answered in a tone of surprise and self-satisfaction. 'Curious how one can never get rid of primitive reactions!'

'In that case you have everything to gain. You'll get six or seven pounds from any dealer for my suit, and that will make up for your own clothes and the quid I'm going to borrow off you.'

'I haven't got a quid,' he said.

'I'll make it two – if it isn't in your trouser pocket when you hand 'em over.'

'Damn you! They're too long for you.'

'Too wide, but about long enough. Hurry!'

'Look here,' he protested, 'how do I know you won't leave me here stark naked?'

'You don't know. And if I have to leave you here, it won't matter.'

'Well, if you want to be hanged—' he began.

'You bloody fool!' I answered with gusto. 'Don't you realize I'll be hanged for High Treason, anyway?'

That really broke through his arrogance, and he sounded ready to panic. I certainly did not want hysterics, so I passed my own trousers in his general direction to restore mutual confidence and asked for his own. They had the quid in the pocket, too – as well as some small change that he was in too much of a hurry to remove.

He was restive during the afternoon. I do not think he had ever sat still for so long in all his life. Whenever we heard 'Erbert's voice droning away in the hall below, he was inclined to make little noises – accidentally as it were. I had to remind him that, since he had no use for patriotism, he had nothing to lose by keeping quiet, and that if he didn't I had a wooden mallet handy.

After nightfall we walked out together, and in the cathedral close I said good-bye to him with apologies. I felt inclined, as the older man, to tell him to mend his ways, but under the circumstances he was hardly likely to care for my opinion. I merely impressed it on him that if the police got hold of me through any information of his I should tell them to check the fingerprints inside the collecting-box with others on their files.

'Howard-Wolferstan,' he replied, 'I sincerely hope you get away. I want to read some morning that you have been liquidated with every possible Russian refinement.'

I put my faith in his drawing-board and sketches, which I held carelessly open on a level with my chest, as if I were just on my way home, deep in thought, from an evening's work. For the rest, my face had three days' scrub on it, and I arranged my hair to make myself unrecognizable to a casual glance. After all, a woman can change her whole appearance, and character as well, by monkeying with her hair, so why not a man? I have always worn my own neat, parted and rather long over the ears. I wetted it from a puddle – for no

49

one could tell the difference between grease and water in the dark – and then made it look as if it were only kept out of my eyes by continual, nervous movements of the fingers.

I simply trusted to different clothes and different bearing, and whether I was ever closely examined by police I do not know. Keeping my eyes helplessly on my sketches, I made little effort to avoid lights or people, and tried to keep an even, innocent pace until I was clear of the town. Then I took to open country and footpaths, moving fast but very cautiously south-east, and by two a.m. had the best part of twelve miles between myself and Saxminster.

I was impatiently hungry. Impatiently rather than physically. Wine and a pound of biscuits – to say nothing of a substantial slice of cake – are quite enough to keep a man going for fifty-six hours so long as he is well-fed to start with. I have known much worse. But I had to think, sanely and impudently. You can't do that on an empty stomach. And at the beginning of June the English countryside produces absolutely nothing to eat: no berries, no harvest.

I had asked my nihilistic friend in the cellar what he did when he was broke and really hungry. 'Pinch milk bottles, of course,' he replied, as if everyone knew that. To swipe the baby's milk off the doorstep before the family woke up was a crime entirely in keeping with his character. But what of it? My own crime fitted my character, too – or at any rate my upbringing. A fat and sleepy lamb. I cut him up with my pocket-knife and built a small fire in the middle of a copse and grilled his chops, inadequately, on the ashes. It was an anxious business, but, when there was light enough to see smoke, only red embers and a pleasant smell remained.

Burying all traces of my sheep-stealer's feast, I lay down out of the wind and considered what on earth was to be done next. My strong impulse was to make for the nearest port,

Bristol or Southampton; but it stood to reason that the ports were just where the police net would have the closest mesh. An experienced stowaway who knew all about seamen's pubs and seamen's papers might be able to slip through, but I did not think much of my own chances. London, then? But hadn't I read that all wanted men tried to disappear in London? And how the devil did one live in London – apart from pinching milk bottles – with no money and no identity?

I think what really influenced me against the life of a fugitive in a town – certainly as sordid and depressing in reality as in imagination – was the grey village down the hill towards which my feet were pointing. It was just waking up, and satisfying to all senses. I could smell the wood smoke drifting up from the new-lit breakfast fires and hear the distant clink of a bucket where some honest woman preferred her well water to the tap for making tea. The harmonies of English summer sights, which affect me more deeply than any ingenious arrangement of sounds, led from movement to movement, each one expected and yet individual: the colour of roofs, the early-morning mist on water, the flowers in the rectory garden, the long shadows of hedges and elms on meadowland, the leaping green of hill turf.

Damn it, I thought, if I am going to hide, let it be where I can enjoy myself! And if I am caught, at least I shall have a few pleasant days to remember. I knew what I was talking about. I'd had ten days in gaol. And during all of them I was keenly conscious of the pleasure which my memories of a May night and Dr Cornelia were providing.

So I was all for staying in the country, so long as I could quickly put a good many more miles between myself and Saxminster, and then find a quiet spot in which to grow a beard. Movement was the difficulty. Any simple alteration of my appearance would pass in the dusk, but to travel in daylight by public transport or to trudge along the roads was asking for trouble. I had not seen a paper since my escape, but I had no doubt that my photograph was now familiar to every reader of English between Land's End and Alaska. There had been no such sensation since the reappearance of Chris Emmassin in Moscow. For headlines I expect I beat him. He had only deserted, whereas I had escaped from the magistrates' court in broad daylight with – for surely one could trust the newspapermen to add it – all the atomic secrets of the nation.

Lying on the hillside and poetically digesting the loin of that unfortunate and unrationed lamb, it occurred to me that since I was a communist to the whole world except myself, I might as well get some help from my fellow outcasts. True, I only knew one, and him by hearsay – poor Cecil Reyvers, who kept a bookshop in Saxminster. He sounded like a local joke, more resembling a harmless atheist or anarchist.

Down in the village the red box of a public telephone glittered in the morning sun and tempted me. The police, against their better judgment, would probably be keeping an eye on Cecil Reyvers' shop, but they could not think the town eccentric of such importance that his telephone would be tapped. Whose signature was necessary to tap a telephone? The Home Secretary? A Justice of the Peace? I could not remember. If done at all, it was probably with a sound John Bullish denial that such an outrage was possible.

I was sorry for Cecil Reyvers, but I was going to larn him to be a communist. I waited till ten to give him plenty of time to arrive in his shop, and then walked down the lane which led from my copse to the village of Kingston Dray. I passed a few people, but they did not pay the slightest attention to a scruffy and preoccupied artist. My disguise was better than I realized at the time. A well-dressed South American type was what my fellow-countrymen were looking for. The newspapers, as I found later, had impressed on the public that I was a handsome Latin. Some of them called me slick, and others called me sinister; but they were all agreed – damn them! – that I was a maiden's dream out of a cheap dance hall. At that period there was no photograph of me available beyond the picture, taken in the courthouse, with the unrecognizable grin, and none in my flat for the police to collect. I dislike photographs of myself. They always make me look too dark.

I found the number of Reyvers Library, and took the risk. When I had him, after an intolerable delay, on the other end of the telephone, I first asked him if our conversation could be overheard. He answered in a testy high voice that it certainly could not, but that he didn't see why . . .

'I have been instructed to get in touch with you,' I interrupted.

'What can I do for you?'

'You have a car, comrade.'

He hesitated. I expect that 'comrade' was what he least wanted to be called in that particular week.

'I have. Who is that speaking?'

'It is unimportant who is speaking,' I answered authoritatively. 'My information is that you are not yet being followed. Is that correct?'

'Yes,' he said, alarmed. 'No, I don't think I'm followed. Why should I be? I never have been.'

'Very well. Be at Kingston Dray in about an hour. Turn up the lane to the copse above the village, and wait under the large oak on the right-hand side at the top of the hill.'

'I'd like to know a little more—' he began, asserting himself.

'You will,' I told him. 'But obey now, and the party will not forget it.'

He did not sound as if he cared whether the party forgot or didn't, but finally agreed to come.

I observed him carefully through the hedge as he sat in his car. He preserved a poker-faced grimness, in which might have been just a shade of self-satisfaction. I had expected some wishy-washy, provincial intellectual with grey wisps of hair curled over his collar and none on his head. I was quite wrong. Mr Cecil Reyvers was red-faced and farmerish. Communist or not, he might turn out to be a regular John Bull. Alternatively, he might insist on his right to receive proper orders. I didn't like it at all. However, it was most improbable that he would dare to give me away.

'Good morning, comrade,' I said to him.

I had emerged from the hedge when he was looking the other way, and was now leaning on a gate as if I had been there, invisible, for minutes. He was obviously startled, but set his face to blank.

'Good morning,' he answered, and waited.

'I am Howard-Wolferstan.'

It was astonishing to see so red a face turn pale. A monstrous improbability like the popular conception of a chameleon!

'I'll have nothing to do with you,' he said. 'I have no instructions.'

'You can't avoid it, comrade.'

'You're a spy,' he began indignantly.

That gave him away completely. He was nothing but a liberal with an intellectual chip on his shoulder – a communist, in fact, just to annoy the stolid society of Saxminster and give himself a sense of martyrdom. Any security officer would have known at once that he was nothing but a pest and likely, if there were ever a communist government in England, to declare himself a tory.

'We do not employ spies,' I replied coldly.

'No. No, of course not. But we are not expected . . . I mean . . . well, it's admitted there is such a thing as patriotism.'

'There is indeed.'

'I am an intellectual,' he protested. 'The party has no right whatever to ask this sort of thing of me.'

'The party has a right to ask anything of you.'

'Then I insist on being instructed in the proper way.'

'You are being instructed in the only possible way.'

He was hopelessly out of his depth. So was I, for that matter. I am sure he should have flatly refused to help me unless told to do so through the usual channels. Yet he could not doubt that I was a communist. The papers had said so, and I myself had said so in court. It would have amused me to ask him if he believed all he read in the capitalist press.

'I won't have anything to do with you,' he insisted. 'I shall resign from the party.'

'You can resign when you like and as often as you like, comrade, but you will obey now.'

'I don't see what they can do to me if I refuse,' he said sturdily.

'You ought to know. You have been engaged on propaganda.'

That was a safe shot – though I doubt if he did anything but talk communism in and out of season. However, he would call that propaganda; so would the party whenever they wanted to make him feel important.

'How would you like it to be spread all over the town that you assisted Howard-Wolferstan?' I asked.

'It would be a lie.'

'Would it? What are you doing here? Why are the tracks

of your car in this lane? Where did you tell your office that you were going, and why aren't you there? You ought to know that we have ways of giving information to the police.'

'Nonsense! You couldn't prove it, and you have nothing to gain by it.'

'Nothing to gain by it, comrade? Nothing to gain by punishing disobedience?'

'I'll denounce you to the police myself,' he said.

'No, you won't. Whatever else you may be, you are not a traitor to your class.'

Cold sweat was dripping down my ribs. I could not have continued this duel much longer. But it was near the end. I had him completely bewildered.

'That's true,' he muttered, and then shouted at me: 'But you leave me alone!'

'Oh, be logical, comrade!' I insisted patronizingly. 'You're not a scab. You'll never go to the police. So you're as guilty as I am from their point of view. You might just as well help me and keep us all out of trouble.'

'What do you want me to do?' he asked.

'Drive me where I tell you. Salisbury, for a start.'

On the journey I did my best to make him feel that he was a gallant party member serving the peaceful future of the world; his mind had to be kept from brooding on divided loyalties and kindly, understanding policemen. But in spite of all my courtesy and eloquence I could not strike a spark of enthusiasm out of him. Of course it did not help matters that he should have to make some slight pecuniary sacrifice for the party. At Salisbury I made him buy me an oilskin coat, a cooking-pot, matches, torch, shaving things and a comb and mirror. And when we arrived at a promising lonely track, which seemed as good a destination as any, I relieved him of his spare cash and gave him a receipt for it.

I never like to part from a man on bad terms, so I thanked him with noble emotion, and asked him if there were anything at all the party could do for him.

'Yes,' he said. 'They can allow me to resign.'

I assured him that they would. I think it quite certain that they did – the silly, sturdy, little man!

Where he left me was the edge of Cranborne Chase. I remembered that remote bit of country from twenty years before when I stayed nearby with the wife of the headmaster of my progressive school. *Honi soit*. She felt that I must be lonely in my holidays. The thickets of the Chase seemed to me fairly safe to inhabit while letting my beard grow. That was what I wanted – a short, black beard to go with the drawing-board, thoroughly untidy like the rest of me but with the dirt of the careless rather than the tramp.

At least three weeks of discomfort would, I reckoned, be necessary; but not much more, for this Mediterranean chin of mine needs shaving twice a day. My poor mother's family were quite remarkable for the luxuriance of their beards and whiskers, and the speeches which issued from those romantic and usually political coverts impressed out of all reason the clean-shaven Church and the merely moustachioed Army. Long before the communists ever thought of it, my ancestors lived by the theory of continuous revolution; but they weren't such damned fools – for they had all had good classical educations – as to believe that revolution settled anything beyond the temporary question of who was going to pay the taxes and who was going to spend them. Even in my few months of youthful craziness I agreed with them. What I was after then was the unity of Europe. My communism was a mere exasperated protest like that of poor Cecil Reyvers.

My short stay as a wild man of the woods in Cranborne Chase was intensely unpleasant. It rained. I caught a cold.

And although my chosen square mile was uninhabited it had disadvantages. There was some kind of school nearby, and small, excitable boys were always popping up in unexpected places. Fortunately they never for one moment kept their mouths shut, and gave me ample warning of their approach. There was also a gamekeeper, eternally playing nursemaid to pheasants and partridges, and accompanied by dogs. I gave up attempting to use the ground in daytime. I made myself a chimpanzee platform in the heart of a glorious evergreen oak, stocked it with stolen sacks to give some warmth and only came down at night to do my foraging and cooking.

There was not much to cook – a few carrots from cottage gardens and the eggs and squeakers of wood-pigeons. Their nests were plentiful, and often within reach of a ravenous climber. I just managed to endure ten shivering days, but could stand no more of this forest euphemistically called temperate. I still had no really convincing beard, and abandoned the project. Instead, I gave myself a bald head – it took hours of experimenting with a safety razor to arrive at the effect produced by nature – and sideboard whiskers down to the lobes of my ears. These connected with the growth of hair which starts close under my eyes, and changed my high-cheekboned, narrow face to a square one.

This gypsy-like appearance was out of keeping with the original character, so I thought myself into a more swashbuckling part – the frank and loud Bohemian, easily sure of hospitality and with a taste for free beer rather than stolen milk.

I had spent nothing, so, when I took the road, I had some nine pounds in my pocket thanks to the generosity of Mr Reyvers and my companion in the service cellar. This wealth was reduced to three when I had bought an army pack, a few oil paints, a folding easel and a couple of canvasses in

Shaftesbury. I preserved the portfolio of sketches in case I were ever asked to draw. I can't. I draw as primitively as a child of six. But someone in authority once told me that the child's was the correct approach to abstract art. So I decided that abstract art would be my line. I did not expect my work to interest a dealer – unless I signed it Howard-Wolferstan – but hoped it would be good enough, in any emergency, for a baffled public.

I felt reasonably confident, for the newspapers had dropped me. They and the public were obsessed by the search for a gentleman who had ingeniously drowned his wife in four inches of water, and I don't suppose the average reader, confronted by photographs of both of us, would have cared or remembered which was which. Meanwhile, I wandered north through Wiltshire, sleeping rough, eating cheap and discreetly wasting time until it should be assumed that I had left the country.

On the fourth day I came to a village green where a cricket match was about to begin. A tent was set up, the pitch marked, and the home eleven waiting for the arrival of their opponents. I settled down on the grass to watch, for it is a game I have always enjoyed. Sheer skill. No violent and unseemly exercise. No freezing with cold or getting rubbed in the mud. And it has about it the atmosphere of *fiesta* – not of red and gold, but of green and white. Cricket, paradoxically, is the English diversion most likely to be appreciated by any lover of the Spanish way of life.

This was the perfect afternoon for it, warm and windless, with the wicket drying after rain and white geese wandering from common to pond like a solemn party of selectors on their way to the bar. The home eleven was true to village form. Six of them were local gentry in ancient, yellowing flannels; four were dressed as they pleased; and one wasn't there at all. The captain was a tall, fair fellow, who seemed altogether too diffident and indecisive. A type too common in our countryside. The squire without land; the parson without a congregation; the former colonial servant with nothing to serve. It matters so little what they do that they cannot help showing they are aware of it.

'Lovely day, sir,' I said as he passed me.

His eye fell on me with alarm and disapproval. However, I was evidently settling down to be an interested spectator, so he could hardly be impolite. He continued with me the anxious debate which he was carrying on with himself.

'But I daren't put 'em in if we win the toss,' he objected in answer to nothing. 'We might never get them out.'

'They're all that good?' I asked.

'County second eleven, most of them.'

'All the same, on that drying wicket—'

'I know, I know,' he said desperately. 'I know.'

'Let me bowl,' I suggested. 'You're a man short, aren't you?'

He was more alarmed than ever. I might be respectable, but I was dirty.

'O'Reilly had a bald head, too,' I encouraged him.

That made him smile.

'What's your name?' he asked.

I had not really decided on a name, and he took me by surprise.

'Michael Bassoon,' I answered. 'I'm a painter.'

I was hopelessly out of practice, but I thought I could probably bother the reserves of a second-class county after a wild over or two. My medium-paced off-break had always been phenomenal, though more impressive to a spectator than a steady bat. I could never keep a length, and it was not much use to make the ball jump sideways like a startled hare when it pitched as a long hop.

The game was short and brutal. I took six wickets for nine, and we had our opponents all out for something under fifty. But it was too soon. The pitch was as treacherous for us as for them. We scored thirty-nine. I nearly decapitated a goose with a six into the pond, and was clean bowled trying to do it again.

After the game we retired to the village pub. When the diffident captain had supplied me with a pint, he frightened me into hiccups by remarking:

'I've never seen an off-break like yours since Howard-Wolferstan's.'

'Good Lord, you mean the spy!' I exclaimed.

I cursed myself for my intemperate longing to play cricket again. My reply must have sounded wildly unnatural, but the tone, I suppose, passed as surprise and interest.

The name caught the attention of three or four other members of the team who were standing at the bar alongside. That was what the captain intended. He could at last claim some serious attention.

'That's the man! But I don't think he was a spy.'

'Did you know him?' I asked.

'Oh, I knew him very well at Oxford. No more sense than a monkey! I can imagine him robbing a bank, but he never cared enough about anything to be a real communist.'

A libellous character! Still, I must admit that at the age of twenty I had not reached the responsibility of later years. He did not know me. He had merely heard of me, and very inaccurately. We may have had friends in common. But he had evidently watched me often enough playing cricket, and, talking to a stranger, it was a forgivable social lie to claim my acquaintanceship.

'He admitted that he *was* a communist,' I said.

'My own speciality at that age was black magic,' he answered surprisingly. 'One would look back on those things with shame if they weren't so absurd.'

'But then what was he doing at Moreton Intrinseca?'

'After women, of course. That was his hobby.'

I regretted that I could not show my indignation. Women have never been of great importance in my life. I delight in them immensely, yes. But I have never been under the influence of one woman for more than a month.

'At least,' I said, 'it is one of the few hobbies which can be enjoyed by both sexes.'

That amused the party. Howard-Wolferstan was forgotten in the excitement of having amongst them a lecherous Bohemian straight from Chelsea. The cricketers listened to indecorousness as fast as I could invent it. It's odd that the English should always consider that painters have the morals of stud bulls. I find it hard to believe that the creative mind can live in a state of excitement so continuous as that of the average business man.

Among my audience was the wicket-keeper. Courtesy demands that even in the private papers of a Traitor the name I give to him should be false. But a name of some sort I must use, if only for my own convenience. Flesh, character and name seem to be equally essential for solidity. Leave out the first, and you get something which interferes with the second law of thermodynamics. Leave out the second, and you have an exhibit at an agricultural fair. And without a name you have an unsatisfactory reality, as of some haunting woman once seen and never forgotten.

Robert Donolow – that's the wicket-keeper – was a farmer and looked it. He was a man who could look any part so long as it called for a good presence and an honest geniality. He had been, I gathered, a diplomatist. The same face, with a

little more pallor, would have suited that cheerful profession
equally well.

'Where are you off to?' he asked.

I answered that I was going nowhere in particular, and
that if I couldn't find a cheap pub I should put up at a cottage.

'Why not come back with me and stay the night?'

In such an atmosphere of bluff good-fellowship I could
not possibly refuse; yet the invitation was somehow suspicious. Even admitting that I was well-spoken, intelligent and
could bowl, I was not the sort of person whom I myself – if
I had been myself – would have invited home without an
ulterior motive. I was unkempt, probably disreputable, and
there was no evidence whatever, beyond the portfolio, colours and folding easel, that I could paint.

I got into his battered estate car, and for the first couple of
miles we discussed the match. Then, after a pause, he asked
me:

'Are you a modern painter?'

I replied cautiously that my art was purely abstract.

'You mean that if you paint a cow, it doesn't look like a
cow but the sort of thoughts one might have about a cow?'

It seemed safe to agree to this.

'I hoped you would,' he said. 'Of course one is often wrong
to judge by appearances, but I somehow felt you belonged to
the *avant-garde.*'

He was a bit out of date, but I was not going to tell him
so. The real *avant-garde* – to go by the few shows I had time
to see in London – dressed like stockbrokers.

'And can I guess what your pictures represent?' he asked.
'Or do you have to explain them in words?'

'I don't have to,' I answered, 'but I find it helps if I do.'

'I wish you would tell that to my sister. She paints, too.
But she won't explain. She says it doesn't matter. Oh, you'll

have a lot in common,' he added. 'She's very lonely down here.'

His glance begged me to be polite to her. He need not have bothered. I had every intention of keeping the conversation firmly fixed on her own paintings.

His farm turned out to be a pleasant, rectangular Regency house, which looked as if it had once been the vicarage. Separated from the house by a semi-circular gravel drive was a formal lawn surrounded by flower-beds, in which his sister was bedding out geraniums. It seemed a very harmless pursuit for so advanced an intellectual.

'I've brought Michael Bassoon back with me,' my host announced – and added more feebly when it was clear the name meant nothing to her:

'He paints.'

Veronica put him in his place, answering, 'Oh, yes?' with a casually offensive lift of the voice which implied that her brother might be easily impressed by sideboards and a folding easel, but that, for her, artists worthy of serious consideration were few indeed. However, she shook hands with me cordially enough, and waved away the trivialities of gardening.

She was fond of gestures which were rather larger than life. No doubt they had grown upon her in the cut and thrust of youthful argument. She was, I suppose, about forty, with an arrogantly classical face which must have tended, when she was a girl, to limit her love affairs to those prescribed by the duty of self-expression; but at her present age it was possible to feel sorry for her, and to note that her profile was magnificent.

When I had had a quick bath – or as quick as could be considering the time spent scrubbing the dirt from the bathtub after removing it from my person – I found drinks laid out in the living-room. Robert Donolow's hospitality was excessive from the start; when his sister appeared he had already ensured that my mood should be genial. Severity was still her keynote. Veronica was all black silk – a vaguely Chinese effect – from neck to ankles. The distance between them, though agreeable, was far too long.

As I was now shining with soap and gin, she decided to give me the benefit of the doubt.

'Michael Bassoon,' she murmured. 'Now, of course I've heard the name, but I don't quite—'

'One has to be dead,' I told her, 'before the dealers will publicize one's name.'

She liked that, so I felt on safe ground. The trouble was that I could not be sure how London painters talked. I had to back my knowledge of Ecuadorians. Apparently there was no noticeable difference.

'And what's in a name?' I went on. 'That lovely thing, now' – I pointed to one of the remarkable splodges of colour on the walls – 'I don't know who did it, and what does it matter? It exists in itself.'

'What would you call it,' she asked suspiciously.

I carried my gin across the room, and looked over it at the picture.

'The Composer,' I said.

After all, Latin America is rotten with painters as good as Veronica and I knew what to look for. There was an ink-potty splash of blue in the left foreground and a thing which was certainly an eye with another thing which was probably a finger. The blue exploded north-east into an effective fountain of red and yellow pyrotechnics.

Veronica looked at me with respect, and a refreshing suggestion of humility.

'The Analyst,' she said. 'I painted it.'

It seemed to me that there was little in common between

a Composer and an Analyst, but evidently there was enough for me to relax. So long as I was not expected to discuss technique, I could carry on as an imposing authority. I kissed her hand. Robert Donolow beamed. We had some more gin.

Dinner was simple – cold beef in quantity and an excellent local cheese. Veronica, who was now addressing me shortly as Bassoon, took over the conversation and ignored Robert. He didn't mind a bit, and kept filling our glasses with a youngish but insidious Burgundy. He was a delightfully unselfish brother, entirely content so long as Veronica could spread her wings.

When she had left us alone with another bottle – for she held by convention to that extent – I complimented him on his care of her.

'I say, old boy, can she really paint?' he asked.

He was not in practice and his speech was getting thick. Evidently he seldom treated guests as he was treating me. But I was no longer suspicious of his motives.

'Just as well as I can,' I replied.

'Very fond of her,' he said, 'but farm not the right place for her. Can't afford to give her an allowance, you see. So got to put her up and put up with her, put, put. Am I talking too much?'

I assured him that he wasn't.

'Shu-shuperfluous female,' he went on. 'Poor Veronica. Takes it out of me a bit. I've got to see to the cows. You go and talk painting.'

He grabbed a vast pair of Wellingtons from a corner and tripped over himself into the night.

Veronica was in the living-room, smoking far too many cigarettes. She supplied me with coffee and brandy, and begged to see a Bassoon – a real Bassoon with which I myself was pleased. It was no good showing her the studies of ecclesiastical architecture done by my predecessor between collecting-boxes, and I flatly refused to be responsible for his other work; but fortunately I had one of my own. The amount of alcohol which her brother had poured into Veronica had, I hoped, overloaded the centres of higher criticism. In any case I felt confident – for my mood was expansive – that the work was up to our common standard of originality.

I had painted it in oils while sheltering from the rain in a barn. What I was icily trying to do was to express a remembered colour: that of an Indian-dyed magenta skirt which my *mestiza* nurse used to wear on holidays. I captured it – at any rate towards the outside of the patch – and set it in a lot of emerald green straight out of the tube. I carried my unique painting around in a frame with a piece of cardboard across, because it would not dry. I had not realized that if you intend to keep walking without any fixed base, you must use watercolours or draw.

Frame and all, it was only intended to divert the eyes of policemen from my face. I propped it up on the mantelpiece for Veronica's approval. My magenta patch looked rather like a horse, so I christened the picture Ploughland. She stood back and gazed devotedly. I thought she would – especially after I had explained that I had tried to paint a childhood memory. The field – that was me. My nurse – that was the horse. And the field was green because it had been ploughed the year before.

She swept over the coffee tray with a magnificent gesture, and ignored the damage with a still finer one.

'Bassoon,' she exclaimed, 'I would give anything to be able to afford that! It is the most exquisite, uninhibited infantilism I ever saw.'

'It's yours for a fiver,' I said.

'You can't!' she cried. 'You can't let it go for that!'

She was serious. I tried to give it to her. I made every possible disclaimer, short of shoving it into her arms and covering her with magenta and green. To my horror she extracted five pounds from her bag and forced them on me, protesting that it was robbery and that she should be ashamed of herself. She almost persuaded me that I was an unconscious genius. I can only hope that she was right. Certainly it would have been quite beyond an expert painter to produce such uninhibited infantilism.

Little sister's face was gay with enthusiasm and worship when Robert Donolow returned sleepily from the cows. He never said – didn't even imply – what he must have thought of her purchase. I wonder what made him give up diplomacy for farming. He looked as if he were about to give us or art in general his blessing, refrained, and staggered off to bed.

We followed shortly afterwards, Veronica talking incessantly of plans for my future. There was no opportunity for me to open my mouth. I could well imagine that, as Donolow said, she took it out of him a bit. And I could not even get away at my bedroom door, for he had placed me opposite her at the end of an interminable passage.

Having kissed her hand when it was not bedtime, I couldn't very well avoid doing it again when it was. I hardly lingered over it more than courtesy demanded, but the delay gave Veronica an occasion for dramatics. What gesture she meant to make I do not know. It started off as Candida patronizing her poet; it became regretful – though somewhat alarmed – dismissal. And then she burst into tears. It was most awkward. All her severity had been dispelled by art and Burgundy, and there remained nothing but the classic profile. What could I do? I took the line of least resistance.

In the morning I was tormented by my Latin conscience. It is entirely different from the English conscience. I have both; so I know. A pure Englishman, finding himself in my position through little or no fault of his own, would have bothered about Veronica as Veronica. That was as nothing compared to my remorse at having seduced, if one may call it so (and my Latinity did call it so), my host's unmarried sister. It was a breach of hospitality of which I should never have suspected myself capable.

Veronica, very wisely, had said her farewells and did not appear at breakfast. I was left to face her brother's eyes as best I could. They were still honest and untroubled. He helped me to kidneys and bacon, while I congratulated him on the excellence of his liquor which had left us with only the merest trace of headache. He discussed the morning's news and offered me three different sorts of marmalade. I could only think of my appetite with shame.

Did I want a lift anywhere? No, I did not. I should walk gradually westwards, I told him, into Somerset. He saw me to the door, still with his fatherly expression, helped me on with my pack, lent me a map and said good-bye. And only then, as he relinquished my hand, did he say:

'Be a good fellow, and write to her from time to time, will you?'

The perfect manners of him! The gentle depths of immoral, iniquitous hypocrisy! The basic English desire for peace in a comfortable home! I understand them, even admire them. But I cannot conceive why he should have been so sure that I was a person who, even after the deliberate undermining of his principles and that carefully arranged contiguity of bedrooms, would have permitted himself so to outrage all proprieties.

I wandered across Somerset in the character of Michael Bassoon. As I looked poor and my approach was cordial, I managed to get a few odd jobs. I spent a couple of days hoeing turnips, and the best part of a week replacing a stable-man on holiday; but my appearance was so unconventional that no employer thought of offering me a permanency. In fact, Michael Bassoon was becoming a bore. Economically he was a mere parasite. He could not hope to exploit his genius for abstract art in the country, and he was incapable – though warmly encouraged – of painting an inn sign in return for drink and lodging. There was nothing to be said for him except that he was unhesitatingly accepted for what he wasn't.

That was important, for the newspapers, after forgetting Howard-Wolferstan among the excitements of rape, murder and a millionaire who, cautiously avoiding both, had been divorced for the eleventh time, decided on a noble outburst of British indignation.

WHAT ARE M.I.5 ABOUT? Even I could have told the patronizing columnist what they were about – checking up on my past and leaving to the police the routine job of finding me. WHAT DOES THE FOREIGN OFFICE KNOW? Well, they bought that. It was extraordinarily silly of them to pretend that they knew anything. Then came the LIFE OF HOWARD-WOLFERSTAN on Sunday – a romantic bit of fiction which the public were exhorted not to miss. I had been a bullfighter. I had lived by my bow and arrows among the Indians up the Marañon. My main source of income had been the export of dried heads to Russia from secret airfields in the jungle. I could spot that the correspondent in Ecuador had been pulling his editor's leg, and I was homesick for the party at which these joyous adventures had been concocted for me.

My English career was fairly accurate. It had been so simple. School. Oxford. Cricket. And two years in London as what they called a 'clubman'. But then came the inevitable accusation. During the war, with Christopher Conrad Emmassin, I had been successful in Penetrating the Secrets of British Intelligence.

Hell! Chris and I were much too busy trying to preserve our own secrets. When he turned up in Russia, he could, I suppose, have given them some information about political security – such as it was – in the Andean Republics; but for his new employers that would be the least of his assets. All they got out of poor Chris's desertion was prestige – and a thoroughly overworked and unbalanced brain which never had a chance to recover its quality.

All this nonsense was accompanied by the same old photograph, touched up with different lights to give it a bit of novelty, and some poorish snaps sent over from Ecuador. One showed me in wild country and wilder dress, but did capture my normal expression. I dared not abandon my disguise, slight though it was, and if I had to keep it, bald head and all, then there was no better man to back it up than Bassoon.

Meanwhile I had obeyed Robert Donolow's modest and touching request – it was the least I could do – and written a discreet letter to Veronica into which, I trust, she could read as much affection as she required. She replied to me at the Post Office, Yeovil, in an overmanly style, ignoring the ephemeral accidents of life and enclosing a cutting from some art monthly which she had covered with indignant exclamation marks. She said that her brother had had a casual visit from a picture-dealer named Finster who claimed to know me well and wanted to get in touch with me. As they did not then know my address, they could only tell him I was somewhere in Somerset.

This was alarming. My first impression was that the enquiry must come from the police, and I cursed my folly in playing cricket and allowing a possible identification by my individual style of off-break. On second thoughts, however, I saw that this Finster had nothing to do with the law. If police wanted to talk to Bassoon, they had only to alert local stations and Bassoon would be picked up in ten minutes. Nor could anyone have been put on my trail through cricket, since the captain of the village eleven had claimed to know Howard-Wolferstan personally. Therefore I was not he.

No, the chances were that Cecil Reyvers had reported his adventure to higher authority. He knew that I was in the west country; he knew that I intended to paint, either for fun or for cover. The immediate impulse of Reyvers' committee or cell would be to give information to the police. But that they dared not do. They had two very awkward hurdles to get over: that Reyvers had, however unwillingly, helped a spy to escape, and that I might be taking instructions from Olympian heights far above their ken. The Olympian heights themselves would be doubtful. They had to run me to earth and find out.

The more I thought of this explanation, the more likely it seemed. I was still a member of the party – which would startle them as much as it did me – and I had been caught prowling around an atomic monastery in the dead of night. What they would want to know very badly was from whom I had my instructions. It would never occur to them that I hadn't any. It was inconceivable that a communist should act without instructions. I began to realize that, so far as the party was concerned, I was in a very strong position indeed.

But the risks were unlimited. Rather than meet this Mr Finster, it was wiser to destroy Michael Bassoon – to drown him or let him disappear on a railway journey. I could make him into a filthy old-fashioned tramp with a week's beard. That, however, probably meant that I should be caught in an unfamiliar world of welfare workers, labour exchanges and police, all so anxious to reform me that one of them, sooner or later, would hit on my identity.

As I could think of no safe or reasonable alternative to Bassoon, I decided to play out the comedy with Finster. It might be a risky gamble, but no worse than standing my trial for High Treason. And at least any enjoyment there was would be mine, whereas if I were compelled to listen to learned counsel trying to persuade himself and a jury that I was innocent, all the enjoyment would be his. The more I considered the comrades, the more I liked them. They might be only too glad to smuggle me on board a ship, and if I did not care for its destination – and I probably shouldn't – a port had far wider possibilities than the fields of Somerset and that intolerable man, Bassoon.

After reading Veronica's letter, I strolled out of Yeovil into the pleasant meadowland to the north of the town, giving plenty of time to any interested persons who wanted to catch up with me. My movements since leaving the Donolows had never been in the least suspicious or concealed, so I reckoned that I ought to have been spotted in Yeovil. But nobody followed me on foot or bicycle. Nobody examined me from a car.

Evidently Comrade Finster, picture-dealer, had managed to lose the scent. Perhaps he was plain inefficient, or more familiar with industrial districts than the west of England. And I suppose I was not easy to find without asking too many questions, which had to be avoided.

So I returned to Yeovil, stopped at a shop that sold artists' colours, introduced myself as Michael Bassoon and bought a tube of white. I chattered away for half an hour as if I owned the place, and left the proprietor in no doubt at all that I was on my way by Ilchester to Glastonbury, and intended to paint the countryside as it had never been painted before.

Even after laying this trail it was a couple of days before the hunt got on to it, and if I had not spent hours idling by the roadside I should have passed well beyond Glastonbury. At last, while I was sitting on the bench outside a pleasant little pub and eating a lunch of bread and beer, a car drew up.

Two men got out. One was a sharp-looking, earnest rat of a man. At a quick glance you would have put him down as a disillusioned schoolmaster. The other was larger and smoother, with the air and dress of a minor civil servant. He might have been an income-tax collector or the municipal slaughterhouse manager. I don't know which of them had passed himself off as a picture-dealer. Probably the schoolmaster. There was nothing of the glossy capitalist about him, but no doubt he could talk theory, whether of art or politics.

It was he who opened the ball – briskly.

'Mr Bassoon?'

'I am.'

'I am going to ask you to accompany me to the police station.'

'What for?'

'On suspicion of being Howard-Wolferstan.'

'Cut it out, comrade!' I said. 'You've been the hell of a time picking me up. Sorry, but I shall have to report that there was not the slightest difficulty whatever.'

This was the line I had intended all along to take, but the sincerity in my own voice surprised me. It had been raining off and on for thirty-six hours, and I was nearly out of money.

'You – you are Howard-Wolferstan then?' he asked.

'Of course I'm Howard-Wolferstan, you fool. What have you arranged for me?'

The larger man then took a hand. He was pointedly

neutral. I think he was not sorry – after some days of working with him – to hear his companion snubbed.

'You must understand,' he said, 'that we are only concerned, so far, with your identity.'

'Then get on back and be concerned with something more practical,' I told him. 'It's the merest luck that I haven't been suspected yet. Now, I'm going to stay at this pub until you return with proper orders for me. And you'd better give me some money.'

'We have no—' began the schoolmaster.

'Of course you have no authority. Can't you ever think for yourself, comrade?'

'Is two quid any use?' asked the other, impatiently.

'It will do for the bar bill,' I said. 'You can pay the rest when you fetch me.'

'We shall be back to-night,' the schoolmaster declared, trying to be sinister.

'No, you won't. I shall be very lucky if this intolerable muddle is straightened out by to-morrow night. Now, get on back to London and report!'

I patted them on the back to show that there was no ill feeling and shoved them into their car. Then I picked up Michael Bassoon's stage properties and managed to get a room at the pub just before closing-time.

The fact that all decisions would now be taken for me induced a sense of delicious relaxation. The merits of communism as a rest-cure have never been fully realized – except theoretically and by professional psychologists. It is not a thought which would occur to party members, like myself, who must pride themselves on their dynamism. I dined on bacon and eggs and whisky, slept till ten in the morning, bathed luxuriously, had a chicken killed for me and ate the whole of it. I will not say qualms were entirely absent, but the party peace was far better than continuing the safe and objectless life of that tramp Bassoon.

Another car turned up the following evening. This time the schoolmaster was not in it. The minor civil servant had as his companion an altogether more efficient type. He had a round, fair face; he never smiled as if he meant it; and he certainly was not English – though his trace of accent would not have been noticeable if one had not been waiting for it.

I took them up to my bedroom and ordered drinks. The new, alarmingly genuine comrade put his gin down in one gulp. I nearly told him that he should never do that in public if he wanted to be taken for an Englishman, but decided that bluff, when I used it, should be more subtle.

He went pretty straight to the point.

'I am to give you this letter,' he said. 'We have been holding it for you for some time.'

The envelope was beautifully non-committal, addressed in a semi-educated hand and properly stamped and postmarked. When I opened it, I grinned.

'You recognize the writing?' asked my new comrade.

'Chris Emmassin,' I answered.

I have not the letter by me. It vanished with all the other papers of Bassoon. But the wording was very close to this.

My Dear Cousin

It's of course obvious to me now that all the time we were working together your true loyalty was where mine now is. Your discretion astonishes all of us.

But, as no one knows better than you, too much discretion may lead to an honest worker being deceived by someone cleverer than himself.

Your uncle and aunt are genuinely sorry that they lost sight of you. There have, of course, been quite a number of changes in the family since you last saw us in 1938, and it is quite possible that your particular friends are no longer with us. Assuming that you acted in good faith, uncle tells me that you need have no fear of his resentment and that he is prepared to give you a good job in the business.

If this letter manages to find you, I expect some of the family will be getting in touch at the same time. My advice to you is to trust them absolutely.

'Are you prepared to obey orders?' asked the professional.

'With delight and relief, comrade.'

'Have you any papers you wish to hand over to us for safe-keeping?'

'My dear fellow, I got rid of them long ago!' I answered with a pretence of astonishment.

'Impossible! You were searched when you were caught!'

'But inside the place. Before I was caught. Surely you know that?'

'To whom?'

'Comrade,' I replied reproachfully. 'You really must know that I am not authorized to answer that question.'

'Oh, damn the lot of 'em!' said my other comrade, suddenly becoming more English than international. 'Get him away first, and let them settle up their own bloody muddle afterwards.'

The foreigner looked up rather sharply at this. Even I shook my head in a deprecating manner.

They paid my bill, and we drove amicably to London, reaching Hammersmith after dark. Then came the inevitable plunge into melodrama. I was invited with unnecessary sternness – conventional probably – into the back of a closed van from which I could see nothing. The minor civil servant drove away the car in which we had come. He did not shake my hand. My experience of English communists leads me to believe that they would form a most unsatisfactory fifth column.

Where we drove I have not the slightest idea – certainly well out of London, for after we were clear of traffic we had a fairly uninterrupted run of some twenty minutes. I was hurried straight from the van into the back door of a country house. I had only a glimpse of a stableyard before I was firmly directed – my companion being behind me – through the stone-flagged passages of the basement and into a very comfortable suite of bed-sitting-room and bathroom. There were books. A London evening paper was laid out, neatly folded. A cold supper was on the table with all the necessary drinks. It looked as if I had only to press the bell for anything I wanted. So I could, the comrade informed me; but he alone would answer it.

When I was formally called in the morning and the curtains drawn back, I saw that my room might once have been the servants' hall. The window was barred and looked out on to a narrow, sunk yard on the far side of which was a thick privet hedge with more greenery beyond. This made the room very dark, though no worse than in many a hotel. My attendant advised me not to use artificial light in daytime. I could be sure, he said, that no one was allowed on the other side of the shrubbery, nor could anyone see through it; but it was as well to be on the safe side. He was much more cordial. My behaviour must have met with approval in high quarters.

Chris Emmassin's letter showed me that the game was going as I wanted – provided that the pace did not become too fast for me to keep control of developments. I had been right to assume that, with a changed regime feeling its feet, it might be some time before all the vested interests of the

Russian secret services could be sorted out. Even in my limited experience of Hitler's cloak-and-dagger during the war I noticed that the more secret organizations there were, the less each one knew of what another was doing. As an old member of the communist party, presumptions must be all in my favour. No one would ever admit that all trace of me had been lost. Therefore it had not been lost. Therefore I must have been employed by somebody. But by whom they could not tell until I should be interviewed – which God forbid! – on such a high level that I had to answer.

I kept up an appearance of being confident and grateful; but conversation was not encouraged. The meals were admirable, and the choice varied. The kitchen must have been working for a number of more important persons than myself. I fear that the concealing of a notorious secret agent in the basement was a gross breach of diplomatic privileges.

On the second day, after breakfast, my gentleman's gentleman turned himself disconcertingly into policeman.

'My orders are that you must let your hair grow,' he said.

I refused. I very badly needed my bald head and facial decorations whenever I should be on my own again. But he was adamant.

'I see what they mean,' I told him. 'If I am recognizable as Howard-Wolferstan, I shall be entirely in their hands. But I've got no great faith in the organization on this side. If they slip up and I am arrested as Howard-Wolferstan, where are we then? You report what I say and cable for instructions.'

He went out without a word; and his unknown boss must indeed have passed on my comment by cable or wireless, since I heard no more for a couple of days. It delighted me that the matter of Bassoon's bald head had to be dealt with right at the top. I suspected that they would send for orders if I refused to eat my pudding. However, I lost the trick in the end, and the hair had to come off my cheeks on to my head.

As a hide-out for someone whom it was desired to treat, for the time being, with respect, the accommodation was admirable; on the other hand the solitary confinement was calculated to seek out any weakness of nerve. I assumed that I might be under observation even when alone and controlled my impatience. It was not difficult to pretend, even to myself, that I was a rescued and grateful spy. I was being given just what I had missed as Bassoon – good food and drink and comfort.

My attendant would not give me the slightest indication of when I was likely to be put on a ship. It occurred to me that, when I was, I might not know very much about it. I caught myself tasting the first mouthful of every dish with exaggerated suspicion, until I decided it was folly; there was nothing whatever I could do to prevent myself being drugged or poisoned, so I might as well enjoy the only sensual pleasure I had.

My guess at their methods was quite correct. I remember taking an afternoon nap after an excellent bottle of Roumanian wine. I woke up to find myself on the bunk in a long and very narrow cabin. My coat, brushed, was hanging on a hook. My shoes, cleaned, were on the floor. I was still wearing sweater and trousers. As a Very Important Personage, I could only admire the care which had been taken for my well-being. There was a nasty taste in my mouth but no headache. I might merely have fallen asleep in an easy chair after a rather too self-indulgent lunch.

Discretion, however, seemed to have been overdone. The cabin was three feet wide and twelve long, built – to judge by its slight curve – against the side of the ship within a false double skin. It was ventilated from a shaft and lit by electric light.

I climbed over the foot of the bunk – the only way in and out of it – and explored. A door at the far end led to a neat washbasin and lavatory, and in the middle of the long inner wall was a sliding door, which was locked. There was a very narrow settee, comfortably upholstered, and on the opposite wall a collapsible writing-table about large enough for making notes on Marx with the book open, or drafting one's last will and testament.

I could hear the ship's derricks working, so we were evidently still in port. I had arrived where I wanted to be. But never had I envisaged such cold efficiency. Gone was my chance of vanishing overboard or of creating, at the chosen moment, such an embarrassing distraction that I could slip away to some other ship without anyone daring to use force or mention my name.

The only comfort I could find was that Chris Emmassin might be right and nothing whatever would happen to me. After a searching interrogation I should be dismissed as loyal but a lunatic, and permitted to live out my life in some minor and respected employment. That cabin, however, that three-foot space between white-painted steel walls, was not conducive to optimism. I panicked. I greatly desired to press the bell-push above my bunk.

After a wash and a severe reminder to myself that analysis was more fitted to the Latin mind than misty and Atlantean terrors, I did my best to analyse. With unreasoning pessimism cleared away – and all optimism going too – it became perfectly clear to me that I was bound to spend the best years of my life in confinement. Assuming that there was any choice, in what country was confinement preferable? If I had to choose between the over-scrubbed respectability of an English gaol and a prison camp in the tropics I should unhesitatingly choose the latter; but a prison camp within the Arctic Circle, ten thousand times no! Very well, then. The ship, under God and the Master, should reach her destination, but I, under God and in despite of the Master, would not. I pressed the bell. At least it should bring the usual excellent service.

Almost immediately the door of my cabin slid back, and an officer entered in the uniform of the mercantile marine. My first impression of him was that he was a European – that is to say, his face had some meaning in it and his smile was casual. His features were sharp and sympathetic. A pleasant type of customs officer he might have been, experienced in catching the wrong 'uns and welcoming to the rest; or, discounting the effect of his uniform, a wide-awake shopkeeper with a fine sense of the idiocy of the public.

'You feeling O.K.?' he asked in serviceable English.

I said I was, and congratulated him on the excellent arrangements for my embarkation.

'Not bruised, no?'

I felt myself over. My hips were in fact bruised, but I had not noticed it, putting it down to discomfort caused by the narrowness of my berth.

'You need the doctor?'

My answer to that started off our relationship on the right foot.

'We don't want to bring him in if it can be avoided,' I replied.

He laughed, delighted to find that I appreciated all the reasons for my journey from nowhere to nowhere.

'My cabin is full of straw from the crate,' he said.

'Shall I help you to clear it up?'

'Very kind. But don't make a noise. No one knows you are here. Only me and the captain.'

He beckoned me through the sliding door, and we passed out into his cabin through a wardrobe and between his hanging clothes. A dash for the outside? England and stand my trial? I decided against such berserk childishness. One is so much more likely to find safety by playing on human nature than by offering it violence.

I had come on board in a crate. The crate had been delivered to this officer's cabin, and removed after he had unpacked me. There were bits of straw all over the place. He bolted his door on the inside, and we swept them up with his clothes-brush and our fingers.

'When do we sail?' I asked.

'Any time now. You would like a drink, no?'

He poured out a couple of stiff vodkas.

'To the heroism of you and such as you!' he said.

It was positively embarrassing. I had not been treated to that sort of thing since leaving South America. I replied modestly that I had only done my duty.

'What about exercise when we are at sea?' I suggested. 'I don't want to spend a week down here.'

'My orders are that you are not to be seen.'

I replied that I would not insist, but that it did seem to me to be carrying security too far.

'I have orders,' he repeated, putting on the proper face for orders, 'to treat you with respect, so far as you will let me.'

I emphasize the pleasant side of the man, because at the time it was uppermost in my mind. I had been expecting that my guard would turn out to be a tough egg with the gun on his hip barely hidden and a reminder to me in his eyes that nobody was innocent till proved guilty. This lively and impressionable officer was a surprise. It was obvious, however, that he was policeman rather than purser – or whatever his tabs meant – and with full power over me.

We heard steps and voices in the alleyway outside, and he had me through the wardrobe and into my cabin with one smooth movement which was effective and not discourteous. I had no time – nor was it necessary – to ask him what would happen if I did not let him treat me with respect.

It was Saturday evening when we sailed. The beat of the engines appalled and condemned me. Even so, I did not wish to be Michael Bassoon again, sitting on the banks of whatever river or estuary streamed past our bows and painting magenta water. I was weary of that oaf. He was a sort of purgatorial existence which could lead to no definite issue, neither freedom nor a prison cell, until I broke away from him of my own accord. Still, I was very sorry for myself. The slow drums of the engines beat for an Englishman who, though somewhat hybrid, remembered with a truly national sentimentality his schooldays and Oxford and those last few months which had culminated so romantically and disastrously in Dr Cornelia. That darling, shut up among her scientists, obsessed me. It was hardly fair to Veronica. But Veronica was fact. I will not say plain fact. That would be both ungallant and untrue. There is, however, an indescribable elegance of passion, an aristocracy of desire, even if expressed by nothing more than a little dalliance, which remains in the memory long after facts are forgotten.

When the ship was lifting to more open water, my attendant turned up with a good solid meal. I do not know how he accounted for it to cooks and stewards. They were probably conditioned not to ask questions. In government circles there must, after all, have been a fairly constant flow of full trays emerging from kitchens into the unknown, and returning empty.

He was pleased to see that I was a reasonably good sailor – the position of that bunk would have given him a lot of work if I hadn't been – and after dinner he invited me out into the more convenient space of his cabin. He locked the outer door which was already bolted, and put the key in his pocket.

He was a Latvian. That accounted for the Scandinavian liveliness which kept breaking through his solemnity. His name was Karlis, and he was a lieutenant of the M.V.D. Before the war he had been, he told me, a policeman in Riga – a specialist in port control – and always pro-Russian. It had been obvious to him that a little nation of two million would not be allowed indefinitely to cut off a country of two hundred million from one of its chief ports. He said – I don't know with what truth – that between the wars a majority of Latvians thought as he did. So, after the occupation, police with reliable records had been encouraged to retain their jobs. While he could not pretend to a solid background of communism like me, he swore that he was completely loyal.

'We cannot all be leaders,' he said. 'We must be content to do our duty.'

'You know all about me?' I asked.

'They told me you had worked abroad as a secret agent, and that you were arrested and escaped. That is enough for me.'

Because he spoke English and had made a number of voyages as ship's security officer, he had been chosen at the last moment and put on board at Riga with orders to be my escort on the return passage. I was again impressed by my own importance. But it stood to reason. Nobody knew what I might say if I were given no help and brought to trial in England. Nobody could be sure that I was not an outstanding agent with a mass of useful information.

I brought up the question of exercise again and asked

85

Lieutenant Karlis if he could not pass me off as a passenger. We were now on informal terms and he gave me a better reason than mere orders.

'Impossible,' he said. 'There *are* passengers.'

They were a mixed bag. Eight English. Two North Americans. An Indian and a West African. All tourists of varying shades of liberal thought. It was Karlis' job to keep an eye on them as well as me.

'When they return, comrade,' he asked, 'will they be under police supervision?'

'Of course,' I replied, for I didn't want to risk offending his mythology.

'But they only want to know the truth about our country.'

'Don't romanticize, comrade! They only want to confirm whatever they believe already.'

'You do not approve of tourists?'

'Certainly not,' I answered sternly. 'And especially when they think themselves qualified to report on truth. This month's truth must always be different from last month's truth.'

He asked me to say that again. He probably had orders to report on my conversation and was very decently giving me a second chance.

'But it is so,' I told him. 'Truth is merely a question of party administration. In capitalist countries what the government says is true and what the opposition says is a lie, or vice versa. The public have no means of knowing which of them is right. Our system is more logical. Since we have only one party, we obtain the same result by the use of the time-factor. This month something is true which next month is a lie.'

'I never thought of that,' he said. 'I wish I understood things as you do.'

When I had passed back through the wardrobe and gone to bed, I was encouraged by this conversation. With my prestige as high as it was, the card to play was muddle. Professionals, of course, would turn me inside out in a couple of minutes. And Chris Emmassin, if I ever had the misfortune to meet him, would make things worse. I knew him. He was loyal to his friends. He would go to the stake for me, and the result of that would be disastrous. We should deservedly work side by side at blasting a canal across the North Pole. Muddle, for what it was worth, had to be played before the ship reached Riga.

The presence of those eager and liberal-minded passengers seemed to offer hope. I saw how I could start to use them and what some of the results would be, but I must admit I did not attempt to foresee the full developments. It was, of course, un-English to take drastic action when its outcome could not be prophesied, but the political instinct of the Latin has always been to blow up what exists and then profit by the falling fragments.

Karlis told me that we should disembark at Riga on Thursday morning. During the Sunday and Monday I made it my business to win his entire confidence. I showed myself nervous at the least noise. I was reluctant to come out of my cabin into his and demanded his assurance that there was no risk. My caution seemed to him very natural. I was reacting from the stress and dangers of my escape, and anxious lest something go wrong at the last moment. He no longer put the key in his pocket when he locked the door. What earthly chance was there that I should try to leave our secure and comfortable suite? I was being rescued, wasn't I?

His free hours when he liked to let me out and talk to me were in the afternoon and late at night. He was sleepier in the afternoon. At night he did not care whether he slept or not, and would sit up till any hour drinking whatever he could lay his hands on for us. He even made a half-hearted attempt to educate me to tea-drinking.

What I wanted were five minutes on deck while the passengers were about. I plotted for my minutes by keeping him up most of Monday night, and, next day, by forgetting to eat my lunch until he returned from his own. I pretended to have been fascinated by a turgid – and inaccurate – English commentary on Engels which he had lent me.

In order not to lose the pleasure of each other's company we took my lunch through the wardrobe into his state-room, and shared a carafe of vodka. I really laid myself out to entertain him, charming him with true tales of Indians and vanished cities above the jungles of the Rio Napo – or at any rate told to me as true. He produced brandy to help my reminiscences after lunch, and again partook freely. After that he could hardly keep his eyes open.

'You have a nap,' I suggested, 'and I'll clear the tray out of the way in case anyone wants to come in.'

Before he could get up, I walked through the wardrobe with the debris of my meal and pretended to slide the door of my cabin behind me, clicking the latch with a finger.

He fell asleep almost at once. I gave him a few minutes' law, and then passed through his cabin, opened the outer door and closed it silently behind me.

At the end of the alleyway was a flight of stairs leading to the main deck. I took them swiftly, seeing no one. On the main deck, near my end of the port alleyway, were two cabin stewards. They caught a glimpse of my back as I dived for a wash-room, passed through it and emerged on the starboard side. There I was close to a companion which led to the promenade deck. At the top of it I was stared at by an officer, but he was some yards away and did not feel sure enough that it was his business to question my identity. And then I saw a row of six deck-chairs with four passengers occupying them. That was what I wanted. I flopped down in an empty chair and wished them good afternoon.

They looked at me with some surprise. I was still wearing the clothes I had taken from my immoral friend in the chapter-house cellar. They had been cleaned while I waited for embarkation, but were pretty disreputable. The half inch of stiff hair on my head gave me the villainous appearance of a Prussian officer or a North American adolescent.

'Been upset by the sea?' asked one.

'A little,' I answered. 'I've been through a lot, you see. I am Howard-Wolferstan.'

A chance to say those devastating four words was the sole object of all my deception of Karlis. If I could remain free long enough to repeat them to a few more passengers, so much the better.

They fairly jumped. Their deck-chairs creaked with horror.

'The sp—' began one, and stopped out of a vague feeling of respect for the flag under which he sailed.

A North American and his wife appeared from down below and hesitated opposite to us. Their arms were full of political philosophy and glossy magazines. I had obviously taken one of their chairs. I got up and apologized.

'Well, say, it's Mr— er—' replied the American, rightly convinced that he knew my face.

'Howard-Wolferstan.'

As he held out his hand, the name registered. His manners were equal to the shock. It is curious that a people whose language and politics are of British origin should have developed an impervious, artificial courtesy which belongs to the Mediterranean.

'That's very interesting,' he said. 'Very interesting, indeed.'

His wife's attractive eyelashes flapped with astonishment. I could hear her mind working. She was frantically reminding herself that I was an inevitable part of what she had come to study and that it was unpardonable to be surprised because French villages had few water-closets, because the English drove on the left of the road, because Howard-Wolferstans had backsides which would fit into deck-chairs.

She was one of those slim, long-legged, wide-shouldered beauties. With the genius of her female compatriots for making the very best of whatever they have, she was wearing a long travelling cloak and hood, grey lined with scarlet, which gave her the theatrical gallantry of a young Hussar officer inspecting his vedettes. I made a mental note of that cloak.

'*You* mustn't believe all you read in the papers,' I told her.

She disengaged her eyes with an effort, and then her hand. She gasped that she would be very glad to listen to my viewpoint.

That made six who knew that Howard-Wolferstan was on board. Fortune presented me with a most useful seventh. He came breezing round the deck, radiating confidence as if the ship were his own constituency. He was that markedly independent labour politician, Elias Thomas Conger, and his face was familiar to me because I so profoundly disliked him. Whenever I – and half the population – get worked up over some act of governmental stupidity or injustice, that professional champion of the oppressed hurls himself unwanted into the fray, and at once transfers all our sympathies to the side of the oppressors.

I slapped him on the back and called him by his Christian name. When he had hopelessly committed himself – I was 'old man' and 'my dear chap' to him in less than half a minute

– I told him who I was. He turned his back on me and fled without a word. I don't blame him. One has to live. And he would never earn a thousand a year at any other job.

Out of the corner of my eye I saw the captain approaching, so I bowed to the company and ran down to Karlis' cabin. He was still asleep, unconscious of the disaster which in a mere five minutes had changed his life. I locked the outer door and returned through the wardrobe to my cabin. I was inclined to laugh and drip sweat simultaneously. I don't think it was hysteria; the two physical reactions were both unavoidable. I lay down, and allowed the situation to develop without me.

It was seven in the evening before Lieutenant Karlis came bursting in on me. The news had been long in reaching him. It had to cross so many discreet gulfs of silence. The passengers could only talk of their horrifying experience among themselves. The officers and crew knew nothing about me. And the captain, while he had unofficial knowledge of my presence on board, possessed only limited authority over Karlis and probably hesitated to ask questions out of turn. He must have guessed that the stranger whom he glimpsed was Howard-Wolferstan, but if I were on deck it was Karlis' business, not his.

'You have been out?' Karlis asked incredulously.

I said that I had several times told him I felt the need of fresh air and exercise, and added, with a beautiful mixture of innocence and superiority, that I couldn't see it mattered. I was safe now, wasn't I?

'You are mad!' he cried. 'I must send them a message what you have done. They can only give me one reply.'

He was touchingly distressed at the thought that he would have to shoot me or drop me overboard.

I assured him that whatever orders he got my execution

would not be among them. I had thought out the moves as far as that.

'You have twelve passengers on board,' I said, 'all knowing my face from photographs and all prepared to swear, when they get back to England, that I was on the ship.'

'It does not matter what they say,' he insisted wildly.

'But you must be very careful to point out the position, comrade. This question will go before the very highest committee, and I think you'll find they give great importance to what the passengers may say.'

He looked at me with resignation. He sensed already that this was a duel between myself and the party over his wretched body. The shape of the cabin helped to give me a moral advantage. I lay back on my bunk with a cigarette, while he could only stand at its foot as if he were my valet.

'You will be punished in the end,' he said gloomily, rather implying that there was little point in avoiding it now.

'If the party so decides,' I answered. 'But you, comrade, well I'm sorry, very sorry that I have had to sacrifice you. But I'll do all I can for you.'

He broke out sobbing, and cursed either me or his fate in some expressive language which I presume was Latvian. He went out, and in his agitation forgot to shut the door. I shut it for him – but decently, after he had left the outer cabin.

Half an hour later he shoved my supper tray into my hands and vanished without a word. He looked harassed. He was already at the receiving end of the wireless messages from Riga. I don't know whether they were yet relaying Moscow's comments, but what Riga had to say was probably bad enough.

At midnight he put in his head to assure himself that I was still there.

'Well, was I right?' I asked.

'You are to be kept alive at all costs.'

'Is that why I have to spread my butter with a spoon?'

'Those are my orders.'

'Quite right, comrade. Don't forget to remove my razor!'

He pocketed it with another tom-cat curse in Latvian. There were times when the self-renunciation of the Russian was entirely overcome by healthy Scandinavian irritability.

'I warn you,' he said, imposing himself in the only way left to a policeman, 'that there is a sentry outside my door with orders to let no one pass except me.'

'Very proper, Karlis. It is essential that I should not be disturbed.'

'You are enjoying this!' he accused me.

'Comrade, I must smile or weep.'

I got him to talk a little, for, after all, the poor fellow had nobody's shoulder but mine on which to lay his head. The captain washed his hands of the whole business. Riga was sending contradictory messages at the rate of one every half hour. They were even asking Karlis, a police officer of no importance, for suggestions as to how the situation could be remedied; but, just like civil servants anywhere else, were unwilling to commit themselves by explaining exactly what the situation was.

'Comrade, if they do not approve of my showing myself to the passengers,' I said, 'there is only one remedy. All the passengers must disappear.'

'But I am not a specialist,' he protested. 'I have not been trained for that. And I have not enough ammunition.'

'Chuck 'em overboard in the dark!'

I was not, of course, serious. It was unthinkable that the naïve eyelashes of the tall American should be lost at the bottom of the Baltic. And nothing would drown Elias Thomas Conger. He would inevitably have floated up the

Thames to Westminster. I was merely underlining the effect of my afternoon's work: that it was quite impossible to stop the passengers' mouths without getting rid of them.

'Signal that I offer to help you,' I suggested.

'Very well.'

This proposal of mine that all passengers should be liquidated stopped the ship – literally stopped it. On Wednesday morning, with only two hundred miles to go to Riga, the engines were silent, and we rocked gently on the summer sea while my fate was discussed, I like to think, by the entire cabinet. Whatever they did to me, the passengers were still there to swear that the spy, Howard-Wolferstan, had escaped to Russia on a Russian ship. That simply could not be allowed. On the other hand, tempting though the solution must have been, there was no way of ensuring that all passengers met a convincingly natural death.

We were still motionless on Thursday. The captain, I heard, was unapproachable in his rage. Lieutenant Karlis and I recovered our old intimacy – so far as intimacy was possible with a haggard man living in a nightmare. The passengers and crew were told that the engines had broken down.

Karlis was receiving no more wireless messages now, but the silence on that silent ship was all the more ominous for that. The storm out of Asia was about to break upon our heads. Even I, the mischievous and unsquashable louse in the pants of the gods, wished that I had ceased from tickling.

It was my move, however. I had played for it, and I had to make it – though the occasion had arrived much earlier than I expected. The august irresolution was so unending that a little help from me might be decisive. I took his bottles away from Karlis, wrote a message for him and told him to translate it into Russian and send it off. He stared at my draft with eyes that were beyond reading.

'Comrade,' I explained to him, 'I am ready to make the supreme sacrifice. The only way out is for the ship to put back and for you to hand me over to the British police.'

'But they will torture you,' he said.

'I am brave.'

He made an appropriate gesture of heroic admiration.

'But you know too much.'

'No, I don't,' I told him. 'Remind them that I don't know where I stayed after my escape. I don't know when I was taken on board or by whom. I can be landed as a stowaway and disowned. Don't you see the propaganda value? The glorious People's Democracies have nothing to do with espionage. We work for peace by cleaner methods than the fascist hyenas. Got it?'

'What about your own organization?' he asked.

'Purely personal. I think they'll see that by now.'

In the last forty-eight hours every scrap of information must have been collected – to the exclusion of all other business in the radio rooms – from any and every department which could conceivably have employed me, and it must have become obvious that I had never been employed at all. Whatever my insane motives, there was nothing of importance I could give away if brought to trial.

'But me? Advise them what to do with you?' Karlis protested.

'You are not advising them, comrade. *I* am advising them,' I replied superbly.

We knocked my proposal into his own officialese, ready to be sent off to Riga whence it would ascend, without a doubt, straight to the heights. Karlis' attitude of reverence, even in his use of both hands to hold the final draft, was indescribable. He might have been some simple Ecuadorian Indian whom I had persuaded that he was able, via the local police post, to send a telegram to God.

The interval between my helpful suggestion and the reply was short – a mere twelve hours. At two a.m. on Friday I was woken up by the ship's engines, and shortly afterwards Karlis hurled himself through the wardrobe into my cabin.

'Your sacrifice,' he panted, 'your sacrifice has been accepted. We are returning to London.'

I was relieved but not surprised. That message from the ship, zealously relayed, must have fallen like manna upon the blotting-paper of those harassed men at the centre of their spider web. It was delightful to think of them – for who does not enjoy the role of benefactor? – wiping the sweat from chewed moustaches, complimenting themselves on their clarity of vision and wandering off arm in arm to punish the vodka and the sandwiches.

O eloquent, unjust and mighty Muddle! As I look back to that moment from my ignominious but distinguished present, I cannot resist a digression in praise of Muddle, for digressions, however unpardonable in a literary man, are historically proper to a Prisoner in the Tower.

Muddle, most powerful resort of the individual against the State, and yet how prostituted! With what ingenuity do we avoid taxes, when with the same weapon we might destroy the complacency of politicians! This world of technicians and economists is more vulnerable than any which preceded it, for there is more to muddle. Inject into it, with all the appearance of legality and innocence, the logic of Alice in Wonderland, and you shall find the planners groping in a world of your creation.

Yet remember always that the answer to Muddle is Violence! When my maternal ancestors were at last compelled to produce the accounts of their provinces or the nominal rolls of the quarter-strength regiments for which they drew full pay, they created Muddle but were careful to preserve their distance and some few rounds of ammunition that would fire. I, too, was assisted by geography to maintain my imaginary but unassailable status. In western countries the risk that the exasperated will resort to violence is slight. And yet, even if the chosen victim of your nuisance be but a municipal sanitary inspector, do not commit it, however great your necessity, before his face!

My fate now depended upon whether or not the captain had been instructed to wireless to London his true reasons for putting back. I thought it probable that the matter would be taken out of his hands. First secrecy, then drama with the utmost publicity – that would be the usual line. Karlis confirmed that I was right. The scandalous presence of Howard-Wolferstan on board was only to be divulged at the last moment.

For two days I gave Karlis no trouble at all. I was a model prisoner, helpful, resigned and silent. It was an easy part, for I needed rest. It was also sound psychology. Karlis had to have plenty of time to think about himself, not me.

He became more and more melancholy, sunk in a monosyllabic Slav depression. He would not let me into his cabin again, but used to sit with me and say nothing when he collected my empty tray. As soon as I thought his nerves were about ripe, I began to work on them.

'A costly business,' I remarked regretfully. 'Fuel. Delay of cargo. And then the poor passengers.'

'They are being given free air passages,' he told me.

'More money and trouble. How unjust life is, comrade! All this expense because I had to take advantage of your afternoon sleep.'

'But why? Why? That is what I do not understand,' he cried.

'You do not need to understand,' I answered gently. 'There have to be some of us who are only expected to obey. But it isn't bad, being a miner. You mustn't believe all you hear. The State is humane. You get enough calories to enable you to work and a little money over. Think of me – tortured, beaten, rotting in a capitalist prison and then thrown out upon the streets to beg.'

He pounded his fist on the wall in indignation. When it was not his duty to be stern, he was easily moved by emotion.

'And escape from the ship before I am landed is impossible,' I said.

So it was, unless I could persuade him to go with me. Together we might have a chance.

'Yes. There is no way out. It is my order to hand you over to the British as a stowaway,' Karlis answered.

I left my bunk and sat side by side with him on the settee. I meant him to feel that we were partners. I said bitterly that I could never be any more use to the party and that at last I was entitled to look after my own interests. He put on his blank, Slav face. He saw what I was driving at, all right; but was afraid to commit himself to what might be a trap. It was hard to believe that a communist hero would countenance desertion to the West.

'Comrade, think for a minute!' I begged him. 'I am sacrificed, finished. My only hope is to live out my life as a peasant in South America.'

It was a good moment to bury my face in my hands and weep. I can do that quite convincingly. I have only to imagine that I am making a manly speech to a Latin audience, and to repeat to myself the nobler sentences of my peroration.

'After causing all this trouble,' I went on, raising my streaming eyes to his, 'after thinking I knew better than the party, after all this deviationist activity, what will be my fate? For the sake of old comradeship I may be allowed to live, but I shall never be trusted. No report of mine will be believed. When we talk now, we can talk as freely as one corpse to another.'

'I am a servant of the people,' he answered firmly.

'Yes, Karlis. But you have no political convictions.'

'You could guess that?'

I begged him not to be alarmed. Old political hands like myself were accustomed, I said, to dealing with men who were not fit for the party, but whose loyalty was undoubted so long as the cash was there on pay-day.

'The first day I met you,' I added, 'I knew that you preferred Riga before the war to Riga now.'

'Is life in England as good as Riga before the war?'

I assured him that it was, though personally I doubted it. You can't honestly advertise as enjoyable to a foreigner a country in which – to use the jargon of economists – it costs a man-hour to buy a drink, and that without reckoning insurance and income tax.

'I would be followed and killed,' he said.

'Not important enough, my dear Karlis,' I replied, dropping that damned 'comrade' for good. 'In England it costs a disproportionate amount of money and planning to have a man killed. You mustn't believe all you read.'

'Chicago—' he began.

I reminded him that Chicago was not England, and that, anyway, his impression of it was thirty years behind the times.

'You've been in the police all your life,' I told him, 'and you know as well as I do that if a man's society isn't that of potential murderers, he can rule out the chance of being murdered. Like everything else in the world, as we communists know, it's just a question of economics. You can be done in cheap if you move in the proper circles. And if you don't, the cost is prohibitive.'

'But would the police ever let me go free?'

'Yes. Ask for sanctuary as a political refugee. Don't try any nonsense about wanting to free Latvia. They'd see through you at once. Just put it on the grounds of self-interest. Say you would be shot if you went back. That's the sort of thing which impresses policemen. No damned nonsense about being converted from this to that!'

He asked how he would live, and I assured him it was easy. Lieutenants of security police were rare birds as refugees, and he could sell the secrets of the M.V.D to the Sunday papers.

'I don't know any,' he said.

He was really being difficult. But fortunately I had not got to explain the capitalist world from the beginning. After all, he had lived most of his life in it. At last I convinced him that an M.V.D lieutenant had only to sign whatever the newspapermen put in front of him, and correct the grosser errors. So long as he did not bite the public, it would never let him starve.

That finished our Sunday night conversation, and I went to sleep at last, feeling sure that I had persuaded him.

But on Monday morning he was back in dejection again. He moaned that he could not be a traitor, that an honourable worker like himself should take his punishment rather than run away. I didn't believe a word of this. Nor did he, at bottom. His scruples, however, were quite genuine enough to make him hesitate until it was too late for action. Time was running short. We should be off the Nore before dawn on Tuesday.

When he had left me alone, I tried hard to make some sort of mental plan of his character – a far harder task than planning action. Character does not lend itself to attack by pencil and paper. One can only close one's eyes, and let the personality of the opponent spread itself all through one's imagination.

The trouble was, I felt, that I had been too flippant, had displayed too freely – in order to gain his confidence – the sardonic bitterness of a man with little hope. It had worked up to a point. I had persuaded Karlis that my own motives were straightforward and purely selfish; but for him self-interest was not good enough. There was sufficient Russian in him to make him unhappy unless he could persuade himself that he was serving an ideal rather than avoiding punishment.

The only bromide I could prescribe was weak. It may be that I lack the common idealisms myself, and therefore do not readily sympathize with those who need them. After lunch, however, I did my best. I told him that he represented the Plain Citizen, not anti- and not pro- but patriotic. How valuable he could be, how helpful to peace and goodwill, if he could convince the enemies of his country that nine-tenths of the Soviet Union thought as he did! How pleasant if they could see with their own eyes that a lieutenant of the M.V.D was not essentially different from a friendly security officer anywhere else!

He seized my hand.

'I will do it,' he said. 'You and I together!'

It was too emotional a reaction to be trustworthy, but I had no time to waste. I took him straightaway into a committee of ways and means, and began to explain to him what his story must be: that Howard-Wolferstan had escaped from the ship in spite of him, and that he knew he would be severely punished.

He objected to that. The official story was that I was a stowaway. How then could he say that he had been on board looking after me?

'You were on board for normal security duties,' I told him. 'After the stowaway was discovered, you were naturally put in charge of him.'

He would have none of that either. It wouldn't stand up for a moment under interrogation, he said. Where had I hidden? How had I come on board? He could never answer those questions satisfactorily in front of a skilled interrogator; and he could not say he had been unable to find out the answers.

'All right, then. Tell the truth,' I suggested.

No, he would not. The disloyalty was too rank. To escape to the West was legitimate; but to say that I had been deliberately smuggled on board was treachery.

'Comrade, it is all too big for us,' he sighed. 'We can only suffer.'

He picked up my tray and turned to go. He was not even dramatic. There was finality in his drooping shoulders. The practical difficulties, from his policeman's point of view, had overwhelmed him.

Only then did I have a flash of real inspiration. It should have occurred to me long before; but I had been so content with the immediate effects of my intelligent suggestions to the Kremlin that I had not bothered to follow them through to their logical conclusion.

'Have you realized, Karlis, that the captain has orders to put you under arrest and hand me over to the British police himself?'

'How can you know?' he protested angrily.

'Experience, just experience. Only you can show the police where I was hidden. Only you know that the government story is a lie. Only you know what really happened and the messages which went back and forth. And only you have anything to gain by giving it all away. You will not be allowed any opportunity to talk to the British police. In fact, I don't think you will be allowed to talk to anyone again.'

He turned pale as the certain truth of this hit him. He stared at me as if I had been a fortune-teller of sinister accuracy who had prophesied his death within a week.

'*You* know as much as I do,' he said.

'Yes, but it doesn't matter. I am a spy, disowned and returned for trial. That act of good faith covers any amount of sins. What I say may or may not be believed, but it can't be proved. And when the ship enters an English port again, there will be no trace of this cabin. The danger, Karlis, is you, not me.'

He put down that damned tray he was balancing.

'And I did my best for them!' he exclaimed. 'Didn't I? Do you not think so?'

Indefinite punishment was one thing; certain death, another. The Slav dropped off him and he stood up, as it were, a naked and very indignant Scandinavian. I told him to go and collect all possible information on our movements and time of arrival. He seemed to be angry because the task was so easy. I had the impression that he would rather have gone straight out of the cabin and scuttled the ship.

During the afternoon hours when he usually slept, we shut ourselves up in my cabin. He told me that I was to be put ashore at Tilbury, to save the long and unnecessary voyage up river. We should pick up a Thames pilot soon after midnight and anchor off Tilbury at dawn. We were not going alongside. Those of the passengers who had accepted the offer of a free air passage would go ashore by the customs launch, if it would take them, or by tender.

There was nothing for it but to slip overboard at night. Karlis, a strong swimmer, was unafraid of this, for it did not matter if he were all dripping from the sea when he hurled himself into the arms of the nearest startled policeman; but for me it was essential to arrive dry and respectable, ready for any opportunity which would enable me to disappear among my fellow countrymen. We had to have a raft or a boat and something to paddle it with.

I read him a lecture on the tides of the Thames Estuary. He knew even less about them than I did, so it was easy to convince him that a swimmer was more likely to fetch up on the Maplins than on dry land. I also suggested that it might be as well to let the ship sail before he gave himself up, and that he, too, had every interest in reaching the shore secretly and dry.

He agreed with me, and at once lost heart. He insisted that he had no chance of laying his hands on anything larger than a lifebelt – no rubber dinghy, no float, nothing. And on second thoughts he doubted if we could even get clear by swimming. The watch, in territorial waters, was alert. Members of the crew had been known to jump overboard, but had always been picked up.

'How?' I asked.

'With the launch, of course.'

I pointed out that at least the launch would then be in the water and not on its davits. He seemed to think that I proposed to take it by force – a one-man cutting-out expedition straight out of the sea stories. Even if I had a gun, he said, Russian sailors would die rather than surrender the launch. He grew quite heated on the subject until I convinced him that there was nothing I disliked more than physical violence. The simpler classes of humanity can be disconcerted so much more quickly by thought than hands.

'Suppose,' I suggested, 'that there *was* a man in the water, but not us.'

'And when he says I pushed him in?' Karlis asked.

A valid objection. But he was becoming far too full of objections. I told him to pipe down for a minute while I worked out the first movement.

'Any of the launch crew speak English?' I asked.

'No.'

'Who would command it?'

He calculated the watches.

'After midnight, the third officer.'

'Does he speak English?'

'No.'

'Then we'll push a passenger overboard. He can't explain what happened to him till he gets back on deck.'

Karlis almost shouted that I was irresponsible, that it was no good at all thinking along those lines. He pictured for me the return of the launch, and the English-speaking captain, who would at once have been called, leaning over the flying bridge and asking questions. The mere existence of the captain seemed to appal him. It was understandable. The dual control got on his nerves. The captain was the only person who could put him under arrest, and the only person whom Karlis could neither bluff nor frighten.

'If the captain wasn't easily available,' I asked, 'would the third officer take your orders – just for a moment?'

'Yes – if it looks like something political.'

'And the first officer, who will be on the bridge?'

Yes, he would too. What I had in mind was beginning to take solid shape, though as yet it could hardly be called a plan. Too much depended on the timing.

'You know Elias Thomas Conger?'

He let himself go on the subject of Elias Thomas, who was pest enough to make one sorry for any security officer having the care of him. He had been carrying his loud and jolly voice into the crew's quarters and everywhere else, and seemed to think he had a special mission to report on the conditions of Russian ships. He couldn't speak a word of Russian or any foreign language, but that did not deter him.

'Are any of the passengers about after midnight?' I asked.

'Not normally,' he replied. 'They are very serious.'

I took pencil and paper, and drafted out his orders. After a lot of alteration they ran, if I remember, something like this:

1. Lieutenant Karlis will make an appointment with Elias Thomas Conger to attend a meeting of the ship's political committee. At 0015 hrs Mr Conger will trip and fall overboard.
2. Karlis will immediately give the alarm, and see that the launch is ordered away.
3. At 0016 hrs Karlis will report to the captain's cabin. He will state that he fears Howard-Wolferstan has escaped and dived overboard. He will desire the captain to come at once and examine Howard-Wolferstan's cabin.
4. At 0020 hrs the captain is shut in Howard-Wolferstan's cabin. Karlis will immediately return to the deck. Howard-Wolferstan will proceed to deck independently.
5. Gangway will be already outboard for pilot. Presumably it will be lowered to receive rescued man. If not, Karlis will order it to be lowered. Karlis is to show marked anxiety over fate of Conger. Though a lousy Menshevik, Conger is an important personage.
6. When launch is alongside and Conger has been carried up gangway, Karlis will order the third officer out of the boat and as many of the crew as he can. Orders should be agitated and mysterious. The objective is to leave one man only on board the launch, who will presumably be hanging on with boat-hook.

7. Karlis and Howard-Wolferstan will descend gangway. Howard-Wolferstan stumbles against hand with boat-hook. Karlis takes wheel and opens throttle.

The tone and to some extent the matter of my scribbling appeared to bring out the best in Karlis. The Scandinavian in him was glad to raise his head for a moment above the limitations of bureaucracy. All the same, he found difficulties.

'The first,' he said, 'is that Conger, Elias Thomas, may be drowned.'

I couldn't see at once that it mattered. I pointed out that politicians had at least one thing in common with the proletariat. They replaced themselves.

'But if he is drowned,' Karlis objected, 'the launch may not return for half an hour. It may then be hoisted straight on board. The pilot may arrive. Nothing will go according to plan.'

'Then you'd better prepare a couple of lifebelts and have them ready to throw after Conger. Where will you do it?'

'Right aft on the main deck. The deck-house will cover us and he will fall clear of the propellers. But the rest is harder than you think.'

'Beyond your powers?'

Karlis had no doubt that his orders, in anything which concerned Conger, would be accepted so long as the captain was out of the way. He had special instructions to humour the man, and everyone knew it. His chief objection was that it would be very difficult for me to hide within reach of the gangway, and perhaps impossible for me to get on deck at all. Where I lived was not exactly known to crew and officers, but they were all on the look-out for a mysterious prisoner who must not on any account be allowed free.

'The stewardesses,' I suggested at last. 'If it were a question of searching a cabin, would they take your orders?'

'Of course.'

I reminded him of the tall American and her easily recognizable cloak.

'Can you get that out of her cabin before she turns in?'

He bothered over the cloak more than anything else. The humanities of policemen are most curious. He was so attracted by the grace of its owner that he felt the deliciously gallant cloak was sacred.

'You are much too broad for it,' he said.

'It will do to get me on deck so long as I am careful not to meet anyone face to face – and for running down the gangway in hysterics, eh?'

'Suppose she notices it has gone?'

'The stewardess will be instructed,' I answered patiently, 'to say she borrowed it to take the measurements. She wants one made like it. And get me a pair of her stockings and her bedroom slippers.'

'They are much too small for you,' he protested.

I doubted it. The American's feet were long for a woman, and mine are remarkably small for a man. But on such delicate ground it seemed best to give way.

'The stewardess's bedroom slippers will do,' I compromised.

Karlis went off about his business, and I did not see him again until he brought my evening meal. He rushed out again with an air of importance and mystery. He was getting very weary of being dominated by me.

About ten he came in and reported progress. Whatever he had been grumbling to himself, he had failed to think up any useful variation on my plan. The appointment with Conger had been arranged, and two lifebelts were in position. He had stowed his suitcase and my pack in a locker of the launch, for we could not run down the gangway carrying any sort of baggage. He brought me the American's cloak and nylons, and a magnificent pair of shabby, fur-trimmed mules. Money he could not supply, or so he said. He had a few pound notes of his own, but he would not risk embezzling official funds. He wanted to leave all his papers and money in proper order so that there could be no question of his return being demanded on the grounds that he was a common criminal.

We rehearsed the captain's excited entry into my cabin, and our exact movements; it seemed pretty certain, even to Karlis, that he could be ushered straight into the trap. The lieutenant's nerves were ragged. He had worked himself into a much higher opinion of his shipmates' intelligence than was justifiable.

When he had gone it was my turn to worry. The two hours while I waited in my coffin of a cabin were hard to pass. I had an uneasy feeling that I might look back on them with pleasure as the final period of my life in which any illusion of liberty had remained to me. The hard glare of the light suggested to me that an infinity of such cells lay ahead. My only comfort was a lively bluebottle which had followed some tray of mine in from the kitchen. Its energy, though purposeless, was soothing; and its hum recalled the irrepressible gaiety of the insect world – not a quality that I have ever appreciated when I myself was the handiest food, yet one which dances through all my tropical memories.

Meanwhile I wondered if it had occurred to Karlis that he would do far better to escape without me. No doubt it had. On the other hand he needed the assistance of an able spy when landing in a very foreign country. And then two of us could, with luck, manage the seizure of the launch while one could not.

At midnight I put on the nylon stockings – or what was left of them after I had stretched them over my calves – and the stewardess's slippers. My trousers were tied round my waist. As for my legs, should anyone catch a quick and distant glimpse of them beneath the cloak or when the wind caught it, the masculine imagination of seamen could be trusted to supply all the alluring details which in fact were not there. Then I took up my position in Karlis' cabin behind the open wardrobe door. It swung back against the wall and concealed me adequately.

Zero hour passed without incident. The ship's engines continued to drive us nearer and nearer to the Thames Estuary and the pilot. There was nothing remarkable, I assured myself, in a little delay. It was most unlikely that Conger, Elias Thomas, would permit himself to be pushed overboard at 0015 hrs precisely.

After a very long ten minutes the ship slowed and stopped. At 0032 (or thereabouts) the captain, followed by Karlis, rushed into the cabin, went straight through the wardrobe and flung back the sliding door of the inner cabin. When he was inside, Karlis slid the door home again. There was nothing to it. We then shut the door of the wardrobe. Practically nothing could be heard of the captain's rage. When he began to ring the bell, Karlis disconnected the wire.

'Did Conger get to the lifebelt?' I asked.

'It hit him on the shoulder,' Karlis replied gloomily. 'He went under. It is the end of us.'

'And the launch?'

'Hopeless. The first officer went in it. He was with the captain. They think it is you who went overboard.'

Poor Karlis had found it impossible to let the first officer think that Conger had gone overboard, while telling the captain that I had. The presence of the first officer in the captain's cabin had complicated the plot. All the same, I embraced Karlis with enthusiasm and told him he had made a fine start.

So he had. The position was rather more fluid than I intended, but you cannot expect any imaginative plan to work out in exact detail. All you can ask is that details should conform to the general pattern.

'If you cannot get on board the launch, I must go without you,' he warned me.

That, too, was fairly in the pattern. One death wouldn't be enough for him if he did not get clear of the ship. The M.V.D would have to revive hanging, drawing and quartering for his special benefit.

I said that I would leave the cabin then and there. He put his head round the door, ordered a steward away and told me when the alleyway was empty. I pulled the hood over my head and bolted.

This time I avoided the main stairs and went up two companions fairly far aft. They were carpeted and I could move quietly. I only saw a belated passenger returning from the bathroom and slipped across behind him.

I found myself in the ship's lounge or smoking-room. It was empty, and all the lights were out except that in the bar steward's pantry. Looking aft through the windows, I could see the launch in the beam of the bridge searchlight, which was sweeping the sea around and ahead of it. On the promenade deck was a small group of crew off duty, including what looked like purser and bar steward. They all had their backs to the lounge and me. It was a fair bet that, on the boat deck above, would be a similar group staring aft out to sea and most unlikely to turn round.

The shutters of the bar were down, but the door was open. Evidently the steward had been interrupted in the course of washing-up and checking stock. Glasses were drying. The sink was full of hot, soapy water. In a corner were empty champagne and whisky bottles. I expect the passengers, under Conger's jovial leadership, had been celebrating their last night on board. Such a voyage, after all, was worth a party. That gallant Diana of an American would be able to dine out on her story for years. I can't believe that she has ever grudged me her cloak.

The till was half open. One couldn't expect much. After all, the ship was no Atlantic liner. Still, fifteen pounds and some odd silver were likely to be useful. I also selected a bottle of rum. I should have preferred whisky, but the rum bottle was flat and would fit in a pocket.

My next task was to reach the boat deck where, among ventilators and deck-houses, I could remain unnoticed until the launch returned. I poked out a cautious head to the port side of the promenade deck. It was empty, with that desolate air which a liner takes on when the passengers are in bed, the officers on the bridge and the watch inconspicuous at their stations. I ran daintily up to the boat deck and was at once caught in the ranging beam of the light on the bridge. I was thankful for the cloak and hood which were familiar to everyone. The only reaction on the bridge was, I like to think, regret that I should have chosen an hour when everyone was busy to visit the boat deck alone, in need of comfort and without my husband.

As I expected, there were figures looking aft, and among them two passengers. That was awkward, for I could not at a moment's notice find a spot where I should be hidden from any of them who might turn round, and at the same time from the bridge. The only place was under the bridge itself.

I walked forward. I could not use my own masculine stride, but I was sure that any little feminine trippings would be equally wrong. I tried to invent for my long-legged American an honest walk which would yet be as seductive as possible. In daylight I should probably have looked like an owlishly drunk movie star; but I was in the shadows alongside the beam, and soon beneath it. My wretched acting sufficed, for Howard-Wolferstan, the spy, the sole reason for the return of the ship, was known to have escaped overboard. No one had time to bother with the peculiar walk of North Americans who ought to be in bed.

I took station in a dark corner, almost under the companion which led to the bridge. There I was pretty safe, for traffic passed over my head and away from me, down the next companion to the promenade deck. Close to me was the gap in the line of boats where the launch had hung, the davits turned outwards and the ropes hanging down.

I could not understand what was being said above me, but undoubtedly much of the coming and going was connected with the search for the captain. If that launch did not return soon, it would be assumed that the captain had gone overboard as well, or was locked in a life-and-death struggle with Howard-Wolferstan. However, Karlis was doing his stuff. I once heard his voice, quiet but with an undertone of menace. He was putting the fear of God and the Arctic into the second and third officers while the M.V.D going was still good.

Voices were suddenly raised and excited. The beam shifted. Conger, not Howard-Wolferstan, had been picked up. There was a cheer from one of the passengers aft. It sounded half-hearted. Possibly he had been sitting next to Elias Thomas at meals. The light was extinguished.

The group at the other end of the boat deck broke up and ran down to a lower level. Certainly they were all bound for the head of the gangway, to watch the arrival of the launch. There, too, would be the idlers whom I had seen outside the lounge. The position suddenly alarmed me. How on earth could I push through the crowd and reach the gangway as soon as Conger had been carried up?

The boat deck, being now empty and in comparative darkness, could be thoroughly explored so long as my movements did not attract the attention of the bridge. Someone up there did hail me, but I satisfied him with one of those charmingly debonair American gestures – half wave, half blowing of a kiss – and vanished behind the funnel. Reaching the boats on the starboard side over dead ground, I looked down between two of them and saw that the head of the gangway was on the level of the main deck. Worse than ever. It probably opened into the vestibule by the main staircase, and had to be approached through the alleyways of the passenger accommodation. No quick rush across the open spaces of a deck was possible at all.

I tried the companion up which I had come. Halfway down it, I saw all the lights blazing in the lounge. I had a vision – probably correct – of passengers up in their dressing-gowns and calling for drinks, of the bar steward discovering his empty till, of the genuine American in something diaphanous and dashing, of a general state of wild excitement in which comrades and capitalists alike would be chasing every shadow that moved and howling for my comparatively innocent blood.

I floated gracefully back to the boat deck. Two damned idle seamen, with nothing to do but watch the launch, were in position between the boats exactly where I wanted to be. It was impossible for me to lean over and see what Karlis was up to.

There were only two moves open: to stay helplessly in hiding on the boat deck, or to risk going down to the port promenade deck. That was still empty. Of course it was. The

entire blasted ship's company – those who were awake –
were over on the starboard side. I went down and scurried
along the port rails like little Red Riding Hood about to
be wolfed. The ropes from the launch davits hung over the
sea. There was nothing for it but to accept their offer. I was
not prepared to engage myself among crowds in the well-lit
alleyways. It was better to swim round under the stern and
watch the launch from there. I should probably find myself
adrift in the Thames Estuary, but my nerve for bluff was
shattered.

Cloak, hood and all, I slid down the hanging rope and
took to the water. I swam aft along the side of the ship without being noticed and took refuge, a frightened barnacle,
under the bulge of the stern. Treading water, I stepped on
the uppermost blade of the starboard propeller. That completed my panic. I had to make a serious speech to myself in
English and Spanish – for I find that in moments of child-
ish unreason I naturally think in my mother's tongue – and
assure myself that the ship's engines would not start until the
launch was hoisted up. It took the combined efforts of both
maritime languages to make me stay where I was.

I could see the gangway. Elias Thomas Conger was walking up it and declaiming. He was in no sort of doubt that
he had been pushed overboard. The first officer assisted
him, deprecating with fatherly gestures so gross a libel on
the ship. Then I saw Karlis run down the gangway and into
the launch. He addressed the bridge like a sergeant-major.
Somebody, presumably the second officer, gave an order; and
up came the boat's crew, leaving, as we had foreseen, a man
with a boat-hook.

It was about the only exact detail which we *had* foreseen.
But the framework of the plan had been solid enough – just
– to hold whatever might be rammed into it by circumstance.

The next move was obvious. With my feet on the propeller blade, I jumped as high as I could, hit the water with an honest smack and screamed.

The beauty of the ship was overboard. Floating cloak bobbed up and down. Wet hood clung to my face as I splashed incompetently. The ball was in Karlis' court and an absolute gift to him if he kept his head. After a moment's hesitation – he told me afterwards that he was wondering what to do if I turned out to be the real American – he started the engine of the launch. The hand who had held the boat-hook leaned out to pick me up. Karlis tipped up his heels and flung him a grating. We were away.

On board the ship was plain indecision. Karlis' insistence on nobbling the captain was justified again. The search-light picked us up, and the black cliff of the bows turned slowly in our direction. But Muddle was gloriously complete. Captain not to be found. First officer still astonished that Elias Thomas, not I, had been overboard. Passengers and crew assuming that the long-legged American had eloped with Karlis. And second officer wondering which of the orders he gave or omitted to give would send him to navigate a raft on Siberian rivers. There was nothing much the ship could do except shoot at us – and that, in territorial waters and with passengers on board, was out of the question.

'What did you tell the mate?' I asked Karlis.

'That the launch had picked up the wrong man and that you were still in the water. I had the boat cleared to prove that you had not been picked up and hidden.'

'And he fell for that?'

'Of course. He knew that the rescue had to be properly documented or we should all be in trouble.'

Karlis was certainly a master at spreading alarm and

despondency. He had played for all it was worth the representative of inflexible bureaucracy.

The ship was now moving after us more purposefully. No doubt the first officer had discovered the American and her fortunate husband peacefully asleep in their cabin. We had a lead, however, of nearly a quarter of a mile and were steering straight for the scattered lights on the Essex shore which, I suppose, were around Shoeburyness. When the ship was disturbingly close and all else was blackness, a gigantic buoy loomed up in the dark with the flood tide beginning to pile against it. Karlis could not make up his mind which side to pass, but the current decided for him. Whatever that buoy marked, the ship didn't like it. She went astern in a swirl of white water which accompanied us along some local channel, while the ship herself merged into a mere pattern of lights following the respectable course towards a pilot and London river.

For us, buoys became unreasonably frequent. I still have not the faintest notion where we were, even after looking at a chart. Light buoys and lighthouses winked at us from every direction but the south, and pretty soon they were there too. Whether they marked the Mouse or the Maplins or neither I do not know. There were also bells tolling at us. I imagine that anyone with a map or chart could no more get lost in the Thames Estuary than on an arterial road – provided he knew where he started from. We did not. I think that at one period – there were three feet of water under us and we backed out cautiously – we must have been mixed up with the buoys of the Artillery Range.

I produced my bottle of rum, but it had a cork instead of a stopper. In trying to knock off the neck I broke the bottle. I was not at my best. It seemed to me highly probable that daylight would find us stuck on a mudbank, from which one could neither walk nor swim, with a zealous lifeboat standing by to rescue us when the tide rose again. Meanwhile all we were doing and could do was to play ring-a-ring-a-roses round meaningless buoys. There were so many little lights in the darkness, obeying in their courses the impenetrable laws of Trinity House, that I had a befuddled vision of us upside down and navigating the firmament. I was also cold and wet and, with all the excitement over, sorry for myself.

Karlis was disappointed in me. His own seafaring had been merely as a policeman, and in the tideless Baltic at that. But me he expected to be able, as an experienced spy, to do a few boy-scout tricks or at least to know the marks of the chief entrance to his own land. As it was, I couldn't even open rum without smashing it. The result was that the magic was broken. I became in his eyes a wretched, chilly embarrassment, no longer endowed with the superhuman cunning of years of subversive activities. I was the kind of person whom a policeman instinctively escorts to the nearest block of cells for shelter and investigation. Perhaps he would have done so in most kindly fashion if there had been a handy gaol. As it was, only the sea was open to receive me.

My Scandinavian partner disappeared, and I was left to deal with a resigned and melancholy Russian. The nation – to judge by my very short experience – seems to have a genius for a this-hurts-me-far-more-than-you attitude. Simple souls must find a delicate pleasure in receiving punishment from such nobly reluctant hands. It was Karlis' unwillingness to lend me a pair of trousers which woke me up. I supplied myself with a dry sweater and shirt from my pack, but I had to ask for trousers from his suitcase. I assured him that he would get them back when my own were dry, but he grumbled. I saw his point of view almost at once. It was reasonable. Why waste a good pair of trousers overboard?

I could no longer hope to recover all my prestige. The situation had become too drastically simplified. Karlis had a pistol, and I had not. And how easy his story for the British police! He had escaped fearing the consequences of my disappearance; he had stopped to pick me up under the honest impression that I was the American; I had tried to get ashore through the mud, and been drowned. And of course it would be I who had crept up behind Karlis and Conger and pushed the latter overboard.

My only chance was to stop shivering and to forget immediately that I was a satellite in star flow. A pity. Whenever I am miserable enough for poetry, something always distracts my attention. I reminded myself firmly that it was what the English call a warm July night, and that hearty maidens, well protected by a layer of pink blubber, were likely to be gambolling in the sea off Southend Pier.

Southend Pier. I jumped to my feet and declared dramatically that we were saved: that the fixed light to port was the end of the pier and the revolving light to starboard the Maplin. They were the only two names I could remember. As a matter of fact the revolving light may have been the Nore. God knows what the other was! But I was concerned with humanity, not navigation. The essential was to radiate confidence.

'Keep heading into the tide,' I told him, 'and we'll get clear.'

I stood up in the bows, peering at nothing in a professional manner and giving him at intervals responsible but enthusiastic orders, such as 'Starboard a little!' and 'Port a point or two!' I did not much like turning my back to him, but I reckoned that, so long as he hadn't spotted that I had spotted the regrettable decision passing through his mind, he would certainly want to preserve so admirable a pilot.

Fortunately we hit nothing, though once when I made a particular point of giving him a mark to steer on we slid closely over a bank. I don't know whether he noticed it; but since, on the other side of the bank, there was an obvious channel marked by some dilapidated posts, up went my reputation.

Meanwhile it had occurred to me that light buoys must have ladders for the convenience of whatever electricians and window-cleaners plied their trade among the mudbanks. When we were out in more open water I directed Karlis towards a light, putting in a couple of wide turns to make our approach more impressive. The buoy indeed had a little spidery ladder leading over the curve to the foot of the tripod.

'I want to know the state of the tide,' I explained to Karlis. 'If there's another hour or two before the turn, we'll be able to make one of the little creeks on Foulness.'

'How can you tell?' he asked.

'There's a glass case on top of the buoy,' I said, 'and they put the tide tables in there once a month.'

He seemed a bit doubtful, so I told him that the tables were put there during the war for the sake of torpedoed seamen. He swallowed that.

'And they still do it?' he asked.

'Of course. In England once something has been done, it goes on being done. You've read enough about us to know that,' I added severely.

The tide was ripping against the foot of the buoy. I hung on to the ladder with the boat-hook. I doubted if I could ever make him go on board the buoy. The only way was to let him think that I wanted to go myself.

'Careful!' I warned him, handing him the end of the boat-hook. 'If you don't hold on, the launch will be on the bank before you have time to get way on her.'

The tide obliged by piling up between the launch and buoy, and gurgling loudly.

He did not take the boat-hook from me. He was working it all out. The man on top of the buoy would be perfectly safe till he was picked up by a passing ship; he would also be very difficult to shoot if he kept the curve of the buoy between himself and a man trying to aim with one hand and steer the launch with the other.

'There is no reason why *you* should go,' he said sharply.

'Go yourself then! All I must know is the time of high water on August 4th. But for God's sake don't make a mistake! You'll find the frame directly beneath the tripod.'

He pushed past me and took to the ladder, carrying the end of the painter with him as a precaution. I had no knife to cut it. Regretfully I had to consider assault. A mere technical assault. A rap over the knuckles. I delivered it, with the brass end of the boat-hook, on the hand which held both the painter and the last rung of the ladder.

He did not drop the painter. The Russian gift of withstanding suffering was too great for me. Instead he caught the boat-hook with his other hand – for it was too clumsy a weapon to be quickly withdrawn – and gave a hearty push with it while I was standing in the bows off balance. I went overboard. So did he. It was the end of our partnership.

I was just able to grab the bottom of the ladder with the hook. Meanwhile the launch had drifted away with Karlis on the end of the painter. Eventually he climbed into it, for I heard the acceleration of the engine and the swirl of the propeller. He did not return to look for me. The chance of my having reached the buoy was negligible, and I cannot blame him for feeling that he had had enough of my society.

I sat huddled up beneath the tripod of the light. Morale did not exist. My watch, which had surprisingly lived up to its maker's claims, was still going. It said 3.22. After infinities of cold it said 3.40. The top of a buoy in the loneliness of primaeval waters was the wrong place for a man of my temperament. It would have suited Karlis much better.

At last the sky to the east grew grey and the water was visible as water, and none the pleasanter for that. The tide still flowed. The land was under haze. No doubt the good people of Essex and Kent, suitably clad in dry pyjamas, were congratulating themselves on a warm night with a fine day to follow. I seemed to be rather nearer the Kent shore than I expected and out of the normal track of shipping – or at any rate the track which was familiar to me, who had only seen the Thames Estuary from the decks of liners.

Ships did indeed pass, but too far to the north to notice me waving and capering on my buoy. The capers were limited. There was only room for half a dozen seagulls to meditate in comfort on their digestive processes. At last a little coaster appeared from the general direction of Kent, heading straight for me. I climbed up the tripod and shouted at them. I didn't care if they handed me straight over to the police so long as the station was warm. A faint flicker of the instinct of self-preservation made me yell in Spanish; if I could convince them that I spoke no English, it would give me time to hear what was said about me.

The sea was flat calm, and there was no need for the coaster to lower her dinghy. She came up alongside, and the mate threw me a rope. I chattered back to him in Spanish, took a turn round my chest and was hauled on board.

Rochester Star she was called. She was returning empty from the Medway to Erith, and had a crew of seven – captain, mate, two engineers, two deck hands and a cook. They all had the amazing kindness of the Londoner to anyone in distress. They could not understand a word I said, but they had me stripped in a minute, and my clothes and even my money hung up to dry in the engine-room. Meanwhile I was wrapped in blankets and irrigated with hot, sweet tea – the only time in my life that I ever appreciated the stuff.

I explained in sign language that I had fallen overboard and swum to the buoy, at the same time telling my tale as dramatically as possible in case someone understood the language. But 'Me Spanish' was my only remark intelligible to them.

The engineer on duty was determined to get my story. He was one of those men – it's a commoner gift among women – who refuse to be put out of their stride by mere differences of language.

'What's your ship? Ship? Name?' he repeated.

'Juan García,' I answered, showing that at least I understood 'name'.

He kept on at me. He patted his own ship. He drew a picture of a ship and pointed to where the name ought to be. I remained incredibly stupid, and insisted that I was called Juan García. I hoped that one of them would mention the name of a ship off which I could reasonably have fallen.

'Can't you let the poor bastard alone?' the captain asked, impatiently rescuing me.

He was down in the engine-room, too, leaving the mate on the bridge. He wasn't going to miss a scrap of the first adventure that had come his way in years.

'He'll be off one of them Barcelona fruit boats,' he said.

That seemed to call for a sign of intelligence.

'Fruta! Barcelona!' I chattered. 'Yes!'

But now I simply had to produce a name. I was feeling, thanks to those sturdy angels, very much better and able to think. And it did not really matter what I called my non-existent ship. If good fortune provided a more likely name whenever I was interrogated by some Spanish-speaking official, I could always pretend I had been misunderstood.

'*Cabo Culebra*,' I said, remembering that there really was a Spanish line whose ships all had the names of capes.

The captain was delighted. For one thing, he had succeeded where the engineer had not; for another, he knew all the lines which regularly traded in and out of London and he had been tied up alongside Cabo boats. He told his assembled crew – all of them except the mate and a deckhand had now found their way to the engine-room – that the Cabo owners provided free wine. The crew were much impressed, except the cook.

'Nasty stuff,' he said. 'That's 'ow they fall overboard.'

The captain would have none of that. He rightly said that it made no more difference to them than water. He had evidently enjoyed hospitality on a Cabo ship. He turned to me and remarked shyly, for he was no linguist:

'Veeno? Bong?'

'Bong!' I answered.

'You come along o' me, my lad,' he said and winked.

I obeyed him with alacrity. He could make me understand English a lot quicker than the engineer. I hope his stock with the crew went up.

He led me, wrapped in my blanket, to the tiny saloon and produced a bottle of port. I seemed destined to port in trouble. There were gin and whisky in the locker, but he was giving me – bless him! – what he thought I would most like. I made him a speech in which I truthfully told him what I thought of him. He gathered what it was all about.

'That's all right, lad,' he said with faint embarrassment. 'Drink up!'

I put down a full tumbler of port.

'Now if you nip along to the galley,' he added, 'cookie will have some bacon for you.'

I damn nearly understood this, but managed to look blank. He led me up a companion to the deck-house where the galley was. I saw that we were passing a port which, I was nearly certain, must be Tilbury.

'Teelbury?' I asked him, pointing to it.

'Aye.'

My agitated ship was not there. I looked down river. She was not anchored anywhere in the reach. As I dived into an immense plate of bacon and fried bread, I chuckled. The cook looked on benevolently. His opinion of wine might be perverted, but he did not believe in talking while a hungry man ate.

Of course she was not there! I should have guessed it already, if I had been in a mental state to give a damn what happened to her. It was most improbable that the captain – assuming he had now been found and replaced on his bridge – would put into Tilbury before he had received exact instructions what to say. He might be ordered to make a clean breast of Karlis' and my escape, or to sink his ship, passengers and all, or to turn back to Riga. He could not possibly guess. The ship, according to Karlis, had never signalled any reason for returning. All explanations had been left to the Embassy, so that the arrival of the ship and the surrender of the spy might be released to the world like the sudden opening of a cage of peace doves.

This passion for secrecy had landed them all in a glorious hole. That unfortunate captain could not give helpful suggestions to the Kremlin with the impertinence of a Howard-Wolferstan. There was nothing whatever he could do but anchor outside territorial waters, on the excuse that he had missed the tide, and pray that somebody would care enough for him to preserve his sanity. Meanwhile there would be no special hue and cry after me, unless Karlis started to tell the true story. He was unlikely to be so rash until he knew what the official story was.

So I had a chance – as high as an even chance I put it – of landing without being recognized. True, a distorted version of my face was familiar enough to public and police, but I was about to appear from so unsuspected a direction. It would demand a most brilliant flick of imagination to identify an unshaven, dishevelled Spanish seaman who spoke no English with the polished spy Howard-Wolferstan, the smooth type of Latin-American band leader whom those infernal, insular reporters had imposed upon the public.

Both my clothes and money were dry by the time we reached Erith. My blue sweater, ex-Bassoon, was neutral enough for any seaman. The corduroy trousers, although twice dipped in the estuary, were perhaps uncommon, but who could tell what a Spanish sailor would or would not wear? My saviours of the *Rochester Star* accompanied me on shore with the utmost kindness. I was not allowed to wander off alone, simply because they wanted to see their pet in safe hands. I listened to them blankly while they discussed what should be done with me, and rejoiced to hear that they thought the police station too formal. They didn't want to alarm me. It wasn't fair to rescue a poor bastard and then hand him over to the cops. They introduced me to an official of the Seamen's Home, and all shook my hand and wished me luck. I felt a worm for not showing gratitude in a language they could understand, but I am sure they caught the spirit of my Spanish.

I sat in the Seaman's Home office, and had another meal and some more tea while waiting for an interpreter. A grey soul in a grey middle age I thought him when he arrived; but as soon as he started to speak Spanish he began to light up, by degrees, like a slow electric fire – first his mouth, then his eyes and then his hands. He was an excellent fellow who had passed fifteen years of his life in the Argentine. The mere use of the language carried him back to the uninhibited generosity of life and manners which he had loved. Respectable Erith, its dirty bricks, its pubs and its furtive privacies were not, for this precious moment of his, realities.

He spotted my accent at once as South American, not Spanish, and I accounted for that by saying I had spent years in Venezuela. I had to go into details of the *Cabo Culebra* and gave her a cargo of grapes and melons from Valencia. It seemed to me a bit early in the season for both, but I was already committed to fruit. She was far more likely to have had sherry in her holds. As the slightest investigation would show that there had not been any *Cabo Culebra* at all in the Port of London, it didn't matter – beyond reminding me that I had to be clear of Erith before any enquiries could be made.

The Seamen's Home fellow began to be a little impatient at the length and good humour of our conversation, especially as much of its substance, when sketchily translated to him, had nothing to do with the *Cabo Culebra* and consisted of joyous reminiscences. He was anxious to call in the police. The *Rochester Star,* being only a Thames Estuary coaster, had known little and cared less about the clearing of aliens. That formality had to be completed, even if the alien had been roosting on a buoy.

My genial interpreter explained to me that we would now visit the police. I expressed the utmost willingness, but on the way to the station I begged him with tears in my eyes to telephone the Spanish Consulate and ask them to cable my wife that I was alive in case the *Cabo Culebra* had already wirelessed news of the accident. It was a dirty trick to play on him, but I could not help it. I gave him my wife's name and address. I spread myself upon her misery and beauty, describing in fact and with enthusiasm my lovely Dr Cornelia.

We stopped at a post office. I had a feeling that it was going to be pretty difficult to get any sense out of the Spanish Consulate about a non-existent ship at nine-thirty in the morning when somebody reasonably inefficient would be there, and consuls and vice-consuls probably would not.

I watched my poor friend – ah, could I but entertain him in Ecuador! – sweating in the telephone box, and then edged out of the post office and walked to the railway station at a pace which any innocent Spaniard would have considered undignified. After a quick glance at the time-tables, I found that in four minutes there would be a train to London Bridge. I bought a ticket, asking for it in broken English. That was rather more than I was supposed to know; but if I were traced to the station, as within an hour I certainly should be, my little bit of English was not enough to arouse suspicion.

Once in the train, with time to think of long-term tactics, the difficulties overwhelmed me. The Spanish seaman, of no particular importance to anybody, could easily vanish. But Howard-Wolferstan could not. As soon as it was obvious that they were one and the same – which it would be, when those much delayed passengers told their story – the police and M.I.5 would be after me in full force. The dreaded M.I.5 I should call them – though they seem to me to be as subject to human error as the rest of us.

Clothes were the trouble. I was too conspicuous a figure. It was safe to assume that whatever I bought, I could be traced through the place where I bought it. When a description of me was out, the second-hand clothes dealer would be round at the nearest police station in five minutes.

I left the train at Greenwich, and by hanging about for a bit in the lavatory managed to leave the station without surrendering my ticket. In that way I might gain an hour while the pursuit bothered the staff at London Bridge. In Greenwich I counted the colours of the suits I saw on the streets, taking only men of what one might call pronounced middle-class, ranging, say, from foremen to commercial travellers. I found that blue came first – that may have been peculiar to a seaport – with greys and browns following closely; and there were a large number of well-worn suits which one man would describe as a sort of grey, and another as a sort of brown. They were colourless as a piece of wet driftwood. That, then, was to be my choice.

I came on a second-hand dealer in a back street, and bought myself a suit and hat for a couple of pounds. The suit was majority colour and would look respectable for a day or two until the worn cloth ceased to hold the shape ironed into it by the cleaners. I could not imitate cockney dialect with any real facility, and I feared I would attract attention if I spoke cultured English. So again I used a foreign accent.

With my new clothes in a brown paper parcel, I kept to the poorer streets until I came to a chemist's shop. There I bought shaving kit, a bandage and a roll of cotton wool. So to a public lavatory – whence I emerged as a decent citizen who had had a nasty accident to one side of his face. I quietly dropped my old clothes into the ebbing tide. The Spanish seaman had vanished, and Howard-Wolferstan had come back to life.

The bandage, however, was a very weak disguise, and I knew only too well that I must change my appearance again in a matter of hours. I took a bus into London, settled myself down with a paper in the gardens of the Tower – it never occurred to me that I was important enough to become a lodger – and considered the next move.

I had to count that the purchase of clothes and bandage would be traced by the police within a few hours of the identification of the Spanish seaman, and that, if I remained as I was, I should be in a cell by midnight; but without the bandage I was plainly Howard-Wolferstan, whose photographs would be all over the morning papers. With the whole country on the look-out for a man of my build and of dark, unEnglish complexion, life was going to be hell not only for me but for every Arab, Spaniard or Italian who happened to find himself in a town where he was not known. I could not take a train, buy, eat or appear in public at all. Even if I could find a hide-out I had no hope of reaching it.

My appearance had to be changed, but there was no way of turning myself into a fair or medium Englishman. Peroxide? It would deal only with my hair, and make me even more conspicuous. I envied regular criminals with a back room in which to go to ground, and escaped prisoners-of-war with an organization to help them. Then stay in my natural colours and account for my Latin face by some disguise? A turban, an Arab head-dress, a mask – any of them might enable me, with sufficient impudence, to get clear. But the present nameless citizen with a bandage over half his face could not enter a shop to buy comic hats, nor could Howard-Wolferstan.

Despairing, I wandered east along Wapping High Street, although I had had quite enough of ships and docks. I doubt if any fixed plan at all was in my mind. I was drawn vaguely towards the half-way house of dark faces, of lascar seamen and Goanese stewards, towards the only real southern frontier which England possessed. Equally vaguely I was drawn to the ships for South America in spite of knowing that every stowaway would be doubly suspect. All the while I kept my eyes open for any possibility. Much as I distrust violence as the last refuge of the brainless, it would not have been safe for anyone wearing an outlandish oriental costume to meet me in an empty lane.

I stopped to look at a shop entrance and window. Half ship-chandler's and half ironmonger's it was, full of brushes and gear for odd trades. There were new and second-hand chimney-sweeping brushes. I stared at them without re-membering what they were for. And then the vision came to me of the local sweep pedalling along on his bicycle with his bundle of brushes over the handlebars.

To find a bicycle shop was the first and – as it turned out – the longest job. At last I hit one, off the Whitechapel Road, stocked with old bicycles from the reconditioned to the cheap and rusty. Making a careful note of the street, I turned back towards the river to discover a reasonably pri-vate heap of coal. I did not have to go far. Near Shadwell station was a coal-merchant's yard. It was the lunch hour, and there was no one about except a watchman eating sand-wiches in his office. I sneaked past him and dived into a coal-heap as eagerly as a chilly man into a hot bath. In a moment my hands and face were black with coal dust, and my suit moderately dirty. Only moderately. I assumed that a sweep would wear overalls at work.

So back to the bicycle shop, now without the bandage which I had left hidden under the coal. I did not yet look my part, judging by the grins and remarks of the passers-by: 'What 'appened, myte?' 'Must a emptied the truck over 'im!' 'Did yer find the chap what pushed yer, myte?' and so on. It was evident that in the absence of brushes the public took my face to be blackened by coal dust, as indeed it was, not soot.

The proprietor of the bicycle shop said:

'Gawd, you are in a mess, ain't yer?'

That entitled me to be short with him. I could trust my cockney dialect enough to answer:

'Never seed a sweep before?'

After that, with grunts and monosyllables, I made him parade his bicycles for me. I bought one which he had not had time to enamel and renovate. It worked, and it had two wheels and a brake; that was all you could say for it. It cost four pounds.

On my disreputable bicycle I went to the ironmonger's, keeping to my part of an uncommunicative man in a filthy temper. I made a play of examining his stand of second-hand brushes at the entrance to the shop.

''Ere!' I called to him rudely. 'I'll 'ave them three!'

He came out from behind his counter and looked me over. He took me without question for a sweep. That was reassuring. As soon as I was in connection with brushes, the very slight difference between soot and coal dust, which, all the same, the human eye unconsciously perceives, became unnoticeable.

'Fifteen bob,' he said. 'Or you can 'ave the lot for two quid if they're any use to you.'

The lot looked far more imposing, for in the bundle was a set of those rods which fit into each other to push the brush up the chimney. The brushes were too mangy to be of value to any sweep but me. However, I had no intention of mixing with professionals, and a good bundle would look workman-like to the public.

'Thirty bob,' I said.

'Thirty-two and a tanner,' said he.

I closed at that. With the brushes and rods came a couple of straps. I pushed my bicycle round the corner before fixing the bundle to it, for it was probable that the ironmonger knew how it should be done, and would spot me as an amateur if I did not follow the custom of the trade.

I bicycled west along the Embankment with a very open mind. I was untraceable unless I made a gross mistake, and I had about eight pounds ten of the barman's money still in my pocket. But my disguise could not be permanent. I had to sleep somewhere, and presumably sweeps washed before sleeping. They would certainly have to before taking a bed at any sort of lodging-house.

It was soon plain that if I had had the faintest notion how to sweep chimneys, I might have followed the trade till my beard grew. I was hailed three times before I left Whitechapel. I also discovered that a sweep is a talisman. Half-wits try to touch him for luck. He suffers the same secretive and insulting pokes as a hunchback.

It pleased me to cycle past Scotland Yard, and then along Pall Mall and St James in order to pass the club which I had proudly joined in 1938 and used uncommonly little ever since. After crossing Piccadilly I turned up into Hanover Square, and the luck descended where it was most wanted – on the sweep himself. There was a wedding under way at St George's: carpet, awning, a packet of old bitches waiting on the ropes, and an immaculate usher on top of the steps to keep the ring clear for the bride.

Hanover Square weddings must be rare in August. Perhaps the bride and bridegroom could not decently delay marriage any longer. But I don't think so. The bridegroom looked as if his mind was set on anything but his poppet. It's more likely that they got the whole fashionable outfit cheap out of season. The usher, resplendent but baggy in morning coat and striped trousers – surely the Latin habit of marrying in evening kit is more sensible? At least every guest possesses it and doesn't have to hire a pair of pants and pray that they have been disinfected – this usher, arrayed by some Solomon in all his glory, shouted to me with a whoop of joy and rushed me up the steps just before the bride emerged. To think that a sweep should pass at that moment! I even had to kiss the little honey on her cheek. I could have done with her lips. She reminded my starved imagination of Dr Cornelia in court, shy but resigned. The recollection that such things were, was an added incentive towards acquiring as soon as possible the appeal, limited though it might be, of a clean face.

I was offered a quid for that job. The bridal party were all obviously rolling in money, so I looked grateful but respect-fully disappointed – modelling myself, so far as coal dust permitted, upon the attitude of the Corps of Commission-aires when collecting a sixpenny tip from a trouser pocket which looked good for a bob. The usher produced another quid. I could have kissed him, too.

I crossed Oxford Street and rode into Regent's Park, where I set myself and my bicycle down on the grass. I had made some progress since the bench on Tower Hill five hours before. I was no longer Howard-Wolferstan; until I drew attention to myself, no police on earth could make the connection between me and him. But I had come to a dead end. Ride out of London and sleep rough till my beard grew? I didn't like it. The travelling itself was so likely to arouse comment. A sweep had to have a home. He could not be dirty before breakfast and dirty after working hours – or only at the cost of telling continual lies which sooner or later must arouse the interest of police.

I determined to observe Bloomsbury – not the totem worshippers of professorialism, but the large-hearted visitors of colour. It was, I remembered, another frontier between the dark- and the light-skinned. Arabs, Africans and Indians poured from its institutes into the streets of London, with growing knowledge of how to spend the taxpayer's money while continuing to buy his vote. Among these students of political economy I hoped to find a fancy dress.

It cost me a lot of worry and self-suggestion to remain quite still by my bicycle at the south-east corner of Gordon Square. I reminded myself that I was waiting for a customer, that I was a bookmaker's runner in my spare time, that I was summing up from the outside a mass of chimneys for which I had just contracted. But it was no good. I fidgeted. I could not compass the all-embracing stare of the working man who at the moment does not happen to be working.

Several gentlemen from far Asia and Africa passed me. Mostly they were dressed in unimportancies; but occasionally there was a robe or a fine, outlandish hat as prescribed by national pride or religion. I spoke to two of them. They laughed nervously and quickened their pace. At last there appeared a magnificent Sikh, his head topped by a superb turban, and his natty grey flannel suit covered as far as the lapels by a black cascade of beard and whiskers. In answer to my interested examination of him, his liquid brown eyes looked at me with a sympathy which was unusual between strangers of different race and very different occupation. It was the sort of look that I myself might have given to some delicate young Indian rejoicing in the effect of her sari upon Gordon Square – doubtful but definitely interested.

'Excuse me, sir,' I said, 'but if I was to want a 'at like yours, where could I buy one?'

He answered me with another question.

'Don't you say in England that a sweep is lucky?'

'There's them as thinks so,' I replied. 'Wish I could 'ave a bit meself.'

I was taking risks with my stage cockney. I assumed that he could not tell the difference between the genuine and the false.

'What do you want a pugaree for?'

'Sweeps' Annual Outin' and Fancy Dress Ball.'

'I need luck,' he said. 'I'll lend you an old one. Come about ten. Here's my address.'

'I'll be dirty, sir. Got a late job to-night.'

'At the worst – I have a bathroom,' he smiled, still holding me with his peculiarly gentle look.

It seemed an odd remark. Who was I, however, bred in the cheerful barbarisms of Christendom, to decipher the motives and manners under that mass of hair? With American Indians I was at home; but that half-understanding of imperial Indians, which every educated Englishman unconsciously acquires from his reading of fiction and government publications, I did not possess. I was aware that I myself had contributed to any misunderstanding there might be. A man compelled, as I was, to make unconventional enquiries must expect unconventional replies or none at all. My opening moves, whether as sweep or Michael Bassoon, frequently met with an absolute 'yes' or 'no' which prohibited further conversation. There is little point in recording rebuffs. I number only the serenities.

My Punjab aristocrat – for that he certainly was – passed on with a slight bow and smile, leaving me with four empty hours to employ. I walked with my bicycle into the grubby district beyond King's Cross, and bought myself a large meal at an eating-house. It was surprisingly solid and good. To eat well in the London of to-day one must, I think, pay thirty shillings or two; between these extremes lie lakes of custard and gravy, deserts of processed meat and cheese. I could not visit a cinema in my filthy condition, so I settled down in the bar of a small pub. Even there the landlord told me pointedly that I could have a wash at the back if I liked.

Before calling on the Sikh, I explored the neighbourhood of his lodgings. They were in a quiet, shabby street off the Hampstead Road, and most of the houses had notices of *Apartments* or *Bed and Breakfast* in the windows. It looked the right district for an exotic foreigner who had not much money, or, more likely, was not allowed by his politicians to take it abroad. Among the basement walls and bushes of a bombed site I took off my coat and trousers, and gave them such shaking and brushing as I could. The dirt of hands and face had, of course, to remain.

A little after ten I rang the bell, and my host, who lived on the ground floor, opened the door. His sitting-room, in the lay-out of its standardized furniture, was much what the outside of the house led one to expect. His small bedroom, however, gave a startling impression of blood-red and gold. The curtains and the cover of the divan bed must have been importations of his own.

He offered me whisky and a cigarette. He was not, he explained, permitted by his religion to take either himself. He also offered me a bath, which I turned down on the grounds that his landlady would not approve.

Opening a cupboard in his bedroom, he showed me three of his pugarees, wound on some kind of framework and ready for use.

'Choose which you like,' he said. 'You can return it when you come again. But what are you going to wear with it?'

'The old woman's dressing-gown,' I answered.

'Are you really a sweep?'

'O' course I am!'

'Yet you can't help speaking like an educated man occasionally, and you have very beautiful hands.'

I silently blasted him and his acute perception. I was out of my depth. His eyes, less accustomed, perhaps, than ours to be taken in by a mere exterior, had spotted my one mistake. My nails were full of coal dust, but they were long. I hadn't had much time, and one can't think of everything.

'I've been inside,' I answered sulkily. 'They trained me as a sweep.'

It was, I think, evident to both of us by this time that we did not share all each other's tastes. Yet the first charge of sympathy which had passed between us in Gordon Square had reality; we were both opportunists, feeling out quick and devious ways to our ends.

'What did they put you away for?' he asked. 'False pretences? Blackmail?'

''Ouse-breaking.'

He was a most disconcerting panther of a man. He weighed me up, smiling and thinking behind his Assyrian thicket of hair. His eyes shone with an emotion which was either sheer feline cruelty or a sense of mischief, and they never left mine. We might have been a couple of tom-cats, staring at each other motionless in a backyard, and communicating only by imperceptible changes of position.

'You ought to have a beard for your fancy-dress ball,' he said. 'Would you like one? With no chance of being caught?'

'I'm going straight now,' I told him. 'There's money in this trade.'

'Enough?' he asked. 'Or was William Morris right when he prophesied that the most unpleasant jobs would be the best paid?'

'Never 'eard of 'im!'

'Ever *'eard* of the Sikhs?' he asked, emphasizing my inefficient assumption of an accent which did not belong to me.

I dropped it forthwith. He refused to be taken in, and it

seemed to be complicating the battle – whatever the battle was – unnecessarily.

'All I know is that you may not shave or cut your hair – like Samson,' I answered.

He said that was all I needed to know, and went on to tell me a most scandalous story. A co-religionist of his was also interested in fancy dress. It was his pleasure to masquerade as a woman, so he had preserved his long, black hair, while shaving of his beard and whiskers. In order to give no offence to the faithful during the more normal occupations of his post-graduate life, he had acquired a magnificently fitted false set. I was to be the chosen instrument of heaven which would enter his room while he slept and cause his whiskers to vanish. He would then be solemnly visited by representatives of his family and religion, and shown up as a backslider.

'There is no danger,' added my Sikh. 'Even if he sees you, he dare not tell the police.'

I did not want a beard. I could buy one myself for the Sweeps' Annual Outing and Fancy Dress Ball, now that I had invented it, without arousing any suspicion whatever. What I did want was an excuse for wearing a beard, a setting for it so natural that no one would bother to wonder whether it was false or not. A Sikh turban would do admirably.

'But suppose he sleeps in his whiskers?' I objected.

'You pull them off.'

'They may be stuck on with spirit gum.'

'They are not,' he replied positively. 'They are fitted to his chin and held on by elastic.'

He sketched with an excited gesture a band passing under his turban in front of the ears, and over the head.

I am no orientalist, but my guess was that tinkering with other people's beards might arouse quite unpredictable passions. I also felt that my Sikh was unreliable. He was not so shocked by his compatriot as he pretended to be. He revelled in what he proposed. If he had lived a hundred years earlier, he would undoubtedly have trained his judicial elephant to step with imperceptible slowness upon those who refused his friendship.

The project, however, had too many possibilities to be turned down flat.

'How would I get in?' I asked.

'Down the chimney.'

It's odd how foreigners tend to accept as unchangeable what they have read. My Sikh still thought that sweeps climbed up and down chimneys as in the days of Charles Kingsley, when a second's thought would have shown him it was impossible even for a child. But try to persuade an Englishman that the Spaniards are magnificent seamen, or the average North American that a lord has much less power than a senator!

When I had pointed out the diameter of chimneys, he said that there was a flat roof, easy of access, by which I could reach the renegade's bedroom window.

'Does he sleep with it open?' I asked.

'Oh, yes. He was in the Army.'

'It seems a bit hard on him.'

'Nothing is too hard on him. I hate him.'

He covered up this sudden lack of urbanity by adding:

'I am carried away by my religious feelings.'

'Would they carry you away to the extent of twenty quid?'

'Fifteen. Five when you start. Ten when you bring it.'

'If it's held by elastic, a tug won't get it off.'

'Pull it down, and then up over the face.'

I decided that I would go far enough to earn the first five pounds. I couldn't afford not to. What happened afterwards would depend upon the gods of India; and that did not take me very far, for no doubt there would be at least one to approve the conduct of each of the three parties concerned.

He took me out to show me the flat roof and window. It was well after midnight, for there had been intervals in our conversation, especially in the early part of it, while I attended to his whisky and listened to his charming efforts to put me at ease. Outside the front door, he turned to the left. My bicycle was also facing left. That wouldn't do. The bicycle had better point the other way in case I returned, as seemed very probable, in a hurry. I pretended my brushes were not secure and changed the direction.

He led me round two corners and into a mews or lane which gave access to the back doors of a street similar to his own. It was a very middle-class district, without any prosperity to attract the ambition of burglars or the zeal of policemen, and depending, I suppose, upon London University for its living.

The flat roof could be reached by walking along the top of a high party wall between two backyards. About four feet above the leads of the roof I could make out the rectangle of an open window, a little blacker than the night. I told the Sikh to give me a leg up on to the wall.

'This is where I get the fiver,' I said.

He gave me three, swearing that he had got no more, that the rest was in a drawer at his lodgings. I ought to have come down at once; but, after all, three quid was three quid and I did not intend to give him any value for money.

I crawled silently along the wall and across the roof, and crouched down beneath the open window. When I was satisfied that the person inside was asleep, I stared through the window until my eyes were used to the darkness and I could make out the shapes within. So, very gingerly, over the sill.

The bed was on my left, and furniture, which resolved

itself into a chest of drawers and a dressing-table, on my right. There were no false whiskers lying on either of them. The sleeper evidently took no chances with narrow-minded compatriots.

I had no intention at all of risking tricks with elastic; but when I looked at him it seemed so easy. He was lying on his back. The luxuriance of a black beard was spread out over the sheets. Closer inspection showed the presence of a narrow black band in front of the ears. I told myself that it was folly, and then was overcome by that accursed spirit which forces a man to do what his natural caution dislikes – such as diving off too high a rock or riding along a mountain footpath when you ought to lead your mule, or removing detonators when they have failed to function.

I closed my hands on the beard and tested it. The sleeper muttered. I barely moved it, but I could feel it was not attached to his skin. I faced him, so that with one motion I could pull it over his head and dive through the window. I pulled.

My Sikh's instructions had been quite accurate; but what he did not know or had not told me was that the elastic passed under the bun of the coiled and consecrated hair. I ought to have let go and jumped for safety. So I would have done, if the beard had stuck fast. But the sensation, during that vital second, was so indefinite. The elastic stretched. The bun of hair stretched and gave. The sleeper, still lying on his back, threw up his arms and grabbed hair, not elastic. I was all but away when he twisted on to his stomach and seized my hand. The next moment I was thrashing round the room with what seemed like four tigers and the entire Indian Army, all covered with long hair.

I grabbed a healthy tress and did not let go. His own objective was the precious beard. It could not be fought over and torn so he clamped a grip on my left wrist. That tied us up too tight for very much damage to be done by either side. It was lucky for me. If he had only broken away and charged in again, there would have been a dead sweep in the fireplace in the morning. As it was, he pinned me to the ground, face downwards, and I swear I expected him to bite through the vertebrae at the back of my neck.

We rolled round the room, both of us keeping the silence of evil consciences and neither of us daring to let go of what he had. Since he was trying to break my ribs with his knees, I wriggled half under the bed. He thought he had me then, and concentrated both his hands on my left, which held the beard. I was still hanging on to it because it kept one hand of his fully occupied – if one can talk of a 'because' in the mere reflexes of self-preservation.

The bed itself prevented him from twisting my wrist back and breaking it. Meanwhile, with the whole of his attack converging upon my left hand, he did not notice what I was doing with my right. I managed to take two turns of his hair round the leg of the bed, and secured it with a tangled, desperate half-hitch. Then I let go, and relieved the garrison of my left hand.

It was easy to move the scene of this undignified brawl a foot away from the bed. The jerk naturally disconcerted him. He let my hand go, and grabbed at the knot. For a moment I was clear of all interference. I plunged through the window and over the flat roof. Lights were going on. Several voices were shouting, some in foreign languages. My late enemy, who had freed himself – probably by just raising the bed – was already on the roof while I was running along the top of the party wall. I dropped into the lane and sprinted round the two corners, passing Sikh No. 1 on the way. He must have been waiting in the road and gloating over the bumps and crashes. He, too, began to run after me – not, I think, to pay the twelve pounds he owed me, but to clear himself of all complicity. Or he may have been just bolting for his own front door. I didn't stop to find out. I had visions of being ceremoniously impaled upon a spike of London railings by both of them. He was a faster runner than I, and it was fortunate that my bicycle was facing the right way.

I vanished at top speed, and then rode more sedately in case I met a policeman. I told myself severely that these high-spirited and infantile risks simply must not be taken. I had merely acquired a beard which I did not particularly want, and failed to borrow a turban, which I did. And I had been very lucky to get off with bruises and an aching wrist. If that was a fair example of a Sikh with somewhat effeminate tastes, I imagine that a more normal warrior could tear up the average European with one hand while continuing to comb his hair with the other.

I thought it unlikely that there would be any hue and cry after a sweep, and that the disturbance would be put down to fun and games among Indian students. The offended party could not tell degrees of colour in the dark; he had taken me for an Indian and hissed curses at me in languages which I did not understand. As for Sikh No. 1, having failed in whatever perfidy he intended, he could only pretend that he knew nothing and that I was no agent of his.

I settled down to pass the rest of the night in that bombed site which I had already visited. It was too cold to do more than doze with my knees up to my chin. But discomfort is relative; I had only to remember my buoy of the previous night to feel that I was well off. At dawn I repaired my make-up, which had suffered from the incidents of the night. There was the usual, pathetic fireplace embedded in a shattered wall, with sound, pre-war soot in the opening of the flue.

Exploration of the black brick wilderness around the North Eastern Goods Depot rewarded me with a so-called café which was open at 6 a.m., and a mound of hot bacon sandwiches. The proprietor was curious that sweeps, like railwaymen, should work at night, and bombarded me with questions. I took refuge in my former pose of an honest working man sullen with grievances.

I did not dare read the morning papers under the eyes of another human being. I bought a couple, looked firmly away from my own face on the front page and shoved them in my pocket. The district was short of open spaces in which to read a paper. Eventually I struck the Regent's Canal. There on the towpath, leaning against a filthy wall with the re-volting canal liquid at my feet, I lit a cigarette and read. My reactions were extraordinary – a mixture of fear and amuse-ment which made me giggle aloud. My mechanism was out of control, as if I had been hit hard on the funny bone.

The ship had landed her passengers on the afternoon tide. The party line – it was the only possible line – was to stick to my story that they were returning me as an example of their bona fide love of peace and fair dealing. I had both stowed away and been permitted to escape by the treacherous col-laboration of the anarchist officer who was responsible for security on board.

All this might have made a fine impression if apologies and explanations had been offered graciously and frankly; but of course they were as boorish as possible. Nobody but the British police and Customs had been allowed on board the ship. The communiqué was nothing but a sulky hand-out from the Embassy. None of the officials would reply to questions. In propaganda on both sides of the Iron Curtain charm is rare, for it is a quality in which propagandists are, by nature, notably deficient. Give me my small room in the

Tower – or even the Kremlin – and a printing-press, and I would guarantee to improve manners all round in a month.

Comment was banished to the middle pages, where leaders and special articles were busy attributing all the wrong motives to everyone concerned with astonishing ingenuity. The front page was entirely occupied by the traitor Howard-Wolferstan. The distressed Spanish seaman had been identified; as soon as that friendly interpreter had been reminded of my existence, he, of course, recognized me. The chemist from whom I bought my bandage had come forward at once. So had the second-hand clothes dealer. They were busting with excitement, and their shops had been photographed. Elias Thomas Conger had made a gallant effort to hog a column for himself, but had been swamped by the tall American, who was looking deliciously slim and shy, and exhibiting a shapely leg while seated on her baggage. Of Karlis there was nothing at all. He had not yet been picked up, and his existence was taken with a grain of salt.

The police were giving away everything they knew, so that the public could help. In the stop press of one paper was a paragraph to the effect that a man with a dark face and a bandage over one eye had been seen in Wapping. But that would be the end of the trail. Unless the watchman at the coal yard had seen me – and I was sure he had not – my metamorphosis into a sweep was going to take a long time to trace. Sikh No. 1 might recognize me, even from the film-star photograph, for he had certainly been staring into the question of what I looked like underneath the coal dust; but a sure instinct told me that his life among private friends and compatriots would be, for some time to come, too agitated to invite the unpredictable questions of European police.

Still, a second change of self was undoubtedly due – if there were any possibility of building it upon the magnificent set of beard, moustache and whiskers carefully folded up and stuffed inside my shirt. I retired again to a public lavatory – welcome though they are to any man, they seem to be essential to the criminal – and examined my remarkable piece of loot. It was expensively made by a first-class craftsman out of human hair, and undetectable so long as one wore a pugaree or turban well down to the ears to hide the elastic. A convincing headdress was what I had to buy.

The place to find that was Covent Garden. To pass the time, I walked there, pushing my bicycle. I attracted no attention at all beyond occasional kindly smiles from passers-by and once from a policeman. What swift promotion would have been his, had he stopped to wonder how a sweep could be so dirty early in the day! At half-past nine I found a small theatrical costumier's open. Again I had to take to cockney. I damned the expensive education which had landed me with a class accent. Ordinary, standard, gruff speech would have fitted a sweep perfectly well, but that was far harder to imitate than dialect.

"'Ad an early job, myte,' I said. 'Shan't look like this in 'alf an hour.'

The man behind the counter grinned at me and asked what I wanted. I cannot analyse what it is which makes people take kindly to a smiling sweep – perhaps the mere comicality of his appearance.

'Got to get a 'at for the Annual Ball to-night,' I explained. 'One o' them Indian turbans, like. Knock 'em cold, that will!'

'I can't let you hire it,' he answered.

'Tell you what. I'll buy it, see? And you can tyke it back afterwards. I'll keep it clean if yer wraps it up for me.'

'Got an idea what you want?' he asked.

'One o' them Bengal Lancer 'ats. Size six and three-quarters.'

He brought out one or two from the back of the shop. They were too gorgeous for anything but a pantomime emperor.

'More army, like,' I suggested.

He had a further search and laid four on the counter. One of them, in strong cotton of a faded blue, somewhat resembled that of my Sikh. It also had graceful lines, the lower folds sweeping from the temples down to the nape of the neck. Even in adversity one should not be indifferent to appearances. I am sure that half my motive in handing over Michael Bassoon to communist care was disgust at his oafishness.

This creation was mine for thirty bob, said the costumier, and I could have twenty-five back if I returned it in clean condition. He packed it up for me, and then winked.

'What's the joke?' he whispered. 'You nearly took me in. All perfect but the accent, and that's damn good!'

I winked back.

'Watch the bill at the Palladium in a month's time,' I said.

I bought soap, towel, shaving mirror, and needles and cotton for repairing the stretched elastic. Then, with my odd-shaped parcel of hat slung on the handlebars, I set out on the endless grind of pedalling into the country along the Great West Road. Not too far from London I hoped to find some quiet stream, hidden by bushes, where I could wash and assume my new personality.

It was a weary way for a man short of sleep and not accustomed to bicycling. By two o'clock I had only reached Slough, and still the houses lined the road. I crossed the Thames at Maidenhead and took the road to Cookham. There was no privacy at all by the river. You couldn't expect it in fine weather at the beginning of August. After Cookham I tried the other bank, which looked more hopeful. At last I found what I wanted – a backwater among willows and scrub. It was sluggish, muddy and uninviting to the general public.

Once safe among the bushes I undressed and slid into the water. The opposite bank was marsh, but even so I was terrified lest someone should appear. I was now plain, bronzed Howard-Wolferstan, naked in every sense. I never could get used to the fleeting moments when I had to be myself. I became a cowering fugitive, without anything whatever to prop my morale or amuse my impudence.

I tried on the mass of hair. It was a fair fit, but would be improved if a tuck were taken in the material under the chin. Lying on my stomach in the grass, I sewed away at the tuck and the elastic. Then I inserted my head into its new decorations and put on the blue pugaree, sick with nervousness lest it should stop short of the elastic. It did not. In fact, seen in the mirror, the effect of the whole outfit was princely. Confidence returned.

With better clothes I could have walked into the Ritz; but better clothes were as yet unobtainable. In spite of two windfalls, purchases had reduced my stock to under eleven pounds. I thoroughly cleaned my grey-brown suit – the police, eager to be precise, had helped me by committing themselves and the public to brown – and put it on again. Before I did so, I stamped my sweep's brushes hard down into the river mud. So irrevocable an act gave me a moment of misgiving. The sweep, so long as he kept moving, was safety. But there it was – he couldn't talk and he couldn't sleep under a roof.

I avoided crossing the bridge over which I had come, and followed the road north to High Wycombe. There I bought a small pack to fit my bicycle, a clean shirt and a waterproof cape – more to protect my pugaree than myself, for I could always stop and shelter from rain. No one in all England was in less of a hurry than I. At a Wardrobe Dealer (as he described himself), run for farm-hands who frequented the town on market days, I found a shabby old coat of excellent tweed. That at once made me appear of a social class more in keeping with the splendour of my whiskers.

The next urgent task was to find a small country inn where I could be put up cheaply and comfortably for the night, for I was pretty well exhausted. On the Oxford road I soon came to it and a landlord who, after a moment's hesitation, decided that the gorgeous East could not be alarming if dressed in an honest country coat. Food, alcohol and sleep were heaven. My face was on the television in the bar. I was too tired even to feel disgust for the grinning ape whose photograph they showed.

Morning brought a fresh day's papers. They were more entertaining. Karlis had been picked up, and indignant editorials were shooting down the whole of British security in flames. He had done the incredible – simply proceeded up river, dressed in Russian uniform, steering a launch the name of which was written in Russian characters and, after drying himself out and filling up with petrol, reached Richmond without being questioned by a soul. That, of course, was the kind of thing which could only happen if a man were simply waiting to give himself up; he surrounded himself with a spiritual aura of innocence. If I had tried it, the first police boat would have swooped down on me.

He had sworn that I pushed Elias Thomas Conger overboard. I fear that a distant note of schoolboy giggle was noticeable in the newspaper comment. Otherwise, the police merely announced that he had confirmed the official story. I never heard any more of him than the rest of the public. Apparently the United States asked for him, and we quietly and thankfully let him go. I doubt if he could have been a success; he hadn't imagination enough to earn a good living out of one of their Committees of Public Safety. He would have done better to write for the Sunday papers as I advised him.

In dealing with myself the papers were still severe, though under the bloodthirsty language I detected a furtive shade of admiration, perhaps reflecting the tone of the talk in Fleet Street bars. They could not get away from the fact that I had convulsed the security services of two empires. It was a pity, I gathered, that I had been corrupted by a Latin-American background. Without that, my enterprise might have been directed to the more worthy ventures of the New Elizabethan Age. I spotted the patriotic note. So long as I remained successfully on the run, I should be an Englishman – though monstrously perverted – of the true breed; but the moment I was a convicted traitor, I was jolly well going to be an Ecuadorian.

I found myself painfully stiff from unaccustomed exercise on buoys, Sikhs and a bicycle, so I decided to stay another night at the pub and restore myself to normal. I passed as a well-born Punjabi exploring England on little money. In that part my way of speech aroused no comment, for an anglicized Indian was not expected to have either a local or a foreign accent. To avoid registration as an alien, I stated, with convincing details, that I had been born in London. The only snag I found was the occasional cheery ex-soldier who insisted on addressing me in some jargon of which every sentence ended in 'hai'. I think it was Urdu. I was, however, at perfect liberty to grin understandingly and answer in English.

The next day I went on to Oxford, and strolled in the gardens of my college to complete recuperation. Stobbs, who had been under-porter in my day, was now head porter. When I passed through the lodge in my character of oriental tourist, he was dealing with a newspaperman who wanted reminiscences of Howard-Wolferstan. I listened, pretending to be reading the notices on the board. A very wild young gentleman, said Stobbs with evident approval, not like what they got nowadays. Well, but was he a communist? Stobbs refused to remember, and I had the impression that a pound note changed hands.

'This college,' said Stobbs, ''as changed the King of England, and wished it 'adn't. And if any of the young gentlemen 'ad politics which they wished later *they* 'adn't, it's no business of yours nor mine, because when you've 'ad my experience you'll always know where the best of 'em are.'

The reporter unwisely asked where. Stobbs jerked his thumb at the war memorial and returned to his work.

Pleasant though it was to be again, for a moment, out of the reach of time, Oxford was no place for me. Even in the Long Vac. earnest souls from east of Suez chattered their way from college to college, and seemed eager that I, too, should enjoy their enjoyment. I became weary of hiding up staircases or pretending to be short-sighted. The impression was growing upon me that our small island – at any rate in its more sophisticated towns – was becoming a mere suburb of Asia. We had all the disadvantages of empire, without the power. A social historian might well put it the other way round, but the difficulties of a harassed and bogus oriental would not occur to him.

Plainly it was best to stick to country towns and villages where Punjabis were whatever I said they were. I pedalled north without the expensive lunch which I had proposed to offer myself. It was as well. Clothes and two nights at an inn had reduced my store to four pounds and a little silver.

Along the road, on the blank walls of barns and, as I neared Banbury, on occasional hoardings, were bills of Benjafield's

Circus. They suggested possibilities for the temporary employment of a picturesque Indian out of a job. Nobody could
know less of circuses than I did, but at least I brought a fresh
mind to the business. The only ideas I had had for earning a
living were fortune-telling or casual agricultural labour. Both
were likely to lead to registration with some official.

I found Benjafield's on a field outside Banbury. It was
a small show, combined with a singularly grubby travelling fair. I called at the proprietor's caravan. His wife was
inside, doing accounts in a space about four feet by two, surrounded by pigeon-holes full of files. Her face had that matt
cream-yellow tint of a hard-working entertainer without
make-up, and the rest of her was lean and wiry. She looked
at me as if I were nothing out of the ordinary and told me to
see Fred. I should find him with the horses.

This glimpse of neatness warned me not to underrate
circus intelligence. There was efficiency, too, in the lay-out
and cleanliness of the motor caravans, the power unit and
the horse lines. The fairground caravans, however, had the
melancholy of detribalization. Their inhabitants were content to earn a living by offering the public the very least it
would accept.

Mr Fred Benjafield was bathing the off fore of a *pinto*
liberty horse. He had the keen and worried expression of
a good farmer on poor land – though no farmer I ever met
had his effortless, Caesar-like ability to do three things at
the same time. During his conversation with me, which was
conducted, apart from a first long inspection, entirely over
his shoulder, he never stopped cursing the groom or doctor-
ing the horse.

'What can you do?' he asked. 'Now then? Can't expect the
public just to look at your whiskers, you know!'

'Why not? Put me in a uniform at the door.'

'Haven't got a uniform. What's the matter with you?'

'Broke,' I said, 'and don't want to ask my father for money.'

The mass of glossy hair made me ageless. I could put my age at twenty-five and be believed. The position I imagined had often been true enough before the war – not that I had ever been afraid to ask my beloved father for money, nor he reluctant to give it. But there had been times when I was so ashamed of my extravagance that I laid on myself, as a sort of pleasant penance, a month of very quiet living. That was how the English countryside came to be familiar to me.

'What's your name?'

I had called myself Ram Singh at the pub; but that, I discovered, committed me absolutely to being a Sikh. A little more elasticity was needed.

'Faiz Ullah,' I answered on the spur of the moment.

It was the only Indian name I could remember – a wild quirk of memory caused by horses, for it belonged to a polo pony in Kipling's 'Maltese Cat'.

'Know anything about elephants?' Benjafield asked.

I feared that would come. No one could look at me without thinking of elephants. Still, I could not complain. It might have been tigers.

'I'm better with horses,' I answered.

'Any act?'

'No. Just ride them and groom them.'

'What's so bloody marvellous about that?'

'Well, what's so bloody marvellous about elephants?'

'This is,' he said. 'The public wants 'em, so I have to have a damn useless pair of 'em.'

'What sex?' I asked.

'Female, of course. You don't have male elephants in this business. For one thing, they're unreliable. And for another, you can't have the children pointing at 'em and calling out, "Ma, what's *that* thing?"'

He worked himself into a swift passion with the groom for not noticing earlier the state of the *pinto's* off fore. I felt it was time to assert myself.

'Two female elephants are known as a sisterhood, not a pair,' I said.

'Not in the circus, they aren't. A pair of bitches, I call 'em.'

'What's wrong with them?'

'They can't do a bloody thing except sit on tubs.'

'Well, what do you keep them for?'

'Haven't I told you?' he stormed at me. 'Because the bloody public wants elephants.'

'I'll have a look at them,' I said. 'I used to play around in the elephant stables as a boy.'

He detailed the groom, whose name was Steve, to show me the elephants. It was Steve's business to feed them, and Mrs Benjafield used to show them.

'There y'are!' said Steve. 'That one's Pearl, and that one's Topaz.'

He strolled off and left me to it. There is a terrifying ruthlessness in the circus. You either can or you can't, and they want to find out at once.

Pearl and Topaz were small elephants, about seven feet high at the shoulder; but the two uncompromising backsides which faced me seemed the biggest chunks of flesh I had seen since the death of my great aunt – not, of course, that she had ever revealed herself to me so unashamedly, but my head, as a small boy, was on a comparable level.

They were in a canvas shelter, like the horses, and both tethered by a fore-leg. Pearl was on the left. I pushed my way between her ribs and the canvas, and told her to get over. She got over, and examined my whiskers and turban with her left eye. She was not impressed. She filled her trunk from a bucket of water and squirted it down her throat. I understood her perfectly. The next trunk load was going to be for me if I didn't get out of there. She expressed her opinion of me still more forcibly as I passed behind her to talk to Topaz.

Topaz received me with a squeal of joy. She was much stupider than Pearl. She thought I was the real goods straight from Lahore, and at once investigated my trousers with her trunk. My experience of the Americas suggested that this was not indelicacy, but a search for something which a former trainer used to keep in his sash. If I were wearing the *faja* or sash and had some bulky treat for my riding animal, it would be there that I should put it.

One could not, I perceived, treat elephants as horses. They were too placid and too intelligent. Yet I had no intimate knowledge of any other animal. It seemed best, therefore, to count on sex rather than zoology and to put my trust in their immense and undoubted femininity.

It is a poor excuse when calling on maiden ladies to say that the shops were shut, so I strolled out into the fairground, which was waiting for the evening and meanwhile doing a desultory business with a few holiday-makers and a lot of children. It seemed to me that toffee-apples were likely to be popular with elephants. One could even present them in a vast box tied up with blue ribbon.

I tried to bargain with the stall-holder for her spoiled, or yesterday's, toffee-apples. She didn't 'ave none spoiled, and yesterday's was kept 'ygienic and good as new. She was perfectly well aware that I was trying to get a job with the circus – news travelled from end to end of the community in about thirty seconds – and when I got it, *if* I got it, I could have toffee-apples at the trade rate. I did not tell her I wanted them for the elephants, thinking it best to keep my secrets as an animal trainer to myself, so I paid the full price and removed the sticks.

I returned to Pearl and Topaz with five toffee-apples in my pocket and one in the waistband of my trousers. They had decided during my absence that I was no conceivable use to the sisterhood. At last, by offering my navel to Topaz with the abandon of an oriental dancer, I managed to persuade her into trying again. She removed the toffee-apple, ate it, and promptly discovered the rest. I allowed her two, and moved over to Pearl, followed by the weavings of an affectionate trunk.

Pearl had regarded this undignified flirtation with contempt. She paid not the slightest attention to me, and I was compelled to lay a toffee-apple at her feet. She picked it up and dropped it daintily into Topaz's straw, Topaz wasn't proud. She ate it.

I could not believe that Pearl did not like toffee-apples. Plainly she was just sulking, so I sulked, too, and turned to go. I was half-way between the sisterhood when the finger of a trunk closed upon the back of my collar and gently persuaded me back. I assumed it belonged to Topaz. I discovered, when deposited in front of her, that it belonged to Pearl. I patted her trunk, said it was time to go now, and decidedly went.

No use. I was popped back again at the tea-table. I reminded myself firmly that if she meant mischief she would not be so oddly formal about it. We stared at each other. Pearl's expressive eyes were not malicious. She was not even laughing at me. She was plain disappointed. 'Here am I,' she almost said, 'a fitting companion for an intelligent person, but I still find that gentlemen prefer Topazes.'

In my perplexity Topaz caressed me with her trunk. She was intolerably motherly – now that she was assured of a supply of toffee-apples. Pearl, on the other hand, had something really solid to offer if only I could guess what it was. Had she, perhaps, been taught some bit of broad comedy by the unknown trainer of whom I reminded her, or worked with the clowns? I petted all I could reach, and apologized to her for stupidity. When again I offered her a toffee-apple she was graciously pleased to shoot it down her maw. We left it at that, reserving judgment about each other.

Confident that I was just as capable as anyone else of watching the sisterhood sit on tubs, I went in search of Mr Benjafield. He was supervising the complicated rigging of nets and trapezes. The trapeze artists were with him. A couple of Germans they were – Stoffel and Schatz. I don't wonder that the speakers of that insensitive language feel outlawed from the rest of Europe. *Treasure, trésor, joya* – all have syllables which lend themselves reasonably to a term of endearment. But *schatz,* though meaning the same, sounds like a small piece of machinery. It must, I think, be one of the reasons for the peculiar complexes of Germans – that they are continually using words, the meaning of which contradicts the primitive emotional value of the sounds. However, Schatz was a most attractive girl and fascinated by my whiskers.

'I'll take over your elephant act,' I told Benjafield.

'What d'ye mean – take it over?' he shouted. 'Feed 'em and shovel up after 'em, that's what I want you for.'

I replied that of course I would, but that the chap who lived with them ought to show them.

'Tell that to the missus,' he said.

It was not irony. It was a simple order, and he returned immediately to tightening up a shiny steel stay.

Mrs Benjafield, dressed in a sun-top, a pyjama jacket and a smart tweed skirt, was haggling with a couple of farmers. I had learned by this time that if you didn't interrupt, nothing would ever get said. So I gave her husband's message.

'There you are, you see!' she snapped at the farmers. 'Take it or leave it!'

What they had to see, I suppose, was that she was inordinately busy. They were stunned into accepting her offer.

Mrs Benjafield led me straight over to the elephants. I respected that woman. She admitted she knew nothing of their finer points, and that all animals were alike to her. She could manage anything on four legs well enough to get by with a provincial public. But the trouble was that she performed already on the tight-rope, in a stock-whip act with Fred and with the liberty horses. When she appeared with the elephants as well, Benjafields began to look like a one-woman circus.

I unchained the sisterhood with some misgivings. Topaz, exploring for more sweets, was kind enough to put on a show of affection. They followed us over to the big top, Topaz hanging on to Pearl's tail. At the entrance to the tent, Pearl put out a forefoot as a stirrup, and Mrs Benjafield hoisted herself up by the ear. I expected Topaz to do the same, but she did not – and I was left to the experience gained in my father's elephant stables. I said *Toffee hai*, which sounded reasonably Indian, and pulled Topaz's ear. She got that, and put out a foot. I found out later that I need not have bothered. Ear pulling was enough.

Steve and an assistant rolled the tubs into the ring. I folded my arms, looked inscrutable and prayed that I would not fall off. After half a dozen circuits Mrs Benjafield slid down and struck a pose. So did I. Both animals put their forefeet on the tubs, then all their feet, then sat on them with trunks curled up. That was that – bar a bit of showmanship to make it all look harder. The elephants were bored stiff. So was Mrs Benjafield. They would have gone through exactly the same performance whether she shouted 'Hup!' or whether she didn't.

She asked me if I thought I could take over the act. I replied tactfully that a beard was no substitute for beauty, but if the public would put up with me, so no doubt would the elephants.

The evening performance, which I watched carefully, revealed nothing more except the legal maximum of Mrs Benjafield who sat on Pearl's head dressed as a harem beauty. For a hard-working woman in the late thirties she was not at all bad; at any rate the sultan would have had every right to expect a fulsome letter of thanks when he handed her over to one of his more earnest civil servants as a Christmas present. The elephants were also conscious of their duty to the public. Pearl had a red and silver pad on her head, and Topaz a blue and gold. I noticed that they enjoyed applause.

The Benjafields supplied me with blankets and a pup tent which I pitched alongside the elephant shelter; but after the performance there was no chance at all of getting into it. I had to undress, tether and feed Topaz and Pearl. Steve showed me how to do it, when I explained that our customs in India would probably be impracticable in a travelling circus. After that, Stoffel and Schatz took good German pity on me, and talked to me interminably about the homesickness they assumed I ought to feel. They were trying to show themselves more human than the English; it did not occur to them that the unfeeling English had taken it for granted that I wanted to sleep.

The sisterhood woke up in excellent form. They were impressed, I think, by the fact that I had pitched my tent alongside their own. I had become a familiar smell. So had they. After an hour's work with shovel, straw and wheelbarrow, and another hour of grooming, I got an excellent breakfast. No sooner was that down than Benjafield told me to take out the elephants before the ring was wanted for other rehearsals, and see what I could do with them by myself.

I was in trouble at once. That damned Pearl would not put out her foot for me to mount, so I climbed on to Topaz. She was quite insufferable with girlish pride, and picked up a wisp of straw and repaired her make-up. What surprised me was that Pearl did not seem to mind. She even looked at me as if I had shown a first and quite unexpected flicker of intelligence.

Round the ring we went, Topaz stepping out and Pearl hanging on to her tail as if the indignity did not bother her at all. They went through their tricks with alacrity, and barely gave me time to say 'Hup!' in the proper places.

That was fine. But when I pulled Topaz's ear and she put out her foot for me to mount and lead the procession off, Pearl spanked her – a whack with the trunk which could have been heard in Banbury.

Topaz and I stood about looking guilty. I, at any rate, did not know how to humour this old-maidish temper. I thought that Pearl might consider it her turn to be ridden, so I tried. No, that was not it. I offered her a toffee-apple. She stamped it into the sawdust. She was rocking herself gently from side to side, and her eyes were impatient. I began to think it was a long way to the entrance and started to walk to it, hoping that Pearl would follow, but not too fast. She didn't even try to follow. She reached out her trunk and detained me, just as she had done in her stall.

I reminded myself that if these elephants had not been tame as dogs, the Benjafields would not have risked allowing me to rehearse them alone. But what is logic when standing by the forefoot of an exasperated elephant? I retired delicately to her hindquarters and bolted. I heard four ponderous strides. The waistband of my trousers was grabbed from behind, and I was lifted kicking and helpless into the air. Pearl deposited me upon her back, and curled up her trunk in salute. Nervously I placed a toffee-apple in it. She didn't even try to hold it. I was spoiling the climax of her act. She strode out of the ring, followed submissively by Topaz.

Once outside, she was all over me, and any toffee apples I chose to produce. When I had surreptitiously lifted my beard, wiped off the sweat and stopped trembling (for I defy anyone to remember that charging elephants possibly mean well), I realized that I was being petted and encouraged. I was quite a clever animal who had understood.

In fact I had not. But I was prepared to work for anyone who would teach me a trade and ask no questions. So back we went to the ring while it was still empty. There was a spirit of enterprise in the air. The vicar, as it were, had agreed to the sisterhood's plans for the church bazaar. We dealt perfunctorily with the tubs, and then Pearl trained us in the remainder of the act. My working hypothesis was that I reminded her of some bearded Indian, genuine or bogus, in her past, and that I was expected to do what he did.

After bowing to imaginary applause, I tried to mount Topaz. Pearl hauled me away. Infinitely patient, she insisted that I was not to mount Topaz, while half a dozen times I tried other possible moves. At last I got the right one. I had to pretend to grow angry or nervous and run away. She then caught me by the belt, hoisted me on to her noble head and proudly led the procession out. It was the old trick of a favourite animal refusing to leave the ring until given what it wants, and a most spectacular ending to the act. No wonder

Pearl had been obstinate. She could never have taught the trick to Mrs Benjafield, for Mrs B. wore nothing by which she could be lifted.

Back in the elephant shelter, Pearl and I congratulated each other. Topaz showed no resentment. She had learned over the years that mere tender simplicity could not compete with the temperament of Pearl. I made them comfortable – to keep up with their appetites called for a tractor, not a wheelbarrow – and went in search of Mr Benjafield. He was out at the rubbish tip, killing bluebottles with a stock-whip at a range of ten yards. If those he hit were always those he aimed at, he was a remarkable artist.

'What do I get if I keep your elephants and show them?' I asked.

'Ten a week, and find yourself.'

'Any bonus for a new trick?'

'Depends what,' he said, massaging a bit of potato off the lash of the whip.

'Good enough for the bills. Is it worth an extra ten quid to you?'

'What's your opinion of Pearl, son?'

I guessed the way his mind was running. Pearl, in one of her moods of frustration, might well have shown herself unreliable. He didn't want any risks with the safety of the public.

'Did she ever show any signs of trying to leave Mrs Benjafield in a state of nature?' I asked.

'What?' he roared.

He was no prude, of course. It was just that the absolute respectability of Benjafield's was an unquestioned first principle.

'Picking at her trunks and that sort of thing,' I explained, sounding rather like a headmaster.

'She did have some nasty foreign ways before Mrs Ben-jafield taught her better,' he admitted shyly.

'Just a complex,' I said. 'I've cured it. Now how about that bonus?'

'You can have it, if the act's worth it,' he replied, 'and I'm the judge of that. But I'm a fair man. They'll all tell you.'

He was a bit doubtful about letting me show the elephants on the three o'clock house that very afternoon, but Mrs Ben-jafield, who urgently wanted to be rid of them, backed me up. She would be standing by, she said, if anything went wrong. Her husband showed far more confidence when I tried on a few fancy dresses from the circus wardrobe. I was the right colour all over – a genuine foreign colour it appeared to him, though anyone could acquire it on a Mediterranean holiday.

I chose a pair of acrobats' trunks and some baggy pants of blue silk to go over them. Round the top I buckled a regular lion-tamer of a belt. Pearl could hoist away on that, if I left it fairly loose, without giving me the sensation of being cut in two.

When we entered the ring I must admit I suffered from stage fright. The private theatricals which I had been con-ducting for the last two and a half months were no help at all in facing this goggling circle of white faces. From sheer shyness I hung on to the character of a stern and unbending mahout. Pearl, however, played to the crowd and supplied the comedy. There was a communal gasp from the audience when she chased me and a salvo of relieved clapping when we marched out. Benjafield handed me ten welcome pound notes in the sight of all. He loved a lordly gesture when he had a reasonable excuse to make it.

In the evening we overdid it. While running away I stepped on the toffee-apple which Pearl had flung from her in pretended contempt, and fell full length in the sawdust.

That gave me a moment of complex panic. I was simultaneously afraid that Pearl would step on me and that, if she didn't, she would swing me aloft before I could recover my indispensable pugaree. A passing thought of Howard-Wolferstan might easily occur to some budding detective among audience or performers if the spotlight picked up the black elastic which held on my beard and whiskers.

Neither disaster happened. Pearl was sure-footed, and my hat within reach and back on my head before the sawdust cleared. When we were out of the ring, Benjafield relieved his feelings by telling me off good and proper. Gross carelessness in rehearsal. Always watch where your properties fall. And above all never make the women scream. I had not even heard them. Little Schatz told me afterwards that Pearl had missed me by inches. Pearl would. It was her sense of theatre. She could have missed me by a couple of feet if she had wanted to.

During the following week I relaxed for the first time since my escape from Saxminster courthouse. I thought that I was now set as an elephant trainer, thanks to Pearl. Instead of concentrating on the next six hours and planning ahead for two days at the most, I could dream of a future. Ten elephants. Thirty elephants. Accompany a circus to South America. And freedom.

It did me good. In fact without this interlude of rest I doubt if I could have carried on. As a dejected rogue I was futile, but as a cheerful rogue I felt in character. That first week of Benjafield's was a fool's paradise, yet none the less valuable.

The circus moved up from Banbury to Rugby. At a halt on the way I was smoking a cigarette in Benjafield's caravan and chatting peacefully, when he came out with:

'Mind if I ask you something, son?'

I did not. Fred Benjafield, within his limitations, never talked anything but sense.

'Why do you wear that beard and turban of yours all the time?'

It was no good trying to bluff him with nonsense about my religion. He knew the beard was false. I murmured something about a disfigurement on my chin.

'Any time you want to take 'em off, son,' he said, ignoring my wretched excuse, 'I'd like you to know that in this business we keep our traps tight shut about a performer's properties.'

I was never more impressed by the fact that we are all islands, without the least idea of what is really going on in our fellows' minds. It had astonished me that nobody doubted I was an Indian, or suspected that Pearl and Topaz were the first elephants I had ever handled. Yet the one secret of which I was sure was common knowledge.

It was natural enough. There was no privacy. I had taken all possible precautions, only washing my face at dead of night in what was left of the elephants' warm drinking water. But there had been times in daylight when Topaz had disturbed my beard – she was one of those females who can't help being indiscreet in the display of affection – and times, apart from my accident in the ring, when the pugaree had been knocked half off before I could straighten it.

So far as Benjafield knew, the false beard was only suspected by himself, his wife and Steve – and all three of them passionately minded their own business. But my safety was hanging on a thread. Mr and Mrs Benjafield never read a newspaper from April to October. They had no time; neither had most of their employees. Over in the fairground, however, the chief occupation during idle mornings was spelling out the police news in the popular press.

I had to think quickly of some other trade by which I could earn a bare livelihood without the continual risk of exposing a bit of black elastic. In spite of weekly wage and bonus, I had hardly any money. All had gone in providing badly needed comforts and clothes. A means of living almost at once suggested itself, but I had to get it out of Herr Stoffel and spend, I reckoned, at least a week on the job.

It was not his wife – though that comely young acrobat certainly entered into my plans – but the guitar which he had picked up in Spain. I could not afford to buy it, and anyway, he would not part with it for mere money. He was the citron-blooming type of German, always drivelling about the Mediterranean. He had even learned to play a tune or two, but the guitar was only an instrument of blasphemy in his hands. You have to be born to its music. Even my father, who could sing admirably in his second language, could never accompany himself. I, however, have been used from my earliest years to the guitar passing from guest to guest at any informal party, and I can perform as well as my neighbour – perhaps a little better, for in 1942 I held down a job as guitarist at a cabaret in the port of Callao. That did not do any good to Germans, either.

Schatz at bottom was a complete innocent, without a useful thought beyond new methods of turning herself inside out in mid air; so she could not help a wild and unreal romanticism. The wideness of the world, the lovers who might be at her feet (if only she had time) and the careers she might have followed (if only she had not been superbly good at one) packed her dreams during the two hours of the day – it couldn't have been more – when she was not engaged in practising or cooking or sleep. Consequently she was drawn to opposites. No human being could come much nearer than she to flight; nothing could be more earthbound than elephants. Stoffel was an extremely serious and worthy young blond with hardly a hair on his body; I – well, I need not emphasize the contrast.

I fear that Schatz had already begun to show a tendency to become the third female in my care, but my behaviour was impeccable. This unaccustomed and perhaps unnecessary morality was, I must admit, materially affected by the fact that I never could be sure of enough privacy to take off my beard and wash it. So I smelt abominably of elephant. To gather little Schatz into that primeval forest, or to take it off, would have shown a lack not only of principles but common sense.

After my private decision to leave the circus, I was compelled to give her some encouragement. I told her the story of my life at my father's court. I explained to her – since it was what she wanted to hear – that the West had got civilization the wrong way up. I treated her as a daughter – an engaging relationship which, provided it is not a fact, may be allowed to develop in any direction the interested parties choose. It was all very hard work, and much of it was carried on while filling wheelbarrows, or up the step-ladder grooming Pearl and Topaz.

While we were at Rugby, Schatz spent far too much time in the elephant lines listening to tales of the gorgeous East. One night she turned up in hardly more than she wore for the public. I kept my mind firmly on the guitar and the sexless good-fellowship of the circus, and explained to her that in India we were easily shocked. She called me St Anthony of the Elephants. It was, as Wellington said, a damned close thing, and, by God, I don't think it could have been done if Pearl hadn't been there! Her attitude towards Schatz was much like her treatment of Topaz – friendly but contemptuous. As the flesh and the devil were about to overwhelm me, I took refuge beneath that all-embracing trunk.

When Stoffel complained to Benjafield, I judged that the time was ripe to approach the subject of the guitar. I knew that he had complained because Benjafield had a long and friendly conversation with me in which he pointed out that the morality of circus folk was the highest in all England. I dare say it was. Sixteen hours a day doesn't leave much time for dalliance.

It was difficult to find an occasion for an interview alone with Stoffel. Either the pair were practising or out shopping together, or Schatz was hanging round the elephants. I had to wait for a morning when, owing to a slight coldness between the pair of them, Schatz did her shopping alone. I called at the caravan and bored Stoffel with conversation. After a while I took down the guitar and began to play. I had never dared to do so while any identity was still mysterious; but now everyone *knew* I was an Indian.

Stoffel, surprised, invited me to sing. I replied that I knew no Spanish, only the tunes.

'But how?' he asked.

'I made a study of Western folk music for the sake of my spiritual development. The tunes which come most easily to me must be those I heard in a former existence.'

Stoffel gave this remark his most serious German consideration. I knew he would.

'You mean you were a Spaniard in a previous incarnation?' he asked.

'I am sure of it.'

'I do not think the evidence sufficient,' he said solemnly. 'Forgive me!'

That was as good an opening as another. I explained that my spiritual development was being hindered by the circus, and that I wanted to leave it. Stoffel did his best to keep a polite dead pan, but hope simply leaped into his normally expressionless face.

'You're good,' he said. 'But perhaps you could teach Steve to take over your act.'

He thought I took a pride in my craft. I admired that. He had a one-track mind, but it was a kindly track.

'I could,' I replied, 'easily. But I've no other way of earning a living on my travels – except music.'

'Can you play other instruments?'

'Only the guitar.'

He weighed up the comparative values of his guitar and Schatz. But that is a most unfair way to describe his second's hesitation. He knew what he must do, and the silence was only one of disappointment. He treasured that guitar. It was a symbol of what he would like to be, never could be and wouldn't enjoy if he was. But we are all so made that those are the most difficult dreams to surrender. Schatz and her mysterious Faiz Ullah. Stoffel and his useless guitar. I hope, when both had vanished, they found time to pay a little more attention to the reality of each other.

'I can't give you its value,' I said. 'Only a couple of pounds and an old bicycle.'

Of course Stoffel took it, and I went straight round to see Benjafield. He was hurt. He offered me proper quarters, more money, anything in the way of comfort that the circus could provide. He could not make out why I wanted to leave him.

'Circus morality,' I told him magnificently. 'I do not wish to see two other hearts broken besides my own.'

He patted me on the back and blew his nose. It is astonishing how those tough eggs in the show business can reduce themselves to the intelligence which the public expects of them. Journalists, of course, are the same. Benjafield, with his knowledge of men, could not have believed for a moment that, if I had a heart to break at all, I should talk about it in the terms of a novelette. But the convention was in his blood.

I must admit, however, that I did find in myself a quite unexpected depth of sentimentality. It saddened me that Pearl should hoist Mrs Benjafield again upon her back, and that other hands but mine should be calloused by the hayfork, the shovel and the wheelbarrow. I went out to the fairground and bought them a dozen toffee-apples apiece. Dear Pearl and Topaz, a prisoner in the Tower, about to eat his lunch, salutes you! The chaste kiss upon the forehead with which I bade farewell to Schatz had not the power to affect me of those coiling trunks. It matters not at all that they only represented sensuality in search of toffee-apples. It is in the nature, the too poetic nature, of the male to believe on such evidence that he is loved.

I was now well equipped for the road. I had my last week's wages, and a pack with all necessities and change of clothing. Over my shoulder was the guitar, safely protected from rain in an oilskin case. I strode out happily from Rugby and picked up the quiet, straight lane of the Fosse Way, writing and singing my songs as I went.

I had to write them. It was far too risky to draw attention to myself by singing in Spanish. The papers were again growing tired of Howard-Wolferstan, but they had given him a good run. Meanwhile the police, who had come in for columns of unmerited abuse, were still picking up harmless Latin Americans and asking them to show their passports. So I hit on a really brilliant idea. As I did not dare to use Spanish, I decided to translate my repertoire into Quechua. It was fairly improbable that I should meet anyone who could swear it was not a language of India – since India, I believe, speaks some three hundred – and if I ran into some exile from the high Andes who could speak Quechua or even recognize it, he would be far more interested in giving me a chance to explain myself than in a humourless rush for the police.

Myself, I spoke it with more freedom than accuracy. Some I had picked up from my nurse, the colour of whose Sunday garment had so intrigued Veronica, and the rest from Indian labourers at one of my father's mining camps on the Peruvian border – the only useful asset which ever came out of that concession. But, however bad my Quechua, at least it sounded like a language; when I did not know a word or could not find a rhyme, I invented whatever was required with the correct consonants and vowels. The result was rather as if one were to translate English lyrics into schoolboy French and sing them with a passably good accent.

After a couple of nights in which I learned by heart my preposterous Quechua couplets, I struck down into Stratford-on-Avon to try out my trade. It was instantly profitable, and would have been more so if I had only known how to do the collection. I couldn't take off my pugaree and set it at my feet to receive coins; so the English, not being sure whether I was performing for money or not, hesitated to shower their offerings on the pavement. Some North American tourists, however, had no such scruples. They solved the problem by stuffing money into my pocket. They could not make me out at all – an Indian singing (as they put it) Mexican songs.

One of them, a solid old fellow who looked as if he might have been a colonial administrator, said he betted I came from the Philippines. To please him I admitted it. I instantly found myself being cross-questioned in English and several unknown tongues, and I was not sorry when the police moved me on for causing a crowd to collect. I had learned at the circus to look a policeman in the eye – apologetically, of course. But I dared not take the least chance with the Law in Stratford. There was evidently a tradition that tourists should only be entertained in the name of Shakespeare.

For a week thereafter I practised my art in the villages. The farmers and squires and Birmingham business men who inhabited the grey stone houses of the Cotswolds were resigned to improbable musicians; they had to put up with Morris dancing, harps, sackbuts, psalteries and all other kinds of Olde Englishe music. September began still and golden, the days exquisite for walking, the nights too cool for sleeping out. I had some slight difficulty in obtaining bed and breakfast, for, after all, I was a hairy heathen with no visible means of support; but when I had been taken in I always found a warm interest in myself and my supposed country. I should like to discuss that with an intelligent Indian and find out if he shared my astonishment that the people should accept so strange and foreign a nation as unquestioned partners. History, since we saluted the sub-continent and departed, is taking an exciting turn.

Stratford had given me due warning of the risk of playing in any town big enough to have a resident policeman and a handy bench of magistrates. Yet, when I walked into Chipping Camden on a market day, I could not resist unslinging the guitar. I felt in place, socially and aesthetically. That ancient and lovely wool town cried out that it had been accustomed to wandering foreigners, with money or without, for five hundred years; and those same houses which now enclosed and gave spirit to an Anglo-Ecuadorian pursued for High Treason had looked down, I persuaded myself, tolerantly upon buyers all exquisite from Constantinople or lousy and furred from Moscow.

I had not seen a little town so faultless and receiving since

I left Quito. I placed my guitar cover on the flagstones, with a few coins in it to encourage the public, and played for pleasure as much as for gain. But as soon as I had finished a couple of Asturian *jotas* – they lent themselves more readily to Quechua than the modes of the south – I was moved on by the local sergeant of police. I dutifully moved, but so did a score of my listeners. I was as obstinate as the Pied Piper, operating in the midst of somewhat similar architecture. Three times I picked up my money, slung the guitar and started again in a side street. A modest audience followed me. So, after a decent interval and reluctantly, did the sergeant. Eventually he ran me in.

Name: Faiz Ullah. Address: Nil. Occupation: Musician. I might get off with a small fine, but what I most dreaded was the kindliness of the Law. No one would be happy until assured that I was not in want. However good my story, I should be remanded for further enquiries, and a letter sent to the High Commissioner of India or Pakistan (I had never really decided to which I belonged) with copy to Scotland Yard.

That's what you get for being carried away by generous temperament. I blamed myself for an utter lunatic. One always curses oneself, in trouble, for following instinct instead of reason. Yet Chipping Camden's tolerant mediaevalism did in fact come to my rescue. My subconscious feeling that the character of the inhabitants must be conditioned by the aesthetic appeal of their town turned out to be correct. As the melancholy procession – the sergeant, Faiz Ullah and some small boys – passed a pub on the corner of the main street, two local worthies of influence if not of leisure leaned out of the open window of the saloon bar.

'What are you running him in for, John?'

The speaker had a round face, reddened by Cotswold wind

and some fifty years of good living. He was a shade too casual to be either farmer or landowner. I tried to measure his quality as desperately as any stranded climber hanging from a strange rope. He was solidly of Chipping Camden, tweeds, manner and all, but had an air of the wider world of business. He left his tankard discreetly upon the table inside the pub, whereas his companion was leaning over the window-sill, shamelessly brandishing his beer in the face of the public.

'Causing a crowd to collect, Mr Moleyns,' the sergeant answered.

'Wouldn't he move on when you told him to?'

'He did. But look at the traffic, sir!'

My last pitch had, I must admit, interfered with a sudden and quite unexpected rush of market traffic from the south. That was chiefly the fault of a lorry driver who pretended he couldn't get through because he wanted to stare and listen. The baaing of the sheep in his lorry and the tooting of horns behind had brought the sergeant again.

'Oh, we mustn't be too hard on strolling minstrels in Camden,' said Mr Moleyns. 'And he's good, you know! I've been listening. Couldn't we turn him loose in the car park?'

'Not on market day.'

'Let him play in my pasture then. He won't be breaking any by-law there.'

'Not if you permit, sir. But it wouldn't do him much good,' said the sergeant, his community spirit overcoming him, 'unless we organized it, like.'

'Organize it, Adrian! Organize it!' declared his companion in a voice which covered an entire octave. 'A pastoral of the age of reason! And whence, sir, come your songs?'

'The Spanish Indies,' I answered.

'Do you then ignore the papal line of 1493?'

'Don't worry the poor man, Thomas!' said Adrian Moleyns. 'He means Goa and places like that.'

'Goa, my dear fellow, following, as I have already indicated, the arbitration of Pope Alexander VI, is Portuguese. And these excellent tunes are Spanish.'

'You forget, sir, the Philippines,' I reminded him respectfully.

'By God, so I did!' he answered with courteous vehemence. 'Are you then a Moslem from the Philippines? And the language you sing is—?'

'Of our island.'

His thin, keen face, the cheeks slightly hollow yet glowing with health, had immediately suggested some learned and pleasant profession. The moment he opened his mouth I knew him for a Don. Oxford, instead of being thirty safe miles away across the Cotswolds, was alarmingly present with us. And this was no harmless scientific specialist, but a man of letters. His general knowledge was likely to be wide.

'Does your religion permit the consumption of alcohol?' asked Adrian Moleyns.

'During licensing hours,' I answered, 'it does.'

The don Thomas gave a high hoot of laughter.

'John, surrender to us your prisoner!' he ordered affectedly. 'I claim for him the privilege of a clerk.'

'Now, Mr Rundel,' said the sergeant, grinning. 'I'll let you 'ave him, and glad. But don't you start it all up again, like!'

Thomas Rundel evidently had a reputation for whimsey. Moleyns also put in a word of warning.

'Now, look here, Thomas!' he begged. 'Not before lunch on a market day! You'll only get the poor chap arrested again.'

How I longed at that moment for the right to be myself! Too many months had passed since I had talked to men with tastes similar to my own, and I was abominably weary of the trick which had so far ensured my safety: the domination of others by sheer eccentric impudence. The company of this Thomas Rundel was just what I needed, though I dreaded his perspicacity.

I had a quick drink in the pub with my saviours – quick because Moleyns was a little uncomfortable and suppressed us firmly. He had saved the strolling minstrel for the honour of Chipping Camden, but he was too responsible a worthy to welcome the company of vagabonds. I found out afterwards that he was an architect of immense distinction and that, when it came to housing the masses, the essential choice was between Moleyns-Camden and Corbusier. Any middle course was a mere begging of the question.

Thomas Rundel, full of questions, carried me off to lunch. He was, of course, accustomed to cultured Indians who, when they chose, could be more English than the English; so I did not have to bother with any phoney show of oriental customs. He immensely enjoyed listening to himself, and I was able to get some sort of working picture of him during our short walk to his cottage on the outskirts of the town. In a way he reminded me of Stoffel and Schatz. He swung on the trapeze of his own intellect; and, though it might travel anywhere, he lived in a caravan of books. Never could it occur to him that the criminal world was so close that he might be brought face to face with Howard-Wolferstan. On the other hand what language I sang and to what community I belonged he was determined to know.

The cottage was his refuge during vacations. It consisted of a library, a kitchen, a bedroom and a bathroom. He did his own cooking and, to judge by the omelette he gave me at lunch, he could not have found anybody to do it better. He had a small cellar as well, and skilfully applied its contents to the mellowing of me. His curiosity was far from idle, for his subject was modern languages.

He tried me out unexpectedly in Spanish, which he spoke stiltedly but well. That was a trap I had trained myself to avoid. I showed interest and answered him in the sort of broken jargon that you might hear from a bare-bummed cacique on the head waters of the Amazon. He was convinced that I could do no better and that I had not translated the songs myself.

'Very well, Faiz Ullah,' he said. 'I can tell that your language *is* a language, and I am prepared to accept the fact that it is spoken in the East Indies. But when were these translations made? Who made them?'

I gathered that my island – which had by this time collected a vague population of aborigines, Malay pirates and Indians who had been there since time unknown – was breaking all the rules; it was most exceptional for an Eastern or any other people to accept a whole body of foreign music and put their own words to it. No doubt Thomas Rundel was right. One can hardly imagine that *Green grow the rushes, oh!* would be sung by a Malayan in Malay; if he wanted to sing it at all, he would do so in English. Even in Latin America I have never come across Spanish songs translated into Indian languages. Mexico might have examples, but I doubt it. Opera libretti pass from language to language with the music unchanged, but they merely prove that the process is most unnatural.

Answering his persistent questions was an impossible trial for my nerves when I was longing to enjoy his room and his society in peace. I was continually conscious of that damned beard which was now far from a perfect fit, for my own hair was growing splendidly underneath. Treatment with stiff pomade kept moustache and whiskers flattened down, but the only way of dealing with my chin was to grease the hairs to a point and cut a hole to let it out. The discomfort, if compelled to talk while eating, was a minor, nagging hindrance to concentration.

'But you were educated in England,' he went on. 'And surely, if I am not mistaken, at one of our universities? Perhaps my own?'

I let myself go with the tide of his wine. I knew his type, or thought I did. He would be so delighted by a high fantastical manner that he would pick it up and leave me alone.

'At a co-educational establishment in Croydon,' I answered, 'from which I was expelled owing to the fact that my religion did not permit me to shave. A fine beard upon a youth of school age was too patent a criticism of the basic principles of co-education.'

He laughed and made some fitting and witty reply which I have forgotten. Then, for the rest of lunch, he courteously entertained me with some utterly neutral subject – the Nabob in English literature I think it was.

'I'm off after lunch and shall be in Oxford to-night,' he said. 'But do stay here. You need it and no one will disturb you.'

I had forgotten that men of his type had spent as much of their adult life in the Army as in the Senior Common Room. He had learned to recognize unbearable strain at sight. When I protested at so much kindness to a stranger who refused to account for himself, he answered gaily that learning was its own passport.

That afternoon and night alone in his cottage were heaven. I had at last perfect privacy – privacy to have a bath without fear that someone might be peeking through wall or keyhole, privacy to sit before a fire and read. The Englishman in me revelled in peace, regarding with well-bred amazement the predative and noisy Latin who could stagger from crisis to crisis and retain a balance.

Both of them, however, had the sense to look up the Philippines in an encyclopaedia. My Stratford American, in connecting Spanish tunes with an oriental appearance, had made a really excellent guess. Unless I ran into another American authority, it would be most difficult for anything I said about my island to be flatly denied. There were seven thousand of them, and a whole riot of languages. Better still, there was a community of Mohammedans, called Moros, who had been there since the fourteenth century. Presumably they spoke a corrupt Arabic or Malay, but there seemed no earthly reason why a few families of them should not speak whatever I chose.

I had finished a lazy breakfast and the morning papers when Thomas Rundel turned up, his health and learning reduced to a more common level of humanity by a slight hangover. I thanked him warmly and prepared for the road.

'First,' he said, going to the cupboard, 'we will take a little gin. I'm not going to bother you with any more questions, Faiz Ullah, but I wonder if you would fall in with a plan of mine?'

I replied that of course I would, if it were at all possible; and he explained that he was honorary secretary of a dining club whose members met every quarter to extend their general knowledge in any tempting and original direction, and to commemorate the founder – a bachelor cavalry colonel with half a dozen learned hobbies, who had left £200 a year for the purpose.

'Quite informal,' he assured me. 'A few dons and diplomatists. Some proconsuls and men of letters and archaeologists. And among the guests anything from politicians up. All good fellows. Would you come and play to us?'

'I'm not good enough,' I said.

'Quite good enough for us, my dear Faiz Ullah,' he replied politely. 'It's not a Wigmore Hall guitarist we are after. For example, once we had a Swaziland chief to recite. Some of us wanted to see if we could take down his speech in phonetic notation and read it back intelligibly. And another time we had some early Byzantine music played to us by a French violinist to see what he made of it, and by a Turk to see what *he* made of it. My idea was that we should be entertained by your Songs of the Spanish Indies and allowed to speculate.'

This was to expose myself most dangerously. Yet it might lead somewhere, whereas my present minstrelling, with the chills of November little more than six weeks away, could very well end in police station or hospital.

Seeing me hesitate, he added diffidently:

'I've been making some enquiries about the Philippines, and it would seem that your people must be Moros. Your Arab ancestors gave Spain its distinctive music. And it is at least conceivable that when their descendants heard it again, they easily adopted it. That's one theory. The other is that a Spanish prisoner, for example, married on your island and stayed there and amused himself with these translations.'

He seemed to me to be jumping to conclusions a little too readily for true scholarship; but as my own researches coincided with his I could only accept them.

'We'll pay you or not, just as you like,' he said. 'And either way you will be my guest.'

I had no intention of being drawn into a sort of philological B.B.C. quiz, so I told him frankly that I would not dine with him – too shabby, for one thing – but that I would gladly play if he would first give me something to eat and drink in an ante-room or elsewhere.

'And no questions?' he asked, disappointed.

'Didn't you want to speculate? Besides, I don't know the answers.'

'You know a lot more than you have told me, my dear Faiz Ullah,' he said, 'except the origin of your songs. Very well, I'll keep you a mystery. More fun that way. But may I say definitely that your language is Indian?'

'You may,' I assured him.

The club dinner, Rundel said, would be on the top floor of the *Three Feathers* in Marylebone. Fee, five guineas. Travelling expenses to be paid. I was to be there before nine p.m. or as early as I liked on the 25th September, and the pub would put me up for the night.

For the next fortnight I wandered through Gloucestershire into Somerset, paying my way but making no profit. I was eager to hit on some form of employment which would render it unnecessary to turn up at this dangerous dinner. Once I hired a village hall for my songs of the Spanish Indies and sold shilling tickets. I would have done well if I had not worked up such an all-consuming thirst. I even lectured to a Women's Institute on the Philippines. All tropics are much the same. I was really talking about the jungle coast of Colombia.

Again I was in the newspapers. Poor Chris Emmassin had died of food poisoning while attending some youth league conference in East Berlin. The press, of course, suggested that his death was not an accident. Certainly he would have been an easy man to poison. Chris fussed so much about hygiene and processing and flies that he had lost his natural taste. If you had put a lump of Thames mud in cellophane printed with a guarantee of vitamin-content, he'd have eaten it. But I do not think his employers put him away. He was their show-piece. In my opinion – though I hate to think I was responsible – it was suicide. The Howard-Wolferstan affair, coming no doubt on top of others, had shown him that bureaucrats were as incompetent in Russia as anywhere else, and that he might just as well have stayed in the Foreign Office.

Either way I was the villain of the piece. If you paid 1½d. for your paper, Chris had a simple British heart of gold and had never realized that such men as Howard-Wolferstan could be employed. If you paid 4d., he got the regretful obituary of a brilliant crank, who had had the misfortune to fall under the influence of international opportunists – meaning me again. He came in for a good deal of charitable judgment. It had been bottled up for so long. When you are alive, it is most un-English to be a commissar or a cardinal or a really outstanding crook; but when you are dead the pride of the nation in your achievement may reasonably be shown.

By September 25th nothing – except another damned circus – had offered itself, so I took a train from Bristol to London and turned up at the *Three Feathers* after buying a couple of new strings for the guitar. I recognized the wife of the landlord at once. She must have enjoyed the club's quarterly dinners as much as the guests; in her youth and mine she had been known to all Oxford as a famous cook of traditional English dishes. The place smelt of onions and spices. A noble array of bottles was prepared. I had less misgivings. By the time bellies were full and the feast of reason and music about to begin, comment, though brilliant and imaginative, was not likely to be up to Scotland Yard standards of exactitude.

I had a bath and brushed and repaired my clothes and whiskers. My blue pugaree, frayed and dirty, was getting beyond such first-aid as could be rendered by cleaning fluid and a needle and cotton. Shabbiness, however, would be expected if Rundel told his fellow members – and he was certain to make a good story of it – how he had picked me up off the road.

He arrived soon after seven, dinner-jacketed and in a state of hospitable fuss. We had a drink together and he showed me the *Three Feathers'* dining-room, which stretched the full width of the first floor. Places were laid for some thirty guests – ten at a high table and a similar number on each of the wings. At the bottom of the room was a piano on a dais a little higher than the floor. Curtains, looped back, formed wings just wide enough for a performer to take a quick drink or change his properties. There was altogether too much top lighting for my comfort, and I suggested that we should turn it out and use two candles stuck in bottles. Between them I would sit and play, cross-legged upon a cushion. That gave a composite atmosphere of East and West.

I retired to a deserted coffee-room, where the same meal and the same wines were served to me as to the guests. I did myself well, for if you are not a conscious artist the next best thing is to be utterly unselfconscious – and my instrument, played as I played it, demanded alcohol to drive the thumb. When the time came for me to face my distinguished audience, my only worry was how long I could sit cross-legged.

I bowed to the tables and looked over the guests while they generously clapped my appearance. There was some whispering between a few proconsular-looking diners, and I guessed that they were assuring each other that I was neither Sikh, Hindu, Pakistani or any well-known type of oriental. It seemed best to slam these finicking speculations out of court at once, so I laid into that guitar fortissimo and gave them ten minutes of non-stop *flamenco* in Quechua.

So long as that stuff has the proper fire no Anglo-Saxon

can help applauding it, at any rate after dinner. I retired behind the curtain, where I had laid down half a bottle of Burgundy, and listened to the comment.

A high voice at the top table remarked genially:

'Of course it's one of Rundel's hoaxes!'

So far as I could tell, he did not get much support – for there could be no doubt that I was giving an honest Spanish programme and that the language in which I sang was real and flexible, though very obscure. I might be one of Rundel's colleagues in a false beard, but it was at least as likely that I was a Moro from the Philippines. Two voices of authority boomed through the cigar smoke; one ruled out the Indo-European and Semitic groups; the other, Basque and Malay.

The second part of my programme was less noisy – a few Galician songs of the sixteenth century. I would not have dared to sing the originals for I had forgotten many of the words. That, however, made translation the more simple. The audience listened intently, since it was easier to distinguish the phonetics of the language. One of them began to make me uneasy, for he leaned forwards from his seat half-way down the left-hand table and stared at me. He was about my own age, dark-haired and elegant, and he could very well be a Latin American.

After a bit, he began to grin with obvious private enjoyment and once he laughed outright. Without a doubt he knew my language. It was quite beyond me to translate the delicate nuances of romantic love, and I had used for the ultimate object of the lover's longing – it gave me an excellent rhyme – an extremely coarse and factual Quechua word. I found it comic. So did he.

I was for it. There were only two courses open: to bolt or to bluff it out. I was prepared to defend a Quechua-speaking community in the Philippines – arriving on Kon-Tiki raft or stolen Spanish galleon – but it was too dangerous. The moment somebody mentioned Ecuador, the game was up. No normal man, conditioned by columns and columns of newspaper tripe, could ever again think of Ecuador without remembering Howard-Wolferstan.

There was a short third session to come; but as soon as I had taken my bow I nipped off-stage to grab my pack from my bedroom and go. In the passage I hesitated for a moment, wondering how I could get hold of Rundel and my five guineas. Half a dozen of the diners slipped out, too, among them the man who had laughed. I made for the stairs casually but fast. He came after me.

When we were alone on the landing, he said softly in Spanish:

'You are Claudio, aren't you? Don't be afraid. I won't give you away.'

I did not answer him. I pretended not to understand.

'We haven't seen each other for twenty years,' he said, 'or you would remember me. Salvador Queiroz Ortega, at your service.'

'Salvador!' I cried and embraced him. 'But how did you guess it was me?'

'Who else,' he asked, 'would have the effrontery to sing in such appalling Quechua? That word, Claudio, is only used by the lower class of mestizo miners – and you a descendant of the Incas! And what man of birth ever had such a convincing and completely vulgar style on the guitar?'

I dragged him into my room and shut the door. There I embraced him again with tears in my eyes. I had felt myself, under this continual harrying, growing so old and dull and English.

'Your beard,' he said, 'smells of elephants. What admirable

attention to detail! And how the devil did you manage to grow such a thing in seven weeks?'

I pulled it down and let it snap back again. I had not seen Salvador Queiroz since I was seventeen and he a precocious fifteen. We were never close friends, but he used to admire from a respectful distance my exciting reputation.

'What are you doing in London?' I asked.

'I? Honorary attaché at the Embassy. It's not worth travelling in these days except as a diplomat.'

I was disappointed. There were a hundred Ecuadoreans of family – for we all knew each other – who could be of more use to me. Though unpaid and irresponsible, Salvador was a man of honour. It was unthinkable that he would connive at my escape.

'What do they believe about me?'

'My dearest friend, communism – well, isn't it a little sad, a little laborious? To those who know you, you are more likely to be a curate than a communist.'

'My mother,' I answered, 'intended me for the Church.'

'Wherefore, perhaps, your little flirtation with its opposite? Claudio, what the devil *were* you doing on that Russian ship?'

'Trying to get out of the country. It was the only way.'

'They really believed you had been after atomic secrets?'

'Of course they did,' I replied. 'I told them so.'

He seemed to find that funny. I don't know why. You cannot expect a communist, after all his training, to recognize truth and falsehood. It was far harder for me to persuade Stoffel that I was a threat to his domestic peace.

'What were you really doing at Moreton Intrinseca?' he asked. 'There was mention of women's bedrooms.'

'Trying to make some money.'

He remarked that it had to be one or the other – a coarse

and unjust remark, but I was in no position to resent it – and then slapped me on the back and asked me if I had ever heard of a man called Harry Cole. I had not.

'You didn't know your father used to send him money through the Consulate?'

We heard steps outside – undoubtedly Rundel or a waiter coming to see what was delaying me. After this precious moment of relaxation, I could not recover myself. I looked at Salvador in panic. He was equal to the emergency.

'Quick!' he whispered. 'Lie down! You're drunk!'

It was Rundel. He found me collapsed on my bed with Salvador leaning over me. I rolled over to conceal my hand, stuck a finger down my throat and with a violent effort was sick. I would have taken less drastic action if I had remembered my long beard.

Salvador was magnificent. He introduced himself with true dignity, and in English that was worse than my Quechua.

'Salvador Queiroz, honorary attaché to the Embassy of the Republic of Ecuador, and convited to your deener by His Excellency the Ambassador of Argentina.'

'Yes, yes,' said Rundel impatiently. 'I know. We met at the door.'

'I go out to vash my 'ands. I hear a cry. The Filipino, 'e falls! I peek him up. Too much wine, not true? And so I put him to bed.'

'I say, Faiz Ullah, I *am* sorry!' Rundel exclaimed. 'I ought to have known you couldn't be in training for a show of this sort.'

'Go back to your guests, old boy!' I said huskily. 'Tell 'em truth! Too much hoshpi-hoshpitality. Just want to go to sleep.'

That made, after all, a thoroughly artistic ending to the evening, and I think Rundel saw it. His stray Filipino, needing wine to give of his best, had collapsed under the strain. He went out, promising to return later. Salvador followed him, holding up a finger to me as a gesture that I had not heard the last of him.

I locked the door, and scrubbed my detested beard, congratulating myself on having had the courage to break out of my safe but objectless food-gathering and face the open. It was a big risk which had achieved, I thought, a middling sort of reward. That sounds ungrateful, but the hopes of a fugitive are unreasonably. high. What I had vaguely wanted from my bold appearance among men of my own kind was a contact with the shipping world or a meeting with some learned and cunning soul like Sir Alexander Romilly who could be persuaded of my innocence and advise me. Salvador Queiroz was hardly more than entertainment. His Harry Cole I put down unhesitatingly as a plain-clothes detective who had pretended to know my father in order to get on the trail of my possible contacts.

I heard the noisy break-up of the dinner, and soon afterwards Rundel came up to my room and paid me my five guineas and expenses. I let him find me ashamed of myself and dripping with cold water from the basin. I did not want him to think I was in need of any further attention. He invited me to call on him at his College or his Chipping Camden retreat whenever I felt like it, and whether I were willing or not to answer questions about myself and my language. It is on my conscience that I grossly abused his warmth and kindness. I can only hope that he and his club were rewarded by the amusement and the speculations I provided.

Three notes were left downstairs for Faiz Ullah: one asking if I would sing at some meeting of orientalists, one written in three outlandish scripts with a request that I would let the writer know if I could read any or all of them, and one just stating: 11.30 *tomoro. Statue Pitapan.*

The rendezvous sounded like one of Bolivar's more obscure battles. With my mind tuned to Latin America it took me a few seconds to recognize Salvador's spelling of Peter Pan. No doubt he had found the statue in Kensington Gardens good neutral ground for the avoiding of husbands.

In the morning I left my guitar at the *Three Feathers,* and tried to think myself into the part of a poor but honest Indian student. But I was continually uneasy in London streets. My ancient gamekeeperish tweed coat, to which I had stuck because it inspired confidence in the country, was all wrong in town. I could not meet or ignore the eyes of passing constables as casually as I wished.

I strolled up and down at a safe distance from Peter Pan, meditating the profound philosophies of the East. Salvador was of course quarter of an hour late, and I added another ten minutes to be sure that he was not followed. We occupied two chairs under a plane tree in the open park where no one could overhear our conversation.

We were both less generous than the night before. For one thing, it was morning; for another, there was no humour in the situation. I begged him to get me, somehow, without compromising himself, on a boat for South America. But it was as I feared. He could do nothing for me except to put me in touch with Harry Cole.

'But he's some damned police agent,' I protested.

'I do not think so. After your first escape, this Cole came round to the Consulate and swore you were telling the truth when you said in court that you were treasure-hunting. The consul found him sympathetic. A real little Englishman with guts. He would not explain, and he wouldn't go to the police. He just said that if any of your friends knew where you were, he wanted to be taken to you. The clerk knew him. It is a fact that he received remittances from your father.'

'And you didn't send him to the police?'

'We told him he ought to go to them. Man, we're always correct! But it was none of our business to see that he did. Besides, we have been enjoying the newspapers. An office sweepstake even, on how long you could remain at large! And one isn't sorry to see the famous British efficiency made dust. As a nation, you are too patronizing, Claudio.'

'Somebody has to set the standards,' I protested.

'But do you like them?'

'I treat them,' I answered, 'with respect. For example, I much prefer to be ceremoniously hanged for High Treason after due process of Law than to be stuck up against a wall and shot with rifles which were not cleaned since Monday morning.'

'You were always over-fastidious, Claudio,' he retorted, 'in everything but your morals.'

I did not consider that a boy of fifteen – his age when we last met – was capable of forming any opinion of my morals and, still less, of my tastes. I nearly told him so. I suppose that I was so weary of making calculated use of every human contact that to speak my mind was a barely resistible pleasure. However, I pulled myself together and became eloquent upon the joyous society of my second homeland, and even its soldiery.

'Don't you see? You are one of us, Claudio, whatever your passport says,' he responded generously. 'That is why I am helping you. You have no idea how much trouble it cost me to get hold of this Harry Cole's file while pretending to look for another. Here is his address!'

He handed me a scrap of paper. Harry Cole kept an inn

on the edge of the New Forest – I shall call it *The Tracehorse* – near Brockenhurst.

I thanked him warmly, and he wished me luck. There was no more to be said. Each of us had so very obviously to keep his mouth tight shut about the other that we might have been meeting in a better and more understanding world where one presumes – though a bitter shock it will be for the clergy – that speech becomes unnecessary.

I was right to distrust London. When I returned to the *Three Feathers* to pick up my pack and guitar, I found that the police had been making enquiries about this enigmatic Faiz Ullah who had registered as British.

'What did you tell them?' I asked the landlady – that excellent soul who had cooked the club's quarterly dinner.

'I told 'im of course you was one of Mr Rundel's young gentlemen, and no more of a South Sea Islands Rajah than what I am.'

Astonishing how complexities suddenly straighten themselves out into a simple path of lunacy!

'Well,' I said, 'that was a wonderful dinner. And now I must go home and wash the black off my face.'

I took a train to Brockenhurst, guitar and all, and walked through the Forest – or rather over bare heath which had once been forest – to *The Tracehouse*. It was a small Free House of old red brick, set back from the road at the side of a green or clearing, and looked as if it would provide a decent, unambitious living for its owner. Why my father had wanted to make a pensioner of Henry Cole, Licensed to Sell Beer, Wine, Spirits and Tobacco, I could not imagine; but the pub had that air of growing out of the soil which an exile remembers all his life. In old days I should have written him a description of it that he might enjoy by proxy his lost – yet contentedly lost – England, and told him how I wished we could both have sat with our tankards under the turning oak leaves on a golden evening. As the sign of *The Tracehorse* creaked in the light wind, he seemed very close to me – a dear, welcoming ghost reluctant to leave his enjoyment of earth for such austere choices as bliss or damnation.

It was just on six, and I waited outside until Harry Cole opened the door. He was a lightly built old man, weather-twisted like a thorn on high ground. He might have been an ex-jockey, except that his knees were straight and his feet solidly planted. I followed him into the bar, and he looked at me from behind it with a closed face – disapproving in principle of the presence of Asia in the New Forest. No, he said, he couldn't put me up, but there was a cottage a quarter of a mile down the road where they did bed-and-breakfasts. He thawed a little after he had seen me put down a double whisky, and asked what part of India I came from. I gave him my old line of being born in England to Indian parents.

'Playin' in concerts?' he asked, nodding to the guitar.

'No, just for a living.'

'Ah, we 'ad a sort of German down 'ere once,' he said. 'Used to fiddle in the woods, 'e did, and get the birds to answer 'im.'

His small, bloodshot, brown eyes watched me from a mesh of wrinkles. My speech puzzled him, and he was trying to find out if I hadn't a more respectable purpose than merely playing for pennies.

'They wouldn't answer the guitar,' I told him. 'It's too human.'

I ordered another whisky and asked him what he would take.

'Well, I will 'ave a small one meself with you,' he replied in a voice that expressed his astonishment at finding himself committed to drink with so strange a visitor.

'You ain't played that for a living all your life,' he said.

'No. But I've played it for fun. I learned it in Ecuador.'

He didn't bat an eyelid.

'Where's that?' he asked 'Coast of India, ain't it?'

A most heartening reply! He could not help knowing that Ecuador was in South America, though he might be vague as to its exact whereabouts. His cautiousness could only mean that he was on his guard against questions.

'Mr Cole, did you ever call at the Consulate of Ecuador?'

'And what if I did?'

'Have you anything you would like to tell me?'

'Not if you're a rozzer, I 'aven't.'

'Suppose I was M.I.5? You'll know what that is from your Sunday papers.'

'Then I'd tell yer,' he answered sturdily, 'that ye're wastin' of my muckin' income tax chasin' after spies what isn't.'

'But if you can clear Howard-Wolferstan, why don't you?'

'I'll clear 'im in my own time,' he said. 'And it's only 'im what I'll talk to and without any of you listening either. If you pick 'im up, you send for me.'

'I have reason to suppose that Howard-Wolferstan is under your roof at this moment, Mr Cole.'

He contemptuously hoicked up an old man's ever ready phlegm, and then suddenly got the implication.

'Well, if he is,' he said. ''E'd better be upstairs than in the bar.'

He took a quick look at the innocent evening outside his porch, and then led me up to the first floor and unlocked a cheerless, dusty bedroom which had not been used for years.

'Been all alone 'ere since the missus passed away,' he said by way of apology. 'Sleeps in the parlour, meself. Saves trouble, like. You make yerself as comfortable as what you can, and keep the door locked, see? You and me, we'll 'ave a little talk after closing-time.'

He tried the window blinds and, finding that they still worked, told me that I could safely switch on the light after nightfall.

I threw my pack and guitar on the bed, and dropped into a broken-springed arm-chair. Speculation was useless. It was enough for the moment that Harry Cole evidently had in his old bones long experience of dealing with inquisitive strangers and the Law. So I removed beard and turban and settled down to enjoy the country silence, pleasantly broken by an occasional rumble of deep voices from the bar below.

Soon after eight there was a scratching at my door, and Cole announced himself in a throaty whisper. I did not bother to replace my oriental trappings. I was in his hands.

He entered with a tray on which were a plate of ham, bread and cheese and a tankard of bitter. As I held the door open for him, he edged round me in a quarter circle, staring.

'Cut yer beard, 'ave you?' he asked.

I tossed him the false one. I thought it would amuse him.

'Damme, that's just what your father would a done!' he exclaimed. 'Forty-five year gone, and I remember that smile of 'is like as if it was yesterday. Aye, and what I can see of your face is the spitten image of 'is except that 'e was a white man. As a matter o' colour, I mean.'

I could not resist telling him that I was no darker than anyone else who had lived most of his life under tropical sun, and that on my mother's side there was Inca blood.

'Inkier, was she?' he asked. 'Well, yer father was never one to mind that. Man or woman, 'e took 'em for what they were. So you're the little Claudio, which 'e was that proud of! Well, 'ow time do pass for them as don't 'ave nothing agin it.'

Somebody punched a bell down in the bar, and he silently vanished with an encouraging sideways throw of the head, as if to assure me that it would soon be ten o'clock and closing-time.

Eventually I heard the formula: *Time, genlemen, please!* the reluctant steps on the road outside, the final shutting and bolting of the door and the clink of glass being collected into the sink. Quarter of an hour later Harry Cole brought me down to his parlour. It was, I suppose, filthy; for an old man ate in it and slept in it and had it doubtfully swept out once a week. But there was a comfortable fire in the grate and whisky was on the table. Cleanliness is so unimportant. The interludes in my life which I look back on as most enjoyable must have been watched, with an anticipatory gleam, by the eyes of uncounted mice and insects in unwashed corners.

Harry Cole grumbled about the difficulties of running a pub alone – except for a girl who came to wash up every morning and a barman who helped him out in holiday seasons. This was all conversation. He was creating, without embarrassment, a human relationship before coming to the point.

'You're goin' to 'ave a shock,' he said at last.

I replied that I had had a fairish few in the last five months.

'Ah, but this un is different,' he warned me. 'Your name ain't Howard-Wolferstan. It's Tutty.'

I received this announcement with regret but equanimity. I had no intention of changing Howard-Wolferstan for Tutty. A man's name, after all, is that by which he is known. And I was singularly well known as Howard-Wolferstan.

'Now, what I got to say is this,' he went on. 'Your dad and I was – well, burglars. *You* know, 'ouse-breakers. A mug's game, if you ask me. Still, it was better than workin' in a cheap jeweller's back room and losin' yer eyesight 'cos 'e wouldn't pay for the lightin', which was the trade we was apprenticed to.

'I'd been brought up honest. But yer dad was an orphan, and 'e'd been in one of them 'omes since 'e was five year old. Church of England, of course. That's where 'e got 'is lovely manners from. It was a pleasure to 'ear 'im speakin' to the gentry and then imitatin' of 'em, for gentry there was in them days.'

Cole's accent was Hampshire grafted upon cockney, with the former predominant. I find it wearisome to try to reproduce his words, for one cannot avoid a touch of the comic, whereas his whole attitude was one of warm and admiring sincerity. I could hear his love of my father coming through every burring vowel of his voice. It fired my own. Dear, joyous, respected Don Jaime, what a way he had come from so scandalous a beginning as Jim Tutty! I could see at last why he would never return to England, even for a holiday, and already guess, very vaguely, at his connection with Moreton Intrinseca.

Harry Cole and Jim Tutty got away with quite a number of small jobs and had every reason to congratulate themselves upon their choice of profession. They were not known to the police, and they both had a gift for keeping their mouths shut. Eventually, however, they were run in. My father's orphanage education had been more thorough and liberal than is the custom to-day, and had taught him to think for himself. At the hearing in the magistrates' court he spotted the one weakness in the police case, and, when the pair of them came up for trial at the Old Bailey he chose from the dock an ancient warhorse of a counsel, instructed him in whispers and got himself and his partner triumphantly acquitted.

'You ought to a seed the judge's face!' chuckled Harry Cole. 'But 'elp yerself, lad, without waitin' for me, 'cos there's worse a comin'!'

After that they were closely marked men in London, whom the police intended to shop by fair means or foul; so they decided to keep on the move in the country and to aim at a few big jobs rather than a lot of little ones. My father hit on the idea – not nearly such common practice then – of watching the society news in the papers.

'None o' them film actresses,' Cole said. 'It was all Jerry princes in them days.'

They spotted that their Serene Highnesses the Duke and Duchess of Saxe-Dettingen-zu-Langenschwalbach were due to stay with Sir Edward and Lady Lockinge at their place near Moreton Intrinseca. I saw the house when I was prowling round the district. It is now a racing stable, and paint and woodwork are crumbling away. But in 1908 it was the latest thing in rich bankers' country houses – all gables, red brick, white balconies and solid comfort.

My father reckoned that as the Lockinges had not entertained minor royalty before the whole place would be in an uproar of excitement and disorganization right up to the last moment. What pickings there would be he did not know, but that sufficient impudence would take himself and Cole within range he was certain. Their only assets were two bicycles, a suitcase and outfits of black coat and striped trousers which made them – or at any rate my father – appear upper servants of the utmost respectability.

''E looked that reliable,' Cole told me, 'that if 'e drove up in a 'ansom cab you'd a given 'im a hunderd pounds to take round to the bank for you.'

They changed into clean, stiff linen and their professional clothes under cover of a shrubbery. Then my father, bowler hat on head, introduced himself into the house as the English valet of a visiting German colonel, and to the colonel himself as the valet who had been attached to him by order

of Sir Edward Lockinge. He picked up two violin cases
which belonged to the Hungarian String Band, strolled
majestically out with them to the shrubbery and then got
Harry Cole through the back door as baggage-master and
man-of-all-work to the band. The band, of course, was led
to believe – like the colonel – that Sir Edward had attached
a special underling to them, and Harry was soon at work
helping them to put up their music stands and the screen of
potted palms.

Having established their bona fides quite well to answer
hurried questions in the general rush, they explored the
house. Luck, up to a point, was with them. Their Serene
Highnesses arrived soon after six p.m. Sir Edward, Lady
Lockinge and their guests were all bowing and curtseying
in the entrance hall, and the servants were watching discreetly from the upper windows. Sir Edward, however, had a
banker's respect for material possessions. He had stationed a
private detective in Lady Lockinge's bedroom.

'Ought to a trusted 'er ladyship's maid,' Harry said. 'We
wouldn't 'ave done nothin' to 'er.'

As it was, they found the detective, like everyone else,
gazing out of the window at all the animated flunkeydom on
the gravelled drive and red-carpeted steps below. They asked
him if they might have a look, too, and in a matter of seconds
had him rolled up in a rug, gagged and deposited under the
chintz flounces of Lady Lockinge's bed. Then they walked
peacefully out of the room with Lady Lockinge's gold toilet
set, her diamond tiara and necklace to match and a few odd
rings, all stuffed into a pillow-case. There was nothing to
hide it but the German colonel's full dress uniform hanging over my father's arm. That and his majestic walk acted
as a passport so long as they were among the outbuildings
of the house and could possibly be going to some obscure

room where leather and spurs were polished. They put the stables between themselves and the house, and then had to waste a lot of time reaching the shrubbery by short dashes or on hands and knees. I gathered that, by the time they had changed and recovered their bicycles, their nerves were shattered.

Once on the road, they felt more confident. They proposed to ride straight and hard for the outskirts of London, and get clear of all likely police interference before the alarm went out. But they were at the beginning of the great change from the Railway Age, and not up to date. They had not quite got hold of the speed of the telephone, though they knew that Sir Edward had installed it at vast expense with miles of private poles, and they certainly had not reckoned with police cars. It must have been one of the very earliest which pulled across the road in a cloud of dust just outside the village of Moreton Intrinseca. Harry hadn't a chance from the start. My father shoved his bike between a policeman's legs and bolted up a dark drive and into the trees. The tiara, the necklace and the smaller articles of the gold toilet set were in his capacious pockets. Harry, who was the faster and lighter cyclist, had the suitcase and the heavy pieces.

It was deep dusk, for the month was September and there was then no summer time. My father simply vanished.

'"Go it, Jim!" I sings out. "You got 'em, Jim!" Well, o' course I were excited, like, but I didn't ought to a done that, for it 'elped 'em to identify 'im. I wouldn't tell 'em nothin'. But they knew as 'ow we'd worked together afore, and so there was a warrant out for Jim Tutty.'

Sir Edward Lockinge was then High Sheriff of the county, and raving furious that such an outrage could have occurred at a moment when his banker's ambitions had been satisfied to the full, and there was minor royalty under his roof. The result was that, besides those few primitive police cars, Sir Edward's Daimlers, crammed with more police, converged upon Moreton Intrinseca. Harry Cole told me he didn't know there were so many cars outside London.

They stopped the drives and paths of Moreton Manor. They patrolled the high brick wall over which I had climbed. They searched, perfunctorily, the house, for it seemed utterly impossible that my father could have effected an entry when all the staff was awake and the whole place blazing with light. They remained on the spot for two days, but never a sign of dear Jim Tutty did they find.

Harry Cole got seven years, of which he served five and a half. When he came out, a solicitor's clerk met him at the prison gate and told him that his firm was acting on behalf of a Mr Howard-Wolferstan of Quito, Ecuador, who had instructed them to see that Mr Harry Cole was comfortably settled.

''Oward-Wolferstan, I says to meself, now where 'ave I 'eard that name before? They didn't give yer enough to eat inside in them days, ye see, and yer memory got all mixed up between what you 'oped would 'appen and what *ad* 'appened. And then I remembers it was the name of the bloke what was living at Moreton Manor. Mentioned at me trial, it was. Rented it furnished, 'e 'ad for a year or so, and 'e 'adn't been there more than a month, like, before 'e 'as the police bustin' down the 'erbacious border. So I says to meself: Gawd, if that ain't just like Jim! 'Adn't time to get away with nothin' from 'Oward-Wolferstan, so 'e goes and pinches his name!'

Harry Cole received a hundred pounds then and there, and a letter from my father offering anything up to five hundred to set him up in business. Harry replied that he would take it later, for it was December, 1914, and he was determined to enlist. He had come out of prison with the hot patriotism of the common man as well as an understandable and quite illogical dislike of all Germans from Serene Highnesses downwards. He became a horse-gunner, was twice wounded and ended the war as a sergeant. In 1920, when he was demobilized, my father kept him going for a year and then bought him *The Tracehorse*, where Harry had remained ever since, moderately prosperous and, till his wife died, very contented.

"Course I always thought Jim 'ad got the stuff over to that there Ecuador and sold it safe,' Cole said. 'And it weren't till I read in the papers what you said to the beaks, that you was lookin' in the 'ouse for family property, that I knew 'e 'adn't. Then I sees it all as plain as if it was yesterday. Jim got into the 'ouse and stayed there doggo for we don't know 'ow long while the coppers was lookin' for 'im over 'alf the county. 'E 'id the stuff, meanin' to come back for it when 'e 'ad a chance, but 'e never did 'ave no chance. 'Is description was out, and they was 'ot after 'im. So 'e must a said to 'isself: the game's up, Jim, unless you 'ops it off to somewheres where you ain't known. And so 'e ups and 'ops it.'

That my father had been a burglar was a mere accident of life which might happen to anyone. Neither he nor I had ever had an exaggerated respect for property, and no doubt that casual attitude facilitated my youthful conversion to communism. But I have never been so proud of him. It was enough to warm any son's heart to know that all the way from Ecuador, when it would have been so easy to forget or ignore, he had kept an eye on his less fortunate partner and financed him out of his resources; they were, I knew, nothing much more than bluff before he married in 1915, and even in 1921, when he sent Cole the money for *The Tracehorse*, his father-in-law was still distrustful and kept him pretty short. It was not till I was ten or eleven years old that he had been able to exploit his gifts as a financier, and to live and dress in that flamboyant style which had remained his ideal.

'Did yer find it?' Harry asked.

I told him that I had not: that I had been in too much of a hurry.

'That's the mistake they all makes at first,' he said. 'Just take yer time, like as if you were in your own 'ome. Nobody's goin' to 'urt yer.'

Now that I knew what there was in Moreton Intrinseca Manor, and how it had got there, I was sure that my father had gone up to the attic floor by a staircase which had been perfectly obvious before the Ministry cut off the nunnery wing, and which I, of course, never discovered. The room which he described as the third on the right would, in fact, have been one of those on my left.

'I've a mind to have another shot at it,' I said.

Harry Cole was dismayed. He pictured the Manor as swarming with mysterious operatives. I felt pretty sure that entry would be no harder than before. After all, that detestable security officer, Peter, had caught his man – which was quite enough for the Treasury to refuse to establish extra staff.

'You take my advice and don't go near the place for another twenty year,' Harry exclaimed, 'when all they scientists 'ave run off to the Russians or been 'ung by the rest of us! Then you'll 'ave a nice little bit for yer old age. It's 'ard. I'm not sayin' it isn't. But you know what them ministries are. Keep anyone out of 'is rights, they will, so long as they can blow the 'ole lot of us up.'

'Suppose it was a private house,' I asked him, 'and you were after valuables which you knew would never be missed, how would you set about it?'

'Well, in Jim's time, I reckon 'e'd 'ave made love to the

cook or the 'ouse-parlourmaid. 'E wouldn't a done, mark yer, if it would get the poor girl a bad name, for 'e was always a sport. But if no one was ever goin' to know what was took, where's the 'arm?'

I must admit, while apologizing to her and to myself, that this remark at once suggested Dr Cornelia.

I recounted to Harry Cole the main incidents of my escape and subsequent adventures. Although he had always known why I broke into Moreton Manor, he was bothered by my reappearance on a Russian ship – or rather a buoy in the Thames Estuary – and undoubtedly more at ease when I had convinced him that any other ship would have served my purpose a deal better.

'Not that I believes what I sees in the paper,' he added, 'ever since I read about me own trial. All wrong they 'ad it. Said as 'ow I 'ad got away in the German colonel's uniform. And there 'e was in court for all of 'em to see! Twice my size, 'e was!'

I told him that was my trouble, too. I had provided too much good reading, and, whether or not the men at the top believed a quarter of it, they would have to bring me to trial.

'Ah, and with juries there's no tellin',' he said gloomily. 'But if the bogeys get yer, send yer lawyer straight down to *The Trace'orse* and an inspector with 'im what 'e knows 'as a bit of sense. But I don't mind sayin', I 'opes I shan't be wanted. I don't like talk that 'Arry Cole done seven years – not that it would make no difference to nobody now the missus ain't with us.'

Harry Cole and I arranged that I should stay at *The Trace-horse* for a couple of weeks, by which time my own beard would be square, black and magnificent enough for the sensitive face of Howard-Wolferstan to be indetectable, even unimaginable, beneath it. The staying, however, was to be at night only, for he could not contrive an explanation of my presence if I were seen during the day when it was known that he did not let rooms.

It was a fortnight of appalling boredom. Cole's kitchen garden, at the back of the inn, was surrounded by trees. I had no trouble in passing out, unseen, at daybreak and in returning after the pub was shut; but during the day I had nothing to do except meditate in an oak tree, like King Charles II, or walk aimlessly through the Forest in the character of a harmless Indian tourist. I spent a couple of days exploring Southampton. Down by the docks Indians were common enough – I had, as at Oxford, some difficulty in avoiding conversation – and I proved to my satisfaction that it would be reasonably simple to stow myself away in a ship. But what was I to do when discovered at sea? Any stowaway of my build and complexion, however bearded, would be presumed to be Howard-Wolferstan till he could prove he was not.

No, the game was to follow my father's instructions, and to buy a false passport or somehow bribe my way out of the country when Lady Lockinge's diamonds had put me in funds. For that, I needed Dr Cornelia.

The letter which I wrote to her, drafting and redrafting it during three nights in the solitude of my *Tracehorse* bedroom, was a masterpiece. And it was in all essentials true, for my imagination had constructed a creature whom I could adore with sincerity. She had an astonishing fascination for me. I even sympathized with her liberal spirit. How was the poor girl, shut up in her scientific nunnery, to keep her spirit buoyant and her hand in practice if she did not create havoc among the only available males?

Was there a chance that she would hand my letter and me over to the police? I debated it back and forth under the trees

of the New Forest and decided to gamble on my experience of women. Quite certainly both she and Sir Alexander
Romilly had doubts of my guilt. Cornelia, sure of herself and
flattered, would give me the benefit of that doubt and listen
to what I had to say.

'To see you once again before I leave England for ever,'
I wrote anonymously – though the rest of the letter made
it clear who the writer was, 'I am ready to risk my liberty. I
need your faith so badly, and I beg you to let me explain. At
midnight of October 15th I shall be under the tall chestnut
which overhangs the wall on the north side of the garden.'

I recognized that Cornelia was far too intelligent to be
swept off her feet by the most pathetic and passionate letter
that even I could write; but I knew enough of her tastes to be
sure that she would go half-way to meet an adventure which
promised to be more exciting than the clumsy and dog-like
affections of her colleagues, Horace and Peter. If I asked her
to meet me at a café or street corner in any neighbouring
town, she might refuse. I was prepared to bet, however, that
so deliciously feminine a woman could not – as long as it
wasn't raining – remain in her room when she was desperately curious to know whether her admirer had really come
to so dangerous an assignation or not. She might spend a
restless hour – say, from half-past eleven to half-past twelve
– fiddling at her dressing-table, trying to read and swearing
she wouldn't go, but go she would.

On the night of the 14th I said good-bye to Harry Cole,
and slipped away before dawn on the 15th. He would not
take a penny from me and hotly refused to have anything to
do with the proceeds, if any, of the Lockinge valuables. All
he asked of me was to let him know, if ever I had a chance to
do so discreetly, whether in fact they were still up the chimney. I left him Faiz Ullah's beard and turban as a keepsake.

I spent the morning in Southampton and very reluctantly sold my guitar for fifteen pounds, which was half what the beauty was worth. With the money I bought new shoes, a suitcase and a duffle-coat. In a pawnbroker's window I saw a second-hand gun-case, very worn and battered, but of expensive leather. That, too, I bought. It was a badge of respectability to draw attention away from myself, taking the place of Bassoon's paint-box and easel.

So equipped, and dropping my baggage importantly on the floor, I ventured to enter a barber's. He cut my hair, gave the ends of my moustache a gallant twist upwards and was with difficulty restrained from trimming my square beard to a point. Quite what I was I had not decided. It was up to the public, and I was prepared to fall in with any suggestion. A naval officer on leave, or a farmer of the type of Robert Donolow, or perhaps a yachtsman who didn't much care what he looked like on land so long as he was well groomed. At any rate I was a man of character travelling to or from a weekend's shooting with a friend, and so I could not be Howard-Wolferstan.

I was determined not to hang about Moreton Intrinseca. Careful reconnaissance was more dangerous than none, for I might arouse the interest of one of those friendly fellows who offered drinks to strangers and sent the bill to the Government. So I took a train to Saxminster, left my bags at the station and went straight for my objective by lanes and footpaths. I should have liked to revisit the Chapter House and the Court. So much had happened in the four and a half months since my escape that I felt as if the town were one I had known in youth. However, I resisted the temptation – in case the police believed in the old saying that criminals could not keep away from the scene of crime – and set out, with dusk falling, upon the twelve miles' walk to the Manor.

I always had luck with my weather at Moreton Intrinseca. It was a soft, damp evening not wholly fitted to whirlwind romance, but inviting enough for those who enjoy the English autumn. I walked past the gate of the Manor, hoping that I could slip through, as my father had done, and disappear among the trees; but the porter was still on duty. He had even been fixed up with a uniform and a sort of sentry box. He looked extremely wide awake. I expect Peter used to stalk him through the bushes to keep him up to the mark.

The brick wall had been topped with an extra two feet of barbed wire, making about four in all – a singularly futile and office-minded precaution, for if a man could reach the top of the wall at all, he could easily climb the wire, at the expense of a tear in his trousers, by one of the angle-irons cemented into the coping. He might also have the sense, as I had not, to provide himself with a pair of wire-cutters. But you can't wean the uniformed world from putting its trust in barbed wire, in spite of the fact that hours of military training are spent instructing the young how to get over or under it.

If it had not been for the extra wiring I doubt if I could ever have got into the Manor at all. I followed the wall very cautiously through the fields, and not a foothold or a loose brick could I find. A former garden gate had been solidly bricked up. The old ladies who once owned the house and let it to the real Howard-Wolferstan – long defunct, I imagine – must have had a terror of burglars. That wall was a masterpiece of determined building.

At last I came up against a cylindrical bulk in the darkness and found it to be a solid roll of wire thrown down and forgotten at the point where the new wiring had been completed. I stood this against the wall, covered it with a double thickness of my duffle-coat and climbed up. Even then I could only just get my fingers over the edge of the bricks. An angle-iron helped me to pull myself up. It was really absurd for the Ministry to think they knew more about security than two wealthy old ladies determined to keep out the public.

Climbing over the wire, I dropped with a resounding thud into the grounds of the Manor, and waited for the night to react. Nothing happened – not even a disturbed wood-pigeon. I sucked and bandaged with my handkerchief a wrist upon which the Ministry of Supply had scored its only triumph, and tiptoed over the dead leaves.

It was now a little after eleven. There were lights in the upper stories, and a few on the ground floor. The cloistered scientists, among them my Cornelia, were going to bed. I was on the west side of the house, and I had to come out into the open, where a wide kitchen garden ran right up to the wall, in order to reach the north lawns and the chestnut. My footsteps crunched on cinder paths. I tried to get off them and was tangled up in a maze of soft-fruit bushes. When I found that I was being led nearer and nearer to the house, my nerve began to weaken. I accused myself of utter, rash folly in ever going near Moreton Intrinseca again. I forgot all that I had so carefully debated with myself and the conclusion to which I had come: that without money and with winter coming on my recapture was only a matter of time.

It was my beloved father who allayed this panic. I remembered how, forty-five years before, just a few strides ahead of the police, the house aroused and blazing with light, he had still managed to enter it unseen. Up a drainpipe? Through a window? Down the coal shute? Only his imperturbable courage connected Jim Tutty with the deeply respected Don Jaime Howard-Wolferstan who had watched over me from the cradle to his casual and affectionate death, and was still inspiring me by his example.

With the most exaggerated precautions I slipped silently

through a stable courtyard and then over the lawns on the north side of the house. It was very dark and until I came up against a complicated rose pergola which I recognized, I was by no means sure where I was. After that it was fairly easy to find the chestnut from which I had first descended upon these servants of Apollyon.

The string which I had tied to a twig was still there. I was astonished. A static string still there after so many months of agitated movement. But why shouldn't it be, when I had taken care to make it inconspicuous? I pulled it, and down came my rope. In a moment I was safe above ground, with the rope coiled up in its fork, feeling the confidence of an impudent monkey. If Cornelia brought Horace, Peter or a dozen policemen with her, I could crawl out along the branch which overhung the wall, drop into the field and be away before any of them could get a ladder or run round by the gate.

Seated comfortably in the chestnut, I composed my thoughts to the business in hand. I ought to show, I told myself, a little reasonable perturbation in order to arouse pity, and be ready to drop it as soon as it interfered with the language of the heart. But when I had got my breath back, I found that I needed a very different type of self-discipline. The memory of Cornelia, the certainty that she would come, began to flood me with an excitement which I had not known since my twenties.

About midnight I heard two light footsteps on the leaves and then silence. In the sentimental mood I had created, I imagined her pausing like the usual frightened deer. But I could not see a thing and I kept silence. A moment later that intolerable man, Peter, passed beneath my tree with his great blunderbuss of a holster bumping against his leg, and shone his torch on the wire. I do not know whether he had heard me plunging about the kitchen garden or whether this was the dutiful round of once a week. I am inclined to think it was the latter. He looked too important for a man who suspected trouble.

I had nicely judged Cornelia's period of hesitation. At twenty-five past twelve she appeared without making a sound, and a deal more efficiently than any frightened deer. Looking down on her, I seemed to see a slight movement of exasperation at finding no one to meet her.

'You are infinitely kind,' I said softly.

She jumped, and retorted sharply:

'No!'

'May I come down?'

'It's merely,' she said, 'that I don't like injustice.'

'If *you* believe in me—' I began.

'I have no opinion whatever. I am going by what Sir Alexander said.'

This was magnificent. The tone of annoyance with herself was exactly right. I told her that I was going to drop a rope.

I had only seen her standing up – with dignity – in court, and I was surprised to find that her head came no higher than my shoulder. She was what the English, always unfeeling in their expressions of admiration, describe as a pocket Venus. To modern taste she was far more alluring than any Venus. Where slimness was required, she was tense and delicate; where it was not, she was in the full flower of the late twenties. That such an anemone of a woman should be a Doctor of Science, with metallurgy as her special subject, was astonishing.

She stared at my beard as if it were something which had grown unexpectedly in a sterilized test-tube.

'I don't wonder they never caught you,' she said. 'Only your voice is the same.'

I apologized for appearing in her presence with so much hair, and explained that it was my only hope.

'It looks clean,' she replied remotely.

'I only left Southampton this morning.'

'Have you found a ship?'

'Possibly. But I don't want to go.'

She refused to see the implication and my imploring eyes. I was silent, and did not help her.

'Well, what *have* you to tell me?' she asked.

'I was only thinking that your crucibles must be of moonlight and your alembics of crystal.'

'I don't use crucibles,' she replied, 'and if alembics are what I think they are, I like them large. Please be quick. It's not too safe. The security officer—'

Her assurance failed her. Both of us, of course, were remembering simultaneously that I had been mistaken for the detestable Peter.

'He has gone past,' I said, 'playing Indians. But if you want to listen to my story, I dare say we should be safer the other side of the wall.'

'Will you give me your word of honour that you are not a communist or a spy?' she asked.

'Yes. What I said about myself in court was all true.'

She laughed. Her voice was rather higher in pitch, rather more Kensingtonian than I should have chosen for her, but it was made delicious, when she was at ease, by a lazy intonation with no more self-control in it than a nightingale's gurgle.

'You seem to go in and out of here very easily,' she said.

I climbed up the rope and pulled her into the chestnut after me. Then I transferred the hook to the branch which overhung the wall, and we slid down into the field. Crawling along the branch was not everybody's meat, but she did it without flinching.

'Holidays in the Alps?' I asked when we reached the ground.

'Yes.'

She did not sound enthusiastic. I imagine that men who climb mountains are tired in the evening.

I remembered from my former visit that there had been the remains of a haystack about a hundred yards out from the wall. It was still there, but now rebuilt of this year's grass. Under a tarpaulin was a dry patch which could not have been bettered for telling one's past or exploiting the possibilities of the present.

First, I gave her a brief sketch of my father as he was in his prime. The character seemed to please her. She said that in many ways it resembled what she believed to be my own. Then I told her – without, I must admit, revealing that his name had been Tutty – of the somewhat unconventional career of his youth. I knew she would be no more shocked than I was.

'So you, too, were just a burglar?' she asked.

The tone of her voice suggested disappointment rather than contempt. I protested. I told her that my past had been adventurous but blameless, as she ought to know if she read her Sunday papers and subtracted those incidents which were obviously impossible. So far as I knew, I was merely recovering family property. I had not the slightest idea that my father's title to it was dubious.

'But did you find it?' she asked.

'No. I'm pretty sure that I went to the wrong chimney.'

'And so you want me to help you to get in and search the right one?'

'I never dreamed of it,' I declared passionately.

'But the risk! Alone! You mustn't do it.'

'Are they still ghost-hunting in the attics?'

'No,' she laughed. 'They decided it was you all along.'

That gave me a wonderful opening.

'It was,' I said. 'Twice I was only waiting for a chance just to see you again.'

'I don't know whether that makes your behaviour better or worse,' she replied. 'And I must go now.'

She had flaring nostrils which appeared to be completely uncontrollable. The adorable child! She was as conscious as I of our accidental and unfinished symphony. And a beard was new to both of us. It added, under the influence of the haystack, a sweet and pastoral innocence to our mutual discoveries. I could even accept her romantic point of view when she insisted – and meant it – that time and place were not yet.

'Claudio darling,' she murmured, 'shouldn't you give this stuff back to the heirs of the Lockinges?'

'I should,' I admitted. 'But if they are as poor as the rest of us, think how they would hate to repay the insurance!'

'And won't it be hard for you, if you take it, to prove that it was ever there?'

'My idea was,' I said, 'that we should leave just enough in the chimney to back up Harry Cole's story.'

'We?' she asked.

Cornelia intoxicated me. I don't know how the damned atomic station ever got any work done at all with that little nun of science popping in and out of laboratories. Or can it be that only I found her so intolerably provocative, and that her colleagues thought of her as just a pretty woman occasionally complaisant from sheer boredom?

'Angel,' she said at last. 'But this is utterly humiliating!'

Ah, well, the moment a haystack ceases to be paradise, it must inevitably become a haystack again.

'Have you realized that in a quarter of an hour I can come

back to you with whatever your father left?' she asked.

'I haven't given it a thought,' I answered truthfully. 'And so long as you do come back to me I don't care.'

I meant it. An hour earlier I had realized to perfection what Cornelia could do for me. But whenever I touched her, nothing but Cornelia existed.

'Where am I to look?'

'Is there a staircase to the attics from your wing?'

'Of course there is. It has a door at the top. It's supposed to be locked.'

I felt a pang of jealousy. If the Ministry of Supply cared sufficiently for the welfare of their women workers, that door should have been locked, not merely supposed to be.

'Then go up the stairs and turn to the right at the top. Look in the chimney of the third attic on the right.'

We returned to the wall and the overhanging branch. I swarmed up the rope and pulled Cornelia up after me. Then she slid down into the Manor garden.

'Wait for me in the tree,' she said, as I prepared to follow. 'Don't ruin it all now!'

A man of less mercurial temperament than mine might have squatted in the fork congratulating himself, like a constipated owl, upon his conquest and the complete success of his plans. I thank the Lord that whenever the present is enjoyable I have the gift of living in it. I could think of nothing but the delicious responses and reactions of Cornelia.

She returned in less than a quarter of an hour. I had not even begun to look at my watch. She carried a large shopping bag of basketwork.

'It was still there,' she whispered excitedly. 'Claudio, how marvellous!'

I slid down to her side. Her eyes were dancing with intelligence and triumph. Up till then, in my experience, those eyes had been cold, or half-closed or pools of meaning which had no immediate connection with the higher centres. This was her laboratory look, perhaps. Soot into gold and diamonds was a remarkable transmutation.

'This is what I have brought you to be going on with,' she said.

She held open the bag. In it were two small round jars, a powder box and a small jewel case, which appeared to be of solid gold.

'And the rest?' I asked.

'There were some rings. I left those and the bag in the chimney. It had nearly rotted away. The collar and the tiara I'm not going to give you yet. You're in an impossible mood, and suppose you were caught!'

She was all ready to be humiliated again, the little love! In all my experience I had never met such an exquisite mixture of modesty and abandonment. I would have asked her to marry me on the spot, if I had not feared that she might suspect a sordid motive. A house in Quito was the right background for her, though I doubted if any thickness of wrought iron or any height of wall could confine her curiosity to its proper object.

'Are you sure they can never be traced?' she asked, when she, but not I, had returned to sanity.

'It's forty-five years since my father removed them,' I replied. 'I shouldn't think jewellers keep records that long.'

I was delighted to see that, in any case, the four pieces did not lend themselves to easy recognition. They were felicitously simple. Either Lady Lockinge had been a woman of surprising taste for her day, or she had had a favourite toilet set of tortoiseshell or ivory exactly copied in gold.

'When you have sold them, would we be quite mad to meet in London?'

I replied that, properly managed, I did not think there was any risk at all, and that I would dare anything to meet her anywhere. She said that she wanted to see – reasonably enough – what I was like in my true setting:

'Dance with me. Give me the evening that you would have done six months ago. White tie and tails.'

As a fugitive and an underpaid scientist, we certainly needed it.

'You must be as bored with the present as I am,' I exclaimed.

'No! But with the sort of life we lead, horribly bored!'

I was surprised by the vehemence of her reply, but realized that I only knew the more frivolous and human side of her. It may be that her emotional life was all the more tempestuous because of the reaction from the sober and devoted masculinity of her profession. Even a female scientist who looks like one must experience her strains and stresses, but how much more difficult when both your mirror and your metallurgy give you the satisfaction of faultless achievement!

'Wednesday night,' she suggested. 'And, if you can, telephone me on Tuesday where to meet you. But don't take a risk, Claudio! You're being foolish now. Do you realize it will be daylight in three hours?'

That startled me. I could not afford to be seen walking the roads, especially in that neighbourhood, at an hour when anyone but a farm labourer would arouse curiosity. After a farewell which recaptured for me the sweet desperation of partings at the age of seventeen, I vanished into the tree.

Though I hoped I should never have to return to the Manor garden, I left my rope coiled in the fork of the tree; it might be useful if Cornelia ever wished to meet me without passing through the gate. I made a half-circuit of the wall, and put back the roll of wire where I found it. The shopping bag clinked as I walked. I packed Lady Lockinge's dressing-table set in fronds of bracken and laid on top a number of plants pulled up by the roots from a hedgerow. They would pass – unless some amateur botanist looked at them too closely – as a gift from a friend's garden to my own.

I covered half the distance to Saxminster at a good round pace, stopping only to take cover from two cars and another cautious pedestrian whose pockets looked suspiciously full. Poached rabbits, probably. After that I strode along in a dream of Cornelia, constructing an indefinite future for myself on the proceeds of the diamonds in which her part was still more indefinite.

While I was in this mood, a blasted policeman approached me silently from behind on his bicycle. He wished me a good morning to which I replied instinctively with a good night – and we thereby established that he was going on duty and I was bound for bed.

He got off his bike and walked along with me chatting. What he wanted to say was: *What have you got in that basket?* But he couldn't quite bring himself to do it. I looked respectable. I was well spoken and casual. I might indeed have been a naval officer on leave.

I searched my imagination for what I could possibly have been doing. Those roots on top of my basket were meant to create an atmosphere in daylight. They were no sort of an excuse for trudging along a country lane in the small hours.

'Moon in the first quarter, constable,' I said vaguely. 'I know it sounds silly. But there you are. Possibly you have a garden and yourself believe in sowing and planting with the waxing moon.'

He looked at me closely.

'Cut yourself, have you?' he asked suspiciously, and shone his torch on my face.

'Look here, constable!' I began indignantly. 'Because I like to collect plants—'

'It's all right, sir,' he said with a broad grin. 'No names, no pack drill!'

'But what makes you suddenly think I'm O.K.?'

'Well, you'll excuse my mentioning it,' he said, 'but I should wash all that lipstick off before you meet anyone you know.'

My embarrassment must have rung true. I felt it.

'One goes quite innocently to a garden at dusk,' I explained, 'and before one knows it, it's five a.m.'

'We all get a bit of luck sometimes,' he answered, mounting his bicycle. 'Good night, sir!'

That night-flowering face which could be, if she chose, so drowsy and full-lipped! It was proper that she should have attended to her complexion before coming to meet me, but I now realized that even after her successful exploration of the chimney she had stopped to repair her lips before returning to the tree. Attention to detail was always a marked characteristic of Cornelia.

After this astonishing escape I gave my beard – and the odd spots she had discovered where there wasn't any – a scrub in the first stream I came to. Dripping with water and restored to a keener sense of self-preservation, I took refuge among the willows and clumps of bushes on the bank and watched the sun rise. It favoured the British Isles by clocking in between two glorious crimson-striped clouds and then took the rest of the day off.

I remained where I was, visited only by some squelching heifers, until farm workers and bearded gentlemen in duffle-coats might reasonably be seen about their business. Soon after nine I made my way by field paths and tracks to the outskirts of Saxminster and the station. Full confidence at once returned when I had picked up my bag and gun-case. That precious badge of social standing demanded that I should live up to it by taking a first-class ticket on the London train. I did so – though the extravagance reduced my capital to two pounds – and settled down in a corner seat to sleep.

From Paddington I took a taxi to a small West-end hotel which had the double advantage of an excellent address and of guests so notoriously antique that it was unlikely I should meet anyone I knew. I stopped on the way to buy a hare which I placed on top of Cornelia's shopping bag. It was an odd way for a man of substance to carry his game, but it reinforced the effect of the gun-case and impressed the hotel porter.

I chose to name myself the Hon. Peter Bowshot St John Godolphin. He was an old schoolfellow and intimate of mine, whom I had rediscovered in a primitive little para-dise of his own making, half-way down the eastern slopes of the Andes. If ever a man were completely lost to sight, he it was. He allowed me to help him with a few necessaries, but made me swear not to bring down on him his family or their letters. He wanted to be left in peace with his three Indian wives and his peculiar religion. He tried to explain it to me. I gathered that if you died drunk you flew up unscathed and smiling past the seven devils whose business it was to inter-cept your soul on the way to heaven and to return it in some unpleasant form to earth. He did not want to risk dying sober and being reincarnated as a flying bed-bug. Where he lived, they did fly.

I had had no breakfast and little supper, so morale was low; but after a very edible lunch – though more to the taste of the surrounding dowagers than mine – and some tentative exploration of the wine list, I was ready for the test. Locking the remainder of my valuables in my suitcase, I took one of the gold jars and went round to a respectable pawnbroker in the Strand – the sort of place which a thief would avoid, and a salaried man, unused to pawnbrokers, would hope to find fatherly and understanding.

I was very manly, gruff and embarrassed. I told the fellow some yarn – which no doubt he had heard many times before – to the effect that I should certainly redeem the pledge in two days' time, and meanwhile wanted all I could get on it. He spent some time in the back of the shop, telling me he had to satisfy himself that the article was solid gold. Possibly he was looking up the list of missing valuables and telephoning the police and my hotel. I tried to feel patient and look confident. The risk had to be taken. Eventually he came back and offered me forty pounds. I ran him up to fifty-five.

Now came my metamorphosis into a more solid citizen. I had no time for a tailor, so did the best I could with ready-mades. I was surprised that I could be fitted so well. My experience till then had been only of Cork Street, when I was rich, and slop shops, when I was destitute, with nothing in between. My aim was to appear as Peter Godolphin might – if he had just turned up from foreign parts and bought himself linen, shoes, a discreet tweed suit, bowler hat and umbrella to be going on with.

That was enough for the day, and there was not much left of the fifty-five pounds by the time I had chosen my restaurant and dined. I spent ten well-deserved hours in bed, dreaming of Cornelia so long as I was awake and of nothing at all when I slept.

My temporary borrowing of Peter Godolphin's name was not wholly due to his retiring nature. When we were both about nineteen, Peter – even then a fanatic – was inspired by Voices to believe that by backing second favourites he could restore the family fortunes. He managed, at any rate, to restore his own by having his grandmother's rope of pearls perfectly matched in artificial pearls, and selling the original. He had even supplied himself with a letter of authorization into which the buyer did not enquire too closely. That was the shop I needed. It specialized in the disposal of aristocratic valuables. The proprietor was not dishonest – he would have been rightly horrified at the suggestion – but he was so determined to preserve a reputation for extreme discretion that he never asked enough questions.

After refreshing my memory of Peter's relations from Debrett, I packed in tissue paper the jewel case, the powder box and the remaining jar, and took them round to their new home. I really did not look at all like Peter – except that we were both brown-eyed and dark-haired – and I did not claim to be him. I let the proprietor do all the work.

When I had mysteriously mentioned a certain rope of pearls he fell on my neck, apologizing profusely for not recognizing me under so much sun-tan and such a beard. Sherry was produced in the office, dark-panelled and smelling of silver. Where had I been? South Africa. Was I home for good? For a year to see how I liked it. How was my Aunt Lucy? Moved from Cannes to Bordighera. Six hundred pounds I got from him. He showed some fatherly disapproval when I said I would prefer cash to a cheque, but the request was not unfamiliar to him. I promised to return the following week to allow him to inspect a diamond tiara and necklace which had been left to me by a second cousin.

With all this money in hand and the value of the diamonds to come, winter caused me no more anxiety. I could retire to the country under any name which pleased me and begin cautious negotiations for a false passport – or possibly a genuine one if I could get hold of a likely birth certificate and establish a new identity. But the sooner I was out of London, the better. Though Peter Godolphin enjoyed it, he felt no safer than Faiz Ullah.

There could be no moving, however, until Cornelia's party was over. I bought the necessary outfit, allowing myself an avuncular and adoring smile at her *naïveté*. She must, I thought, have been unduly fascinated by society columns in the evening papers and failed to realize that occasions in October for white tie and tails are rare – if, that is, one has no connection with theatre or charity balls or government contractors.

On the Tuesday, our menu chosen and our table booked, I telephoned her. She sounded overjoyed to hear that I had safely disposed of my father's property and that I was safe. She told me that she would stay at the Westminster Palace Hotel, but that I was not to call for her there. She insisted that she would meet me in the lounge of Claridge's at eight.

The Westminster Palace would not have been my choice for her; but after all she had only the pay of a scientist, and it was cheap, comfortable and handy – one of those enormous, fairly modern joints where everything was slightly spurious, from the glittering cocktail bar, where there was little gin in the cocktails, to the restaurant, where a full complement of waiters served food of tea-shop standard. My instinct was strongly against it. I suspected that the Westminster Palace was just the place which would appeal to criminals in their brief periods of prosperity between one gaol sentence and the next. However, I had to go there. It was a move which Cornelia might or might not be expecting, but certainly would not resent.

On Wednesday afternoon I moved over to the Westminster Palace. I did not use the name of Peter Bowshot St John

Godolphin or carry my gun-case, feeling that one would arouse suspicion, and the other alarm. So I became William Winthrop of Birmingham, by profession Foreign Representative. The hall porter and the reception clerk treated me, after the same searching look, with the same degree of polite contempt. My beard suggested that I had not even a decent wish to win friends and influence people; my choice of the Westminster Palace showed that I had learned nothing abroad.

It was not the right hour to reveal to Cornelia my presence under the same roof so I changed at leisure and went over to Claridge's. A little after eight she irradiated the entrance to the lounge. That was why she had not wanted me to call for her! That was why she had demanded a white tie! Lady Lockinge's tiara crowned her dark brown hair. Lady Lockinge's diamonds hung lightly from her neck and flamed upon – there is no name for that decorative and sexless interval. They covered in barbaric abandon the whole of the space which, in a man, would be occupied by the V of his waistcoat.

Europe stared at her, and whispered that she was of course American. America goggled, and guessed that she was foreign royalty. Her dress was of white lace, matching the roughness of the diamonds and not, I think, outrageously expensive. The sable cape, however, which was slipped slightly back from her shoulders to reveal the necklace, must have made every woman feel that mink was a mere perquisite of film stars. Where she got it from I never knew and could not ask. I suspect, perhaps charitably, that it was a legacy from a wealthy great-aunt, refashioned by the best of furriers in exchange for half the skins.

I rose to meet her. She passed unconcernedly across the lounge with just the right mixture of modesty and of delight in her own appearance. I suddenly realized that my bored and unconventional little scientist had probably attended an excellent finishing school before she disappointed her mother by immuring herself in lecture-rooms and laboratories.

'I couldn't resist it,' she said. 'It's unfair to ask a woman to handle such things and not wear them once.'

'Wear them always,' I begged her.

She accepted this politeness with a smile which I could translate as I liked.

'What on earth do you suppose they think we are?' she asked.

'The sturdy Englishwoman to your left,' I told her, 'the one who has never been the mistress of anything but foxhounds has just conjectured that we are South American millionaires.'

For myself, it was a good guess. I might well have been a jungly and conservative magnate from a remote mining town, taking his pesos through London on the way to spending them in Paris. Cornelia was an unlikely Latin. She was dark enough and exquisitely groomed and of the right proportions; but the anemone face was too dreaming for vivacity, and such a texture of skin could never be found below the Tropic of Cancer.

She looked a little alarmed at mention of South America. She certainly could not afford to be caught hobnobbing with a spy, while covered with unaccountable diamonds.

'My darling,' I assured her, 'is it conceivable that the traitor Howard-Wolferstan, whom everyone knows to be on the run, could possibly be in Claridge's accompanied by such a woman as you?'

I hardly liked to tell her that she was in the same class as a gun-case, a sweep's brushes and a portable easel, but I explained over our drinks some of the invaluable properties

I had used in my escape, and let her draw the parallel.

So on to dinner. I look back, realizing that I was being tested and summed up. Indeed, I realized it at the time. Hadn't she said that she wanted to know me better? But the laboratory in which she was pouring me from tube to tube was so full of warmth and rapture that food passed unnoticed and wine unsavoured. I am half ashamed, in fact, that the essential quality of the evening should be no different from that which would be felt by any imaginative boy entertaining his girl at a coffee stall.

We went on elsewhere to dance. It was ritual, like the preliminary bowing of birds. The question of where I was staying fitted harmoniously into caress and response. She made no comment upon my choice of the Westminster Palace beyond a liquefaction of white lace.

I had just enough sense left to see that it would be wiser, in case of accidents, not to enter the hotel together; so I dropped her outside the door and myself turned up ten minutes later. Her room was two floors above my own. I put on my dressing-gown and negotiated the stairs and passages with caution, having an instinctive feeling that a hotel with so mixed a complement of guests might be ultra-careful of respectability. I was quite right. The shoes which the occupants of her floor had put out for cleaning were all female. I doubt if any of their owners was ever so sure of her own perfection and her sense of timing as to allow herself to be surprised dressed only in a diamond necklace.

All innocently I asked the dark head on my shoulder:

'When do I see you again?'

Not that it was time to go – only the intermediate moment when it is again possible to remember that a future exists.

'My darling, be sensible!' she answered. 'It's you we have to think of – how you are to escape and where you will be.'

I told her that I thanked God for my father, my arrest and my danger because all of them had led me to her. On such occasions it is hard for any man to know how far he is sincere or not. Her response was touching. She was a woman who was overwhelmed by the effect of her own beauty on a lover; it fascinated her as much as surrender itself.

'Do you really love me, Claudio?'

I answered her incoherently. My beard, which had clumsily learned its part upon the haystack, could now communicate to me her delight like the whiskers of a cat. Again my departure was postponed.

'Claudio, tell me the truth!' she asked with a delicious ripple of laughter. 'Shouldn't we be fools to marry even if we could?'

The way she put it was perfection. Her voice formed an alliance between us two against a prosaic world which could never know such abandon. I suspect that she was near to a feminine counterpart of myself. It does not disturb me. I like to think that her tempestuous emotions were just as sincere as her self-interest, though she was much more able to disentangle them than I am.

'Possibly,' I answered.

'And would you be miserable if I married Horace?'

Horace! I had never given him a thought. All I knew of him was that he was tactless, stolid and that her door in Moreton Manor had been left open for him to continue some talk or other.

'You can't!' I protested.

'He'll make a very good husband for me.'

'Are you sure?' I asked.

'That's very ungallant, Claudio,' she murmured and melted herself against me. 'No, I am not sure.'

'Then why marry him?'

'Because he is a brilliant scientist and very lonely and he needs me.'

'I shall go mad with jealousy,' I cried, for some dramatic gesture was essential.

'Darling,' she answered, lifting the diamonds to my lips as if she wished me to leave a permanent kiss upon them, 'I shall be with you every time I touch your present to me.'

It was impossible to tell her what I thought of her. And did I in fact think anything of the sort? Was it conceivable that she had not known I was offering a mere civility when I told her to wear the diamonds always? I am sure of nothing except that her intelligence was as exceptional as her beauty and that my whole character was transparent to her. Indeed I cannot avoid a feeling that I myself had created a pattern which compelled her to hand out poetic justice. Yet I do not think I can accuse myself of ever having exploited the opposite sex – with the possible exception of Pearl and Topaz.

I will not pretend I felt all this at the time. I was shocked and shattered, for after all I had built a whole imaginative future on those diamonds. But Cornelia had created for me a world which had paid me six hundred pounds, which could no longer go so far as hanging me if I were caught, which had granted to me, a helpless fugitive at the onset of winter, herself.

That, however, was of no importance one way or the other. For a descendant of Jim Tutty and of Spain there could be but one answer:

'That's all I ask of it,' I said.

I suppose the tone of my reply was more or less what she wanted, and yet she vanished under her hair and showed unaccountable emotion. I held her close. I could not tell what was going on in myself, let alone in her. I asked her, without much hope of any reply, why she was crying.

'Because I wish that you did love me,' she said.

I think that was the most profoundly feminine remark that I have ever heard.

When at last I left her, it was just after six o'clock. A stupid hour. It was too late to slip unseen back to my room, and too early to mingle confidently in the comings and goings of a fully awake hotel. However, I managed to get clear of her floor without being spotted. That was essential. In the stuffy, threatening corridors of the hotel I realized more fully the risk she had taken for the sake of – well, whatever it was for the sake of. A dowry for Horace? Our helpless mutual attraction? But it is unprofitable now to speculate.

On the floor below there was more activity. A number of guests must have been catching an early train. Clean shoes were being replaced outside doors. Tea-trays were being delivered. My dislike of early morning tea was reinforced. I have never been able to understand why the English insist that a teapot, depressing symbol of the dullness of the day ahead, should be the first object to meet their waking eyes.

I passed the open door of a pantry and wished the two waiters, who had observed me, a cheerful and unconcerned good morning. Another man in the pantry, not himself a waiter and swilling the tea made for his betters, looked at me sharply and came out.

'Excuse me, sir,' he said. 'Are you looking for your room?'

I answered that it was No. 117, and showed him the key. He accompanied me, making remarks about the weather. Evidently he was a sort of house detective. I explained that I had gone up a floor because I could not find the lavatory on my own. Weak, of course – but the excuse would have been accepted in a hotel less accustomed to questionable guests.

Outside my door, he asked:

'You are Mr—?'

'Winthrop.'

He drew a list from his pocket and checked the name.

'If I might see your business card?' he suggested.

'I don't think I have one with me.'

'A letter will do. Anything just to establish that you are Mr Winthrop, sir,' he said, following me into my room.

The sleek, smooth little Westminster Palace floor-walker! Damn him, I had not a chance of getting away with any bluff at all. If I had polished their hygienic flooring with his detestable nose, he would still have been polite and persistent.

'I'm sorry,' I said. 'This was a most unexpected visit, and I don't believe I have anything whatever.'

'Any name on your suitcase?' he asked. 'Clothes? Pyjamas?'

'I am afraid I am not accustomed to have them marked.'

He could not resist his triumph. He had some reason. Where all the police of Great Britain had failed, he, the slimy little crook who had probably been eased out of Scotland Yard as unreliable, had succeeded.

'Make a habit of dressing-gown and pyjamas, don't you?' he said.

He stepped smartly outside my room and locked it.

The game was up. He was so sure of my identity that he was ready to risk being sacked by the hotel. I had known all along that as soon as anyone admitted to himself the possibility that I might be Howard-Wolferstan, I was finished; but up to the present the world had been hypnotized by my stage properties. Here in the hotel I hadn't any. Worse still, ever since the newspaper reports of my arrest in Moreton Manor, Howard-Wolferstan had been associated with dressing-gown and pyjamas. And to any Englishman who, with superior and uplifted eyebrow, coarsely ascribes my downfall to running after women I suggest that a man who cannot worship beauty at the expense of his own liberty is unworthy to enjoy either.

I looked out of the window. There was a sheer drop to the street. With no escape possible I had only one way to save something from the wreck; and that was to shave off my beard at once before a photograph of me could be taken. You can describe a man with a beard as long as you like, but provided you use only words no one can be quite certain how he really appeared. I had to prevent all the waiters and public who had seen me with Cornelia from rushing down to police stations with yarns that Howard-Wolferstan had been entertaining a beautiful spy. Nor did I want that excellent jeweller from whom I had obtained six hundred pounds to be compelled to suspect who Peter Bowshot St John Godolphin really was; he would certainly be proof against the temptation to report to the police if he could convince himself that there was a reasonable doubt. Which was my true motive – love of Cornelia or six hundred pounds? I do not know. Two floors above she may – unless I am completely misjudging her – have been exercised by a somewhat similar problem.

I jammed the bed against the door; and the dressing-table, lengthwise, between bed and far wall. Satisfied that the police who called for me would not be able to open the door more than a couple of inches, I set about the removal of my beard. It was a longish job, for I had only nail scissors. When most of the beard – dying in the full flower of its experience – was in the basin and I had begun to lather my face, the police were at the door and quietly requesting Mr Winthrop to open it.

They had no wish to make a noise in a respectable hotel – especially as they must already have investigated so many innocent Latins in dressing-gowns and pyjamas which they were reluctant to explain – and they talked to me reassuringly while I packed and dressed. My evening clothes, which might lead enquiries to Cornelia, and my new suit I rolled up in a tight ball and tied with string. I tried to land the bundle in the back of a passing truck and missed. Then a bus ran over it and a passing taxi-driver picked it up. I never heard any more of it.

The police outside my door carried on with soothing conversation addressed to Mr Winthrop, in which I began to detect a note of impatience. If their disgusting little colleague were right in his identification, the notorious spy might be destroying his papers or committing suicide; and there was nothing they could do about either.

'Gentlemen,' I said at last, 'if you will now stop pushing for a moment, I will remove the furniture.'

They came tumbling into the room, hotel manager, house detective, plain-clothes detective and two decent London constables trying to look stern. They found me in the old tweed coat and shabby trousers which had served Faiz Ullah so well.

'Claudio Howard-Wolferstan,' I said, 'and at your service.'

Epilogue

by Sir Alexander Romilly,
C.H., D.SC., D.LITT., F.R.S.

WHEN FIRST I was shown Mr Howard-Wolferstan's manuscript and approached with the suggestion that I should write an introduction to it, I rejected the proposal as one which illuminated the enterprise of a youthful publisher rather than his sense of propriety. But, where a preface might suggest to interested parties that I approve a work of which the execrable taste, enlivened though it be by ribaldry, can arouse and indeed deserves nothing but disgust, an epilogue which confines itself to the mere confirmation of the truth of Mr Howard-Wolferstan's narrative may reasonably be considered a duty to the Establishment over which I and my colleagues have the honour to preside.

The interests of a certain former member of my staff appear to have been somewhat wider than I had any reason to suspect, and I will refrain from comment upon her reasons for resignation and her present choice of the Pacific coast of South America as a domicile. Since, however, the integrity and competence of my Establishment have been impugned by the fantastic allegations of the more irresponsible sections of the Press to the effect that Mr Howard-Wolferstan and this former member of my staff are secretly engaged on the construction of a Primary Reactor for the Andean Republics, I think it only proper to point out:

(a) that the lady in question is not a physicist;

(b) that her work was solely concerned with problems of metal fatigue, and their solution;

(c) that, so far as Mr Howard-Wolferstan is concerned, I am of the opinion, while disclaiming both my right and my intention to influence senatorial investigation in the United States of America, that a degree of personal charm, of musical proficiency and of political irresponsibility do not provide an intellectual equipment sufficient to undertake Nuclear Fission.

The unexpected release of Mr Howard-Wolferstan, after he had been held for three months in the Tower of London upon a charge of High Treason, gave rise to comment in which the readiness of a healthy democracy to argue from unjustifiable hypotheses was only equalled by the vehemence, no doubt legitimate, with which they were expressed.

Had this document at that time seen the light, a clearer but not necessarily more favourable view of Mr Howard-Wolferstan's motives and morals would have been available to such leaders of public opinion as are able to read with ease and accuracy. As it was, Mr Howard-Wolferstan being a prisoner on remand, the document was privileged. It could be, and in fact was, handed by him to his solicitor, but might not be divulged to the prosecution and still less to the public. The essential facts, however, were freely admitted in the prisoner's statements to the police and in his markedly cordial replies to War Office interrogators. Both authorities could only advise the Crown that on a charge of High Treason no jury would convict.

The withdrawal of the prosecution, after all the publicity which had attended Mr Howard-Wolferstan's arrest and re-arrest, was indeed difficult to justify. I venture to suggest that a note of gaiety might profitably have been introduced into the explanations to Parliament and public. In this solemn century, however, no government can afford to be accused of light-heartedness; and, while the fear of ridicule may excuse the indefinite and unhelpful nature of the information given to the House of Commons by the former government, it had regrettably little influence upon the scenes which led to the suspension of Mr Elias Thomas Conger and the appointment of a Select Committee.

That publication of this narrative is desirable I cannot admit; but that misconceptions on both sides of the Atlantic have rendered it necessary I do not deny. Mr Howard-Wolferstan's permission and that of a former member of my staff were given with a complacency in which patriotism no doubt outweighed the hope of profit; for their joint recommendation was that the manuscript should be printed without alteration or amendment in order that the internal evidence of its authenticity, provided by both style and matter, should be unassailable.

While recognizing the truth of their contention, the publishers have found such exactitude impossible. To avoid causing unbearable distress to living persons, names have been changed where necessary, and the fugitive's route has been slightly altered.

As regards the extraneous evidence of Mr Howard-Wolferstan's veracity:

1 I have already mentioned that his solicitor received the manuscript directly from Mr Howard-Wolferstan before the release of the latter from the Tower. I should add, perhaps, that the firm of solicitors in question is well known to me, is of the very highest repute and does not normally engage in practice in the criminal courts.

2 The Chief Constable of my County has permitted me to state that on November 4th, 1953, at the request of the Metropolitan Police, search was made in the attic chimneys of Moreton Intrinseca Manor and the remains of a pillow-case, bearing the monogram of the late Sir Edward Lockinge, were discovered *in situ* together with three rings, valued at £105 16s. 8d., and a single diamond which appeared to have become detached from its setting.

3 The Assistant Commissioner of Metropolitan Police ultimately responsible for the investigation has authorized me to state:

(a) that Mr Howard-Wolferstan's account of his movements, where it can be confirmed, has been found to be accurate;

(b) that in so far as his voyage is concerned the information given to the police by Lieut. Karlis tends to agree with that of Mr Howard-Wolferstan, especially in Karlis' second statement given after the death of Mr C. C. Emmassin;

(c) that the sworn statement of the gentleman described in the narrative as 'Harry Cole' is consistent with the records of Scotland Yard, but that, since there is no evidence apart from Mr Howard-Wolferstan's manuscript that the proceeds of the Lockinge burglary were in fact recovered by him and his alleged accomplice, no further action can be taken at present;

(d) that owing to the usual intelligent co-operation between the Metropolitan Police and the Public, Mr Howard-Wolferstan's bandage was discovered in a coal merchant's yard near Shadwell Station, and that brilliant and imaginative work by an Inspector of the C.I.D. led almost immediately to the identification of the sweep. Mr Howard-Wolferstan would have been arrested the following day if he had not unexpectedly changed his appearance meanwhile.

I should add, perhaps, that I have no desire to enter into idle correspondence or engage in controversy. My concern is solely with the facts, not with such interpretation as may be put upon them by communists, anti-communists and other religious sectaries. And, if I may be permitted to finish upon a personal note, it is that I myself, unlike the majority of my uninvited correspondents, consider this earth upon which we are privileged to carry out our duties a most pleasurable dwelling-place. Let that be my assurance to those who flatter my colleagues and myself by supposing that we are not only able but resigned to effect destruction which the infinite dangers of a hostile cosmos have, since the birth of the planet, been inadequate to accomplish.

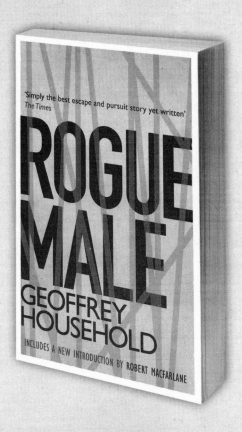

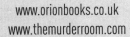